23/12/2014

Howard,

Best wishes,

David Hodgson

CAN I TOUCH YOUR FACE?

By

David Hodgson

First published in 2014 by Berforts Publishing

Copyright © David Hodgson

The right of David Hodgson to be identified as the author of this work has been asserted in accordance with section 77 of the Copyright, Design and Patents Act 1988

All Rights Reserved

No part of this book may be reproduced in any form by photocopying or by any electronic or mechanical means, including information storage or retrieval systems, without permission in writing from both the copyright owner and the publisher of this book.

DISCLAIMER

The likeness of any characters in this novel apart from historical personalities, to anybody living or dead is purely coincidental.

Acknowledgements

I should like to thank my wife, Sheila, my daughters Louisa and Zoe and other members of my family for their help in writing this novel.

© David Hodgson Beckenham October 2014.

PART ONE

ONE

Never tell lies, my Granny told me, it's wrong and you'll certainly be found out. Well, I found out when I was just six years old that being open and honest was not always such a good idea. One brilliantly clear spring day my Granny had taken me to school as usual and left me by the forbidding iron gates. As I wandered through into the playground an older girl, she must have been about nine or ten and whose name I still remember, Kaylie Smith, stopped me and asked why my Granny always took me to school and not my mother.

"Granny looks after me," I explained.
"What about your mum or dad?" she asked.
"They're dead," I said, innocently telling her the truth. It would have been better if I had said they were serial killers and locked away for life.
"Dead?" she replied. "What d'ya mean, dead?"
"Dead," I said, "they're dead. My Granny told me they went to heaven."
A small group of older children had gathered around us. Another girl, Julie Plumb, overheard and chimed in. I still remember the feeling of terror as she loomed over me, her ugly face a few inches from mine.
"Dead?" she queried. "I don't believe you. You're wicked. You're a liar."

"I'm not lying," I protested.

"Liar, liar, liar!" she screamed and some of the other kids joined in. Of course I burst into tears which only made matters worse. Someone started laughing and the awful cry of "liar, liar, dead mum", started up. I tried to run but a whole gang of them followed me round the playground chanting the dreadful words. Fortunately, when the bell rang it ceased and we all filed into our classes. Miss Farthing, my class teacher, noticed my tearful face.

"What's the matter, Sebastian?" she asked.

"Nothing Miss," I replied. I didn't want to get known as a tell-tale. For the rest of the morning I found it hard to listen to what she taught us and was relieved when lunch time came. I met my friend Jason and we went out into the sunshine. Like a pair of greedy, overfed cats, Kaylie Smith and Julie Plumb were waiting to pounce.

"Hello Dead Mum," Julie called. "Have you stopped crying yet, cry baby?"

"Go way and leave me alone," I shouted.

"Ooh, ooh, keep your hair on, Dead Mum," she retorted, "Can't you take a joke?"

Some of her class mates had gathered around and asked her what was going on. "Dead Mum can't take a joke, can you Dead Mum?" she sneered.

I swore at her and lashed out with my fists but she was much bigger than me and easily grabbed my flailing arms. Screaming with laughter she pushed me over. I scrambled up and started to run but they all followed me round the playground chanting those dreadful words. I covered my ears with my hands but could not shut it out. Miss Farthing appeared and rang the bell so the chanting stopped but the damage was done. It became my nickname. Someone would tap me on the shoulder, shout 'Dead Mum,' scream with laughter then run away. Eventually I took to hiding in the toilets during playtime. It worked and for a short while I was left in peaceful if foul smelling solitude. Eventually I was spotted of course, and a group of children soon rushed in, hammered on the door making a deafening noise and terrifying me. Suddenly it ceased and I could hear whispering. After a few seconds a single boy's voice called out: "What the matter, Sebastian, shit yer pants?" They all screamed with laughter and I realised who it was who had uttered those words. It was my best friend Jason. He was leading the appalling chorus. I could not believe he was one of my persecutors. How could my best friend do this? I felt totally betrayed, trapped and helpless as they all jeered and mocked me, and the banging on the door started again, this time much louder. I put my shoulder against the door to stop it opening but they burst through and knocked me backwards on to the floor. I kicked out wildly and caught Jason in the face. He fled, crying and sobbing that he would tell the teacher. I screamed that I would kick anyone else who called me names. Later, I was cross-questioned by Miss Farthing about the incident but I refused to say anything and was given a play time detention. Eventually, however, she got it out of me. She gave the class a lecture about bullying but it just made matters worse. I was accused of being teacher's pet and the name calling just carried on in whispers. I have never forgotten the dreadful feeling of misery and worthlessness I felt. I wanted to die and it still sends shivers through me now to think about it. I hated my mother and father for dying and leaving me alone but I despised myself even more for being stupid enough to tell anybody about it. Was it really as awful as that? Yes it was. I recalled asking my Granny why the other children had treated me like this. She just said I must learn to stand up for myself. I told her my best friend Jason had joined in. Why did he do that? You'll understand one day, she told me. I never did and for a long time I felt totally alone. When I told her this she simply said I had to take the world as it was and get on with life. I never trusted any of those children after that incident and if anyone asked me about my mum and dad I simply invented some implausible explanation as to why they were not around. I told no one the truth and it was many years before I had any close friends. I grew to become a gawky teenager and retreated into the world of books and computer games where good always triumphs and evil is always punished.

My less than ideal childhood now seems a lifetime ago. You must be resilient, my Granny told me. I was and, although I still find it painful to think about, I had moved on. I went to university, obtained a First in computer sciences and now enjoyed my life as a college lecturer. I married at twenty-one but it lasted a very short time. The break–up was not my fault and is another painful experience I've done my best to forget. True, my love life is and always has been a little tangled, but one can't have everything can one? A few weeks ago I celebrated my thirtieth birthday, an event only tempered by the uncomfortable thought that in as many years as I had lived I would be sixty. What would I feel when I was forty?

The First Year Art Show at Waterbridge College where I teach is something I normally avoid, but my good friend Mark was on the lookout for an original painting. He wanted to see if there was anything he might like enough to buy and so we went along to it. It would change my life forever.

Are you Alice Watson?" asked the dark haired man, pointing to my name on the wall by my paintings. I nodded. He had just walked into the room with another man and I noticed he was wearing a navy coloured T-shirt and clean pale-blue jeans, quite unlike the usual unwashed, baggy-kneed ones worn by some lecturers. 'He's probably a bit uptight,' I thought.

"I'm Sebastian Winter," he went on, "but most people call me Seb. I teach here."

I had seen him around the college. He had a reputation among the students. They called him Gucci because of the smart shoes he wore. It might also have been a wish fantasy because he had unnervingly intelligent, soft, brown eyes like an Italian gigolo.

"My friend is thinking about buying a painting," he said.

His companion was a tall fair-haired man in his late twenties and dressed in a smart, grey, pinstriped suit. He looked like an accountant. 'He won't buy anything,' I thought, 'he'll be just like my father – far too careful to waste his precious money on an original painting.' I tried to focus on the book I had brought to pass the time but my nerves fluttered as I tried not to build up my hopes. I risked a glance at them as they studied the paintings but Seb looked across at me at the same time and I hastily concentrated on the page I was seeing but not reading. "Buy, buy, buy," I muttered under my breath. Did he hear me? I hoped not. His look was so penetrating, so disconcerting, it was as if he knew what I was thinking. I lowered my eyes in embarrassment and heard his friend say something - a facetious comment about modern art, no doubt.

"I see your paintings are a series on the six days of the Creation in the Bible. Are you religious?" Seb asked.

"No, I just thought they might sell."

"I'm not sure I really believe you," he replied. He was right, of course. I had chosen the subject because I found the images of the extraordinary myth-like account of how the universe came to be, powerful and fascinating. True I hoped the paintings might sell well. Waterbridge was, after all, a very traditional place. How wrong I had been! The First Year Show was a chance to make a little cash and I was failing dismally. Most of the students had sold work but there were no red dots by mine. Why not? It was very dispiriting.

"I'm Mark, by the way," said the fair haired man. "I really love your work. Do you have a price list?"

That was a surprise. I smiled nervously and pointed towards the leaflet on the far wall. They both studied it.

"Which one are you interested in?" I asked.

"I wondered about 'On the Sixth Day,'" replied the fair haired man. It's very beautiful."

"I agree it has exquisite colours," interjected Sebastian, "and I love all those little animals. I can see Eve but where's Adam?"

"I left him out because he spoiled the composition," I replied. "Adam's not important anyway."

"Very funny," replied Seb, grinning. "What's the matter? Don't you like men?"

'I don't like you,' I thought and ignored the question.

"Leave her alone, Seb," intervened Mark. "It's just a painting,"

"Yes, but what does it all mean?"

"The title gives you a clue if you really think about it," I replied, determined not to be put down by this irritating man.

"The painting is certainly original," he pronounced. "It has a frisson of organic minimalism about it."

"I'm sorry, I've no idea what you're talking about," I replied. He was really beginning to annoy me. It was bullshit, of course. I don't know what he taught. It certainly was not art.

"Neither do I," he replied with a disarming smile. "I read it in a newspaper the other day. I thought I'd try it out on someone. I'm afraid you've rumbled me." At least he could laugh at himself.

"It's five hundred pounds, I see. Is that your lowest price?" asked Mark.

"Well, yes," I replied, rather feebly. My tutor had also told me to name my price and stick to it but the lack of red dots was undermining my resolve. I was very aware that I was no saleswoman. Mark shook his head looking rather doubtful. I wavered. "I suppose I'd take four hundred and fifty," I said, without much conviction and feeling the sale was slipping.

"Candidly, that's rather a lot for a student work. Will you take four hundred?" he asked.

"I'm sorry, no," I replied. He turned to go. "I suppose I would accept four twenty five." I quickly added. He agreed and I told him he could have it on Saturday after the show was taken down.

"Should I come here to pick it up?" he asked.

Seb intervened and said he would collect it to save Mark the drive, explaining that his friend lived at Stowe Minster, about twenty miles away and he was going to see him at the weekend anyway. I gave them both my card. I hoped it looked professional.

"Well, Alice I'll call you on Saturday morning," said Seb. "I could come to your place or meet you somewhere for a coffee. Do you know the Alhambra?"

I said I did and we arranged to meet there at eleven. They wandered off and I heard them burst out laughing as they left the room. I wondered if I had missed something and watched them go before turning back to my paintings, fixing a red dot on the picture I had sold feeling much better. I did not have long to dwell on it because my luck really changed. A smartly dressed woman in her thirties, who had looked at my pictures earlier, returned and introduced herself.

"I'm Sophie Blumenthal," she said, "I'm going to open a gallery in London in a few months showing the work of new artists. I'd very much like to show your work. Would you be interested?"

Would I be interested? To be offered a gallery at the end of your first year at an art school was unprecedented. I'd sold a picture and now a gallery owner was interested in my work. Fantastic!

Mark chided me unmercifully about the lousy lines he said I used to engage Alice Watson in conversation, or as he put it, stand on my head and waggle my toes.

"I look forward to it," he mocked. "And what was all that organic minimalist rubbish?"

"I just made it up. It's sort of crap art critics come up with," I replied.

"You don't even like contemporary art," he said.

"True, but I like to keep an open mind," I replied.

"I know what your real interest is," he said. "You can never pass up trying to impress pretty girls like that, can you?"

Like most people who do not teach in colleges, Mark clearly thought I took advantage of the endless stream of attractive girls he imagined were at my disposal. He was married and lived amongst the almost exclusively male inmates in the Cathedral School in Stowe Minster where he taught. No doubt seeing the temptingly pretty girls here, he might find it difficult to believe that in truth I led an almost blameless existence. Well, I say blameless but that is not entirely true. I enjoyed flirting and the occasional fall from grace. What was wrong with that? We're all human, after all. Nevertheless, I was always careful not to let it go too far.

We went into the college car park and Mark stopped beside his car. As is the habit of old friends, he thought he ought to give me yet more well-meant but pointless advice.

"I saw the look you had when you said you'd pick up my painting," he said. "I've seen it before. She'll give you a lot of grief, believe me. Stay away. Your trouble is you're always looking for the perfect woman. They don't exist."

Mark was, of course referring to my estranged wife. I had married when I was twenty-one and it could only be accurately described as an utter disaster. He had been my best man at our wedding, but I had never told him what went wrong. I met Jackie, a year after I left university. She worked for Sky Television as a make-up artist. Incredibly, our marriage had lasted little more than two weeks. The breakup was definitely not my fault. Why not? Well, apart from a couple of frustrating attempts at less than perfect love making, she simply invented reasons to avoid sex. It was the usual excuses of headaches, she did not feel well, women's problems and all that sort of thing. And when I understandably got cross she upped and went back to her mother. Naturally I was deeply upset and angry about this but eventually they both just vanished, whence by that time I neither knew nor cared. That was almost nine years ago and I had heard nothing since. Good riddance! It may be true that you can't choose whom you fall in love with but you can't choose whom you fall out of love with either. To wind Mark up, I muttered something to him about having to agree Alice was rather delicious. Unfortunately he took me seriously.

He snapped back wearily: "My advice is to stay away from her. It will end in tears."

Did he think I didn't know that? He drove off and I walked back through the town to my lodgings. Mark knew from our university days that most of my relationships were short and ended either with my rapidly losing interest and having to duck and dive to avoid the girl, or getting dumped for someone wealthier, cleverer or better looking. In those days the latter often made me very angry and upset. Of course I was now much more sanguine and did not fret too much when things went awry. Nowadays my sporadic encounters were largely with colleagues, most of who seemed to want me to be a sort of brother or kindly uncle. It did make me ask myself what I really wanted from a relationship and I found it an impossible question to answer with any certainty.

I found myself thinking about Alice. I could not understand why I did not remember seeing her before. She was certainly very pretty and had a sparkle to her personality that was very appealing. I also liked her quick-witted reaction to the rubbish I talked and I enjoyed the repartee. However, the danger signals were clearly there. Consequently I had no intention of trying my luck with her. I very much doubted she would be interested in me in any case, and I thought I would just end up making a fool of myself. While I found her extremely attractive for some reason she made me feel awkward, gauche even.

My encounter with her made me realise how little I really knew about art and I determined to embark on a crash course of self-education. I did not want to appear to be a complete ignoramus when I met her again. Over the next few days I read up in libraries and on the internet what I could about the history of art, impressionism, cubism, abstract-expressionism and all that incomprehensible stuff so that I could at least pretend to show an intelligent interest in it.

One morning I ran into Alice's tutor and asked him about her. He told me that she was a very, very bright girl indeed. She had three A stars at A level including maths. In his opinion, she could have gone anywhere or done anything she wanted. She had been offered a place at Cambridge but had chosen to come here instead. I was very surprised. I thought people who went to Art College did so because they were not much good at anything else and frequently not much good at drawing and painting either. When Saturday came I duly rang Alice and confirmed that I would see her for coffee at the Alhambra Café in the High Street. Because of what the tutor had told me about her high intelligence I felt nervous and not a little wary.

I agreed to meet Seb at the Alhambra because I knew it was always full of mothers with their toddlers and push chairs. I wanted to keep him well away from my digs, which were rather dingy and untidy. I knew very little about him apart from the comment by my friend Gemma that she'd heard he needed watching. So I thought I would be relatively safe in the coffee shop. I found out that he lectured in computer sciences - geeksville as far as I was concerned. People like him usually think fine art is a complete waste of time.

When I arrived at the Alhambra he was already sitting by the window. He greeted me with a continental style kiss on the cheek and ordered an Americano for me.

"Well, did you sell any more?" he asked, looking at me with his trump card eyes and the same intense expression that had unnerved me when I saw him at the exhibition. It made me a little on edge so I tried to avoid looking at him.

"No," I replied, rather too abruptly.

"Bad luck," he said.

"Not really, quite the opposite," I said. "A gallery owner came in just after you left and was very interested in my work. She's starting up a new gallery in Bethnal Green and said she wanted to represent me and show my paintings."

"That's brilliant," he replied. "I'm not surprised, I thought your work was just awesome myself."

Was he making fun of my posh accent? I was unsure. He might be just trying to sound young and trendy. He smiled, I sensed a little nervously, and continued: "The trouble is most people don't understand contemporary art. They are more likely to buy either cheap reproductions of French impressionists or those ghastly pictures of trumpeting elephants to hang on their walls than original work. They're too stingy to buy real art."

"You're probably right," I replied. Why did he make me feel so awkward?

"I think we are living in exciting times," he went on, "the new Brits like Hirst and Emin are really breaking ground. The tent with Tracy Emin's lovers' names was a brilliant idea and I loved her unmade bed installation at the Tate. As for Hirst, I am not sure I would like a sheep cut in half in my living room, but I wouldn't say no if he wanted to give me the diamond encrusted skull."

"Neither would I," I replied, smiling in spite of myself at his silly joke. "I don't suppose any of us would. I'm surprised you know so much about modern art."

"I don't," he said, "I read up about it just before I came here."

We both laughed. He clearly thought being disarmingly honest was a good line. I suppose I was flattered that he was obviously interested in me and I admit I quite liked him but I knew perfectly well he was not my type at all. For one thing he was too old. I prefer men who are nearer my age. I'd had only one boyfriend so far and I met him at a school dance when I was fifteen. We stayed together until just before I came to Waterbridge when he asked me to marry him. When I said we should wait until after college he had promptly dumped me. I cannot say I was deeply upset. At college I went out for drinks from time to time with other students but I had met nobody who really interested me. Most of them seemed rather immature boys and were just there to have a ball for three years at someone else's expense. I doubted that very many had any real intention of trying to make a living as an artist.

"I hear you chose this place instead of Cambridge," he said.

"I'm afraid so. You must think I'm mad."

"Not really. Cambridge isn't for everyone. What did your parents think?" he asked.

"About what?"

"Well, your doing art."

"My mother was quite happy but my Dad was very disappointed I didn't go to Cambridge. I was determined to go to an art college because I'd wanted to be an artist as long as I can remember. My mother tells me she took me to the Tate Modern when I was four. I demanded a drawing book and sat in the gallery trying to copy some of the Picassos on display. Perhaps that was the start, I don't know."

"You did that at the age of four? Amazing!" Seb replied. "I do admire people who set out to do what they really want regardless of the consequences. It would have been easy for you to go to Cambridge and have a comfortable life but you want something more. I think that's wonderful. For people like you art is a true vocation. You're not like the rest of us."

"Oh do you think so?" I said, but he heard the slight mockery in my voice.

"No, leave it out, I'm serious," he replied. "I know it sounds corny, but I meant it. I think artists show us human truths. Van Gogh, for example, painted all those wonderful pictures which nobody bought. He went on painting more and more masterpieces in spite of poverty and starvation, and in the process immensely enriching us all. I think his story has a wonderful spirituality."

He was being really pompous now. "Cutting his ear off wasn't so clever," I retorted.

"Maybe not, but he left the world a much better place for his art. Life is not all about microchips and new technology. Art is what separates us from the animals and enhances our lives, you must think that."

He was obviously trying to impress me so I decided to spin him along and have some fun.

"I quite agree," I said, "but my father doesn't. He won't talk to me to me now, until I see sense, as he puts it. He tried to persuade me that if I took a degree in Art History I could teach and paint in my spare time. That way at least I would make a living instead of expecting him to bail me out all the time. I turned it down. I wanted to be a full time artist. He called me pig-headed and told me I would never make enough money to live on. He now says he bitterly regrets paying for my private education and that I'm throwing my life away on a hopeless dream."

"We should all dream," Seb replied, reaching out and touching my hand. I smiled tragically at him, hardly able to stop myself laughing.

"He said it was up to me to make it pay," I continued, warming to my theme. "Everything in this world has a price is his mantra. He certainly doesn't believe in subsidising art. His view is that art is a criminal waste of public money. He's a banker, you know. He won't help with my fees or student loan and he's told me I'm on my own now."

"Really? It must be very tough for you."

"And now he's told me I can't go back home. They've even let my room."

"Good heavens!" he replied, sounding really shocked. "Surely if he's very wealthy he doesn't need the rent."

"You would think so," I answered. "He says it will pay for his golf club membership. He only got a five million pound bonus last year and is worried this year it will be even less."

"No! You're kidding."

At this I'm afraid I did laugh out loud.

"What's so funny?" he asked.

"Nothing," I said and took a deep breath wondering whether to go on with this entertaining fabrication. Enough is enough I decided. "Sorry, I was just kidding," I muttered, smiling sweetly at him.

"Oh," he said. "So all of that was untrue?"

"I'm afraid so - well most of it," I replied. "It was a wind-up."

Seb laughed and looked somewhat uncomfortable.

"I rather thought it might be," he said and glanced at his watch. "Look, I have to go."

I had clearly offended him. He deserved it yet I felt a little guilty. He gave me Mark's cheque, picked up the painting and I watched him walk off down the High Street. He looked rather crestfallen and to my surprise, I felt sorry for him. Yes, he was trying to impress me with his limited knowledge of art but perhaps he was merely trying to find something we had in common. What was so wrong about that? In a way it was flattering.

I saw him around the college quite a lot during the summer term. He seemed rather cool towards me and I rather regretted what I had done. He was always pleasant enough but kept his distance and I decided I had misjudged him. Perhaps he wasn't such a twit.

She fascinated me even more after that awkward conversation in the café. I became aware that a peculiar kind of madness threatened to take over my every waking thought. I avoided her and tried to supress these feelings, which was not at all easy. For a start there was something innocently sensual about her. Perhaps it was her perfect, unblemished skin and the slightly untidy hair. She was one of those students who no matter what they wear always look stylish, even elegant in a scruffy, Oxfam sort of way. I usually found chat-up lines easy. With her I had none. I was like a tongue-tied teenager. Probably it was the joke she had at my expense but it was more than that. In a way I felt intimidated because she had a vivacity and intelligence about her that both attracted me and kept me at arm's length. She was committed to becoming an artist and it was obvious that she would let nothing stand in her way. And how she worked! Her tutor told me that most art students do very little for most of the year, usually until a few weeks before they are due to be assessed, and then they work like mad to produce something to show. Not her. She often stayed in the Fine Art department till ten or eleven at night painting, trying to find new forms and ideas for whatever she was working on. She had a frightening nun-like commitment. It was obvious she was an exceptional person and not to be fooled around with. The last thing I wanted was to fall in love with her. It was sure to cause too many problems and I would just end up looking a fool. I tried to erase her from my thoughts altogether and carry on as normal. But I could not. It was one thing to flirt and fool around, and I had been no saint in this respect, but at the college I had always avoided anything serious. As a lecturer with a duty of care, as they put it, it just could not be allowed to happen. Who was I kidding?

As the term went on, my sangfroid slowly disintegrated. The less I saw of her the more I found it difficult to stick to my resolve. Fortunately, she made it impossible for me to get too close by seeming to be wrapped in a cocoon of untouchability. We used to come across each other in the building now and again but she was always in such a hurry and not inclined to chat. But for the brief moments I was with her I felt an overwhelming and agonising physical attraction. Her skin, for example, had an iridescent freshness that I found almost irresistible and when I spoke to her I could feel my heart thumping and my insides churning with nerves. We had ultra-polite conversations about how her work was going whilst inside my head a demon voice told me how nice it would be to kiss her sweet soft lips. Yet when she walked coolly away I was relieved that I had once again avoided making an idiot of myself. My ego was still intact and I could still look the other tutors in the eye. I was sure she would tell me to get lost in any case. And I suppose because I was not able to get close, I desperately wanted her all the more. I began to sleep badly. It was just as it was when I was a teenager. I even went off my food. She occupied my thoughts most of the time and it became very wearing. I had to do something if only for my own sanity.

I think it was Bertrand Russell who once said that man had never refrained from any foolishness of which he was capable. He was, of course referring to some lunatic letting off an atomic bomb but he could equally have been talking about love. My foolishness was that I decided on what I thought was a brilliant strategy for survival. When Picasso saw a pretty girl in the street he offered to paint her portrait and I'm sure lots of artists undoubtedly still do exactly that. Why not the other way round? Why should artists have all the fun? I would ring her to ask her to paint my portrait. She was probably short of cash and could do with the money. It was bound to involve a great many sittings, we would be certain to get to know each other better. I would find the real person behind the shimmering beauty, the flaws in her would become apparent and that this would somehow destroy my fantasy. It was a nice romantic idea but of course it was doomed to failure. I picked up the phone then I put it down. She might guess my intentions and see it as a bit sleazy. No, I had to find some other way to stop this lunacy. My resolution lasted little more than a few days before I was unable to stop myself nervously picking up the phone again. Alas my brilliant plan fell at the first hurdle.

"I'd like to commission a portrait from you," I said.

"I don't paint portraits," she replied bluntly.

"I'll pay you for it, a proper price," I said.

"Sorry," she said, "I really have to concentrate on my course work. Why do you want a portrait anyway?"

"Mainly because my Granny wants one," I thought this half-truth, well, to be honest, outright lie, would do the trick. My poor Granny was in a nursing home suffering from advanced Alzheimer's disease. She had no idea who I was these days. I suppose it just might help her to remember me. A bit thin, I know, but it was the best I could do. Alice was unmoved.

"Sorry," she said, "I really have too much on at the moment. No can do," and rang off.

It left me feeling a mixture of disappointment and relief. Why didn't I just ask her out you might ask? Well, I thought I would almost certainly be turned down and did not want to risk the humiliation. I know it sounds old fashioned but ever since my marriage broke up I had always relied upon women asking me out, not the other way round. It sounds a bit pathetic, I know. Experience had taught me that women always made it quite clear if they wanted you to show some interest, and if they did not you were wasting your time.

My next strategy for the preservation of my sanity was to avoid her at all costs and I even took to eating out of the college to minimise the risk of meeting. It worked to begin with and for some weeks I did not see her at all. Just as I had begun to feel more or less normal fate took a hand. One morning she literally crashed into me coming through the door of the college just as I was going out to get some breakfast. The books and papers she was carrying went all over the floor so I was forced to help her pick them up whilst apologising profusely.

"I'm terribly sorry," I said, and then noticed she was crying. "What's wrong?" I asked.

"Everything's going wrong. My painting is a disaster and today I'm supposed to hand in the work I have done so far on my thesis," she told me. "But my computer has crashed and I think I've lost everything."

"Haven't you put it on a back- up disc?" I asked.

"I knew you'd say that. No I have not. I didn't get round to it." She glared defiantly at me and sniffed. "Months of work down the pan and I will have to do it all again."

"That's terrible. Maybe I can help."

"How?"

"Fix the computer, it's what I do. I may be able to retrieve your thesis. I don't just teach Photoshop, you know."

"But if it's crashed, surely all the files have been corrupted."

"Not necessarily. I'll have a look at it if you like."

You might think I was just taking advantage of the situation but that was not my intention. I often helped students out with their grotty old computers when they stopped working. I had no ulterior motive. I would try and repair her computer just as I had done for the others, nothing more and I certainly did not want anything in return. That evening I went to her digs and inspected the faulty machine. The hard disc had gone and I told her I would have to remove it and fit another. I took it into the maintenance department at college and after an hour or two recovered the lost files and saved them on to a memory stick. I replaced the faulty components and set the machine up again. Of course she was very pleased. I treated her as I did all the students and just asked her for the cost of the drive.

"I'm so grateful, I must give you something else in return," she said and offered me one of her paintings. I shook my head.

"Don't you like it, then?" she asked.

"I never charge students," I said.

"You don't like my work, I can tell!" she said.

I protested that I did but she brushed that aside.

"I agree I don't either. I told you my paintings were a mess at the moment. My ideas just aren't working."

Of course I could not resist the obvious opportunity. "What about doing the portrait of me then?" I asked. "A change of direction might help."

"Perhaps," she murmured. "Why do you want one?"

"I told you, it's for my Granny."

"Your Granny?" she queried, her voice full of scepticism. I had been right. She had seen straight through me. I began to feel distinctly uncomfortable. "If it's for your Granny," she asked, "why don't you just have your portrait taken in the Photographic Department? My friend Gemma is doing Photography and she takes superb pictures."

"I think painting is inherently more interesting than photography," I persisted. "These days anyone can buy a good digital camera and it will do most of the work for you."

"I can't agree," she said. "Photos can have a feel and an aesthetic that give a quality that simply cannot be captured in a painting."

I knew I was out of my depth and I wanted to escape but I just blundered on: "Well I think paintings can tell you more about the character of someone. And I'd like something original. You can do me with three noses and four eyes if you like."

"I don't think your Granny would like that much," she observed with what I uncomfortably suspected was irony. I was floundering:

"Well what I mean is that I would like a portrait that is more than just a likeness," I said. "It should also an intriguing painting. You know, in any way you can think that shows my personality."

"But I don't really know you."

"Now's your chance," I told her. "As I said, I'll pay you."

"How much?"

"Two hundred pounds?"

"Ridiculous! Have you any idea how long it would take?"

"A thousand?"

"Now I know you're not serious."

"OK, five hundred."

"No," she said. "I really do not want to do a portrait of anyone right now."

"Oh," I said. "That's disappointing."

"Why?"

"One, because, I think you have a remarkable talent and two, I'm quite sure it'll be worth a lot of money one day."

"I doubt it. Since you don't like the painting I showed you, I'll see what else I can do. But I don't want paying. You saved my thesis and fixed my computer. That's quite enough."

"It was nothing," I replied. "It only took me a few minutes. Another painting will take you hours. I must give you something."

We agreed on a hundred pounds, and as the painting progressed I could not resist popping in to see her. It does not take a genius to work out that doing so would just make matters worse. Naturally, I was the perfect gentleman even though just seeing her turned me inside out. The painting was a bit weird but that was not important. She had got under my defences in a way that I had never experienced before. I simply had no idea what to do. Then she wrong footed me yet again. One day when I arrived there was no sign of the painting. She said she had destroyed it as she thought it was rubbish.

"Sit there," she said pointing to a chair by the window. "I've decided it would be more interesting to paint your portrait."

"But why?"

"I have to do one at some point for my course."

"Oh that's disappointing. I thought you might have found me fascinating."

"In your dreams!" she mocked. She did not know how near the truth that was. "Do you want me to paint one or not?" she asked.

"Yes, of course."

"Well sit down and keep still then."

She was treating me like a small boy, not that I minded. I obediently made myself comfortable in the chair as she put a new canvas on her easel. I sat there feeling very self-conscious until she started complaining that I looked too stiff and awkward and told me just to relax and talk to her. So for the next session I brought two pizzas and bottle of wine with me. It helped, although I was careful not to drink too much. I was happy just being with her and said nothing, plodding on keeping my feelings to myself. She talked a little about herself and I began to know and understand her much better. Because of this I was even more reluctant to tell her how I felt. In the past my experience of falling in love had not exactly been encouraging, apart from the obvious dangers of a relationship with a student. Not that I had any delusions that she might be attracted to me. I was sure I was just a useful face for her to paint for her course. As time went on I grew to like her and I did not want our relationship to come to an end as it surely would once the portrait was finished. After the final session I asked her if she would like to come and have dinner with me as a thank you. I thought she would probably turn me down but she agreed. At the meal she was pleasant enough but gave me no encouragement. Feeling relieved and at the same time a little disappointed I took her back to her digs and to my amazement the whole thing kicked off.

"What took you so long?" she asked, after she kissed me. She was soft, sweet and all the things I had dreamed of. And I thought I understood women!

Seb was not the best looking man I had ever met but he was obviously very intelligent and not really the computer geek I first thought he was. After a little while I began to find his initial boyish awkwardness attractive, which when I thought about it, was odd since normally I could not stand fumbling, nervous men. And he could be charming and thoughtful, for example bringing food and drink to our sessions. He explained he needed something to eat himself, but he obviously thought I could do with a good meal. It was true I found it difficult to find the money to pay for food and I was struggling with the rent. He occasionally brought me little presents like bunches of tiny freesias, which he claimed he had got cheap in the market. My friend Gemma had warned me I was playing with fire. She said those warm, deep brown eyes and long eyelashes fascinated all the girls, which is partly why I kept him at a distance for so long. She told me that I risked getting badly hurt but I took no notice. Why did I give in that evening? Well, mainly because I was fed up with playing games. Had I had fallen in love with him? I am not sure. I had worked very hard all year and it was nearing the end of term. I was fed up with my hermit like existence. I wanted a diversion, to relax with someone who knew what they were doing and Seb was there. I don't really know why I took him to bed - probably too much wine.

After that evening, we met mostly away from the college. I said nothing to either Gemma or my other friends. In any case they seemed far too pre-occupied by their own love tangles to notice mine. Shortly after our relationship started, he took me out for an evening meal in a country pub. One thing had been bugging me ever since he said he wanted a portrait for his Granny. Why his Granny? Why not his mother or father? I had asked him once at the sittings and he avoided answering the question. At the time I simply thought he might have been playing the sympathy card and posturing as the devoted grandson. But it still bugged me. Consequently, after the meal I asked him once again why the portrait was not for his mother or father.

"I hardly knew my parents." he said, looking away.
"Why was that?"
"It's not something I like to talk about."
"I'm sorry, I don't want to pry."
He smiled. "It's fine," he said. "It's a perfectly reasonable question. My mother died when I was very young and my Granny brought me up, that's all. What about your parents. You've never told me about them."
"You never asked. My father is solid middle class English, stiff upper lip, do your duty and all that. My mother's family were from the Ukraine originally. My grandmother came to this country to

escape from communism in the late twenties. Her name was Alisa. I was named after her."

"Really? What was she like?"

"She dressed in tweeds and became more English than the English. She died when I was young so I don't remember much else except that she used to sing lullabies in Russian to me when I was a toddler and give me pretty dolls and toys."

"How fascinating. You've got a little bit of wild Ukrainian in you then."

"A quarter, I suppose. She had a very good voice. I was told she used to sing professionally in the Ukraine but she never did so in this country. I imagine she wanted to forget."

"It all sounds rather exotic to me."

"I wish I knew more about her. I must ask my mother one day."

"You should. I think we should go before it gets dark. I want to show you a lovely view I know near here."

He paid the bill and we went for a walk in the Mendip Hills. The sun was low and as it started to set, the view over the countryside was like a landscape painting, with the trees, hedges, little villages and church spires silhouetted against the sun, gold rimmed in the falling summer light.

"Fantastic," I said quietly,

"I thought you'd like it," he murmured, putting his arm round my shoulder.

"I love the countryside," I said. "It's my dream to have a studio and live in a cottage somewhere like this. I want to walk over the hills and through woods at dawn listening to the birdsong. I want to see the sun go down over a view like this every night. I want to sit quietly by a stream and watch the fishes in the water and the little animals on the bank scurrying around. I'd like to get a sense of the extraordinary power of creation and beauty that nature provides."

"That's a lovely idea," he said. "I'm sure that one day it will happen for you if you want it enough."

"Do you ever dream about what your life might be?" I asked him.

"I try not to."

"I don't believe that."

"OK – making a lot of money I suppose."

"You're such a cynic. I don't believe you. I mean real dreams about what you want."

"Definitely not, it's much too dangerous."

"Dangerous? Why?"

"They might come true."

"Huh! That's too glib. I'm sure you had dreams like the rest of us when you were a child. We all need them."

"I suppose I did."

"What sort of dreams?"

"That I would play football for Spurs and score a superb goal."

I took his hand and faced him. "Why do you always hide behind a joke or a smart remark?"

He laughed and pulled me towards him. "Because I don't want you to find out the shallow man I really am."

"There you go again. You never let anyone know what you really feel do you?"

"That's because I don't feel anything much except how amazed I am to have this beautiful girl in my arms."

"No, no," I said, "I'm not going to let you get away with that. Tell me something more about yourself."

"Give me a kiss then."

"No. Not until you tell me something."

"Like what?"

"You said your mother died when you were young. What happened?"

His expression flickered with pain as he looked away and shrugged his shoulders. "Cancer I think. I've told you. It's not something I want to talk about."

"Oh that's sad. How old were you?"

"About five."

"And what about your father?"

"I don't know, I hardly remember him at all."

"Why?"

"I just don't."

"Why not?"

He ignored the question and pulled me into him. "Don't be nosey," he said. "What about my kiss? You promised." I gave him a little peck on the cheek. "I don't call that a kiss," he protested.

"That's all you're going to get." Of course he ignored that and pulled me to him again.

"I am not to be trifled with," he said, his eyes still laughing at me.

"Tell me more then. I want to know a lot more about you."

He shook his head. "No you don't. I want to talk about you. You're much more interesting than I am."

"Don't be annoying. I want to know about your father."

His expression again changed a little and he spoke rather quietly: "Another day, it's all very boring. I can think of much better things to do."

Alice's persistent questions about my childhood on that idyllic evening did not spoil it but they did bring back memories I have always tried hard to forget. I had told her I did not remember my father and this was quite true. I must have been about a year old when it happened. I know it sounds improbable, but I was told he left for work one morning as usual and didn't return home. My Granny said he worked for the Home Office, although she had no idea what he did. She told me the police said they thought he might have gone abroad or committed suicide but no trace of him was ever found. Obviously at the time he vanished I was far too young to remember anything. After my mother died I have a vague recollection of my Granny taking me to see someone she said was an uncle, although I don't think he was, who she said might look after me. But he apparently refused and so I went to live with her. I liked Granny and I did not mind, although I remember being very perplexed and miserable for a while at what had happened. Oddly, I have no memory of my mother's funeral. I must have completely blotted it out.

My Granddad had been killed in the Second World War and consequently Granny was not very well off. Most of the furniture in the house was rather shabby and there was almost no heating in the house, just a gas fire in the sitting room. It was extremely cold in the winter and I used to scrape off the ice that formed on the insides of my bedroom windows. I remember putting on my outdoor clothes in bed and having chilblains. I was frequently ill and when I was not, I often behaved very badly. My Granny was very strict and believed in old fashioned discipline. When I did something really bad or was rude I still remember the slaps she gave me. She used to tell me what a wicked child I was, and that God would punish me. This frightened me as I had no idea what God would do.

At that age I began to have uncontrollable rages and lash out at everything. Once when Granny took one of my prize possessions away as a punishment I even kicked and punched her in a rage. She told me I was a little monster and shut me in the cupboard under the stairs telling me I could not come out until I said I was sorry. It was very frightening, and while I sat there in the dark sobbing I remember feeling extremely angry because my mother was not there to get me out. I thought I must be really wicked or why else had she abandoned me? I could not understand where she had gone. Granny had told me she was in heaven but where was that? Why did she not come back? After a little while in the cupboard I felt quite alone and unlovable. I screamed and cried a lot but I would not say I was sorry. Granny eventually let me out and sent me to bed without any supper. She did not shut me in the cupboard after that although she used to threaten me with it. At the time I thought she did not love me, but of course she did. Mostly she was kind and no doubt I deserved the punishment she meted out. She believed she had to teach me right from wrong and this was the way to do it. It was how she had been brought up. I realise now that she was probably exhausted and at the end of her tether with me.

The horrendous time I had at my primary school did not help. After the dead mum incident, I started refusing to do my work, began truanting and even stealing from local shops. I was caught, punished severely and my conduct became even worse. I was insolent to the teachers, violent towards other kids and, in short, I became quite impossible. Granny eventually got fed up with my behaviour and the constant complaints, and when I was eight she took me to see another man she again said was an uncle, who was a professor. I think she wanted him to take me on. He was less than welcoming and I remember him glaring ferociously at me. I took an immediate dislike to him. The two of them went into another room where I could hear a big argument going on and another woman joining the row. I suppose she was his wife. Whoever they were they must have refused my Granny's request for we left soon afterwards, and instead she sent me to a Catholic boarding school near Ipswich. I could not understand why. I remember thinking that if she really loved me how could she do this? I felt nobody cared about me and I was just rubbish.

    I loathed the new school. All that religious brainwashing jammed down your throat, prayers and worse several times a day starting before breakfast, bible readings, and teachers who caned you without hesitation if you broke the rules. It was awful. My only consolation was cricket. I found that I was very good at it. I loved being part of the team and the congratulations when I did well. The sports coach was a really nice man who did not shout at me but quietly and patiently showed me the correct way to bat and bowl. Fortunately I had a natural aptitude and learned quickly. In a way it began to restore my self-confidence. I was good at something.

    Some of the kids there were from split homes or their fathers were abroad in the armed services, so when I was asked about my dad I told them he was in Russia working for the secret service and my mother was with him. Amazingly, I was believed and I was left alone. I had found out at a young age that a little harmless invention could be very useful in evading awkward questions and making life a little more bearable.

    Going to the Catholic school did install some much needed discipline in me and I began to do well academically. I endured my time there rather than enjoyed it, and much to my relief when I was eleven Granny took me away and sent me to the local comprehensive school. I think she could not afford to keep me in private education any longer. I was much happier there but I kept everything to myself and just simply made things up if anyone asked awkward questions. What choice did I have? It was either that or constantly face being reminded of what I wanted to forget. Alice had asked about my dreams. Yes, as a child I dreamt, but not of going to the stars in a space ship and becoming a superhero like other children. I dreamt simply of having a family life like everyone else. They all had mothers who hugged them and fathers who played football in the park with them and I keenly felt the emptiness in my life. Fortunately, when I went to university I made good friends and left all that behind me. Admittedly my personal life was a bit of a mess but hey, nothing's perfect is it?

TWO

Continuing to see Alice had its risks, of course. I knew the college authorities frowned upon any member of staff who became involved in a serious relationship with a student. They were aware little flirtations sometimes went on but relied on us not to let things get out of hand. The last thing any Rector wanted was an angry parent hammering on the door. Some of my colleagues started to ask where I kept disappearing to at weekends and I was sure that her friends had some idea of what was going on. You could not keep something like that secret for very long at a college. Consequently, Alice and I were very discreet.

It was the longest relationship I had had for a while but after a few months I had begun to wonder whether some of the magic was ebbing. At first I was very impressed with the brilliance of her mind and the breadth of her knowledge but I had now begun to find it mildly irritating. She seemed to know far more than I did on almost any subject I brought up. If I mentioned English literature, she had read far more widely than me. If it was foreign literature, she had already read the major French and Spanish novels, not like me in translations but in the original languages. Her grasp of art and music went way beyond mine and the only subjects I could compete in were my own computer sciences and the history of war, a speciality of mine. But in neither subject did she show the slightest interest. Our relationship was reaching a difficult phase. We began to disagree a lot and she did not seem particularly happy. I was not sure exactly why and wondered whether it might not be long before I was dumped. Stupidly, I became irrationally jealous of some of her young male student friends. I even thought she might be seeing someone else when she occasionally told me she felt unwell or was too busy with her course work to see me. Of course it was nonsense but I still felt physically sick at the idea of losing her. I knew it would all end one day – but I did not want it to be yet.

Matters did not improve when one morning I received a quite unexpected letter. It was from my estranged wife, Jackie. After such a long time it was a shock, to say the least. She said she wanted to see me about what she claimed was something important. I decided that most likely she had met someone else and wanted a divorce. Sod her! I would let her stew for a few weeks. I had never told Alice about her as I thought it would only complicate matters, but I wondered if the time was coming when I should do so.

Later that evening and quite against the rules of the game, Alice called on me in my digs. Recently she had become somewhat irritable, pre-occupied and difficult to talk to. On this occasion she looked tired, pale and was rather dark under the eyes and I wondered if she was unwell. I soon got an answer I was not expecting.

"I hope nobody saw you," I said. She waved her work folder at me and told me not to worry as it was early evening. She barely smiled at me.

"What's the matter," I asked?

She dropped her grenade.

"I'm pregnant," she said, and looked hard and anxiously at me.

"Oh," I said, but thought 'oh shit!' Pretty inadequate I know.

"How long?"

"Six or eight weeks, I think. The doctor said it was difficult to be certain."

"That's wonderful," I said but the hollow tone of my voice must have given away my real feelings and to my horror she started to cry.

"Seb, what are we going to do?" she whispered, clutching at me, tears streaming down her face. I put my arms around her and kissed her on the forehead.

"Don't worry," I murmured, while I tried to think.

"Don't worry!" she sobbed. "Of course I'm going to worry. My parents will kill me and I won't be able to finish my degree."

"I'll sort something out," I said, trying to put my arms around her. But she pulled away.

"What are we going to do?" she repeated.

"*We* going to do?" I queried.

"Of course we - I didn't do this on my own."

"I need to think," I said.

"Think?" she said and started crying once again. "What's there to think about? My baby is on its way. You can think all you like but it will start to show soon and everyone will know. Think about it! Before long a child will be born, I will be a mother and you will be a father."

"Are you quite sure?"

"Of course I am. I thought you loved me."

"Love?" I repeated, hardly hearing what she said. "Of course I love you." What a disaster! I felt a spasm of real anger as I slowly realised the serious consequences for both of us.

"Have you told anyone else?" I asked. She shook her head. "Good," I said. "You must keep very quiet about this. Don't tell your friends, don't tell anyone. If the college finds out, it will be extremely serious for me. I'll be fired with no references. No job, no income, what good will that do anyone? You must keep schtum about this at least for the moment."

"Do you think nobody will notice?" she snapped.

"Of course they will, in time, but don't say who the father is, at least until I sort something out, for both our sakes."

She looked at me blankly.

"What do you expect me to do?" she asked.

"I've no idea just at the moment. I'll deal with it somehow. I'll think of something."

"Like what?"

"Do you want this baby?"

"I don't know," she said and looked at the ground. "What do you think?"

I took a deep breath. "I have to be honest with you, I'm not sure I want a child right now."

Stupid thing to say really and it lit the cordite.

"Well, you're damn well going to whether you like it or not," she shouted. I tried to quieten her down.

"Please listen to me," I whispered. "Don't you understand? It will be a disaster for both of us if you have this baby. Have you any idea how tough all that will be?"

She burst into tears again. I put my arms round her and tried to comfort her but she pushed me away.

"You obviously want me to have a termination, don't you?"

"I wasn't suggesting that at all. I'm just trying to find a way out for both of us."

"Kill our baby? How could you want me to do such a dreadful thing?"

"It's not really a baby yet. It's just a cluster of cells."

"Cells!" she shrieked in horror.

"Yes that's what it is. Look, I'm just exploring options. Of course it's entirely your decision but maybe you should consider it? It makes a lot of sense to me and it's hard to see any sensible alternative. Can you think of one?"

We both stood in silence, not looking at each other for a good minute. She would not stop crying. What on earth was I going to do?

"Couldn't we get married?" she suddenly asked. "It would be OK then, surely?"

"Get married! I don't think so."

"Why not?"

Why not, indeed? I could hardly tell her I was already married could I?

"I'm not sure I am ready for marriage," I said. "Not like this, anyway."

She laughed hysterically. "Like what, then?"

"Look, it's complicated. I just do not want to get married at this point in my life. I can't explain."

She boiled over. "What's to explain?   Your child is on the way. That will take some explaining. It's that simple."

I shook my head. "No," I said quietly. "I'm sorry, no."

"What about the baby?"

"You could have it adopted. Have you thought about that?"

"Go to hell!" she screamed and rushed out of the room.

I knew I handled it badly but I was shocked. I helped myself to a large whisky and tried to think clearly about the situation. She was carrying my child. She was determined to have it. To make matters worse I was not sure what we felt about each other anymore. As for the prospect of becoming a father, that really alarmed me. I realised I must talk to someone and next afternoon I drove to Stowe Minster to see Mark. He had been having a few technical problems with their music technology computers and I had agreed to look at them.

He was teaching when I first arrived so I wandered through to the garden and sat on a bench on the edge of a small playing field. Some of the choristers were playing football and it was not long before the ball came bouncing in my direction. I stood up and tried to trap it but the ball skewed behind me into the hedge. There was a great cheer from the boys and they all laughed. One lad, who had been running after the ball, hurtled past me to retrieve it. He punted the ball back and instead of going back sat down next to me.

"I don't think Barcelona will want me now," I joked.

"Probably not," he smiled. He was a dark haired youngster probably about ten or eleven years of age.

"What's your name?" I asked quite expecting it to be Tarquin, or something like that. I was not far wrong.

"Tristram," he replied.

"Hello Tristram, I'm Seb," I said.

"Are you waiting for somebody?" he asked. "Have you come to hear us sing?"

"Yes and no, I've come to fix the computers. I'm waiting for Mr Manning."

"Aha," he replied. "I'm the striker."

"I used to play football for my school," I told him. "I was a winger." Tristram blew through his teeth and looked at me.

"My Dad's a professional footballer," he said and added. "He was anyway. He's retired now. He used to play for Crystal Palace. But we don't live with him anymore."

"I'm sorry. That's sad," I said.

"No, it's better like that," he went on. "It is much quieter at home now. They used to shout at each other a lot. I hated it. But my Dad still takes me to watch football sometimes. He said he would teach me some of his tricks but he never comes to see me. He's always too busy."

He had begun to look rather upset so I thought I should change the subject before he burst into tears.

"Are you singing this evening?" I asked.

He nodded. "Will you come and hear me?" he responded. "I'm doing a solo."

"If I've got time," I said.

He looked rather dejected, so I said of course I would love to hear him. He grinned and ran off to join the others just as Mark arrived.

"I see young Tristram buttonedholed you," he said. "He tends to latch on to anyone he thinks might take some interest in him. I hope he wasn't being a nuisance."

"Not at all, he seems a nice boy. He was telling me about his father."

"The professional footballer stuff," said Mark. "It isn't true, you know."

"Really?"

"He just says it to impress people. I believe his father was once a physio at one of the league clubs but now works in a fitness centre in Chelsea. I imagine it's where he met the mother. I've only seen him once. He was good looking in a rugged, broken nose sort of way but when he opened his mouth he sounded like a real yob. I'm sure he appealed greatly to the wealthy ladies of West London as a bit of rough I can't imagine why she ever married him. Tristram is such a likeable intelligent and sensitive boy It's hard to believe a man like that is his father. But clearly the lad has a few problems."

"He seemed normal enough to me."

"Yes and no. He cried a lot when he first came here but he's all right now. He's much more like his mother. I imagine sending him here was her idea. She's the one with the money – she owns a boutique in Notting Hill. She told me his father believed in good old-fashioned discipline and we all know what that means. It always amazes me that whatever parents do to their children the kids still adore them, at least until they grow up."

I certainly knew what old fashioned discipline meant! "Tristram asked me if I would come and hear him do his solo," I said.

"He must have meant his violin solo. He's very gifted. The school orchestra is rehearsing for a concert later. He's playing a Bach solo violin piece in that. Why don't you come along?"

I fixed the computers and afterwards went to hear Tristram perform. I was not really looking forward to it. Squeaky solo violin music is not for me. Seventies rock like Sting, Queen or Phil Collins are what I really like. But I could see that the kid really enjoyed it and played well. I switched off after a short while because my thoughts were elsewhere. What was I going to do about Alice? I felt very guilty about how I had reacted to her when all she wanted was my reassurance. How would the college react? It should not have happened but it had and now I had to deal with it. What's more, with my estranged wife clearly wanting something from me adding to the equation, I felt my life was rapidly descending into the vortex.

The rehearsal ended and as the young musicians left, Tristram looked in my direction and gave a grimace. It was unexpectedly human and made me smile. It was what I needed. He clearly thought I was cool or something ghastly like that. Maybe I was not so awful after all. I had enjoyed talking to him and that had surprised me. Children were normally way off my radar but the possibility of my becoming a father meant that before long I would have a child of my own. If he was like Tristram, the prospect was not quite as alarming as I had imagined.

Mark and I adjourned to the local pub for a pint and a sandwich. On the way there I had decided I was not going to mention anything about Alice to him after all, because I knew exactly what he would say. But I blurted it out anyway. He called me a bloody idiot and asked why I had not taken his advice to steer clear of her?

"Well, you know how it is," I replied. "I never could resist a pretty face."

"What does she think?"

"Well, when she got over the screaming hysterics she suggested we got married."

Mark laughed. "Why not? You could do a lot worse."

"I can't."

"You're not still married are you?"

I pulled a face. "I'm afraid so."

"Boy," he said, "you really know how to mess things up. I thought you were divorced long ago."

I shook my head. "I never bothered. But it may not be as bad as you think." I told him about the letter from Jackie. "She's probably met some rich sucker and wants a divorce."

He laughed. "I'd like to be a fly on the wall when you tell her you are going to be a daddy. I can just imagine what she'll say."

"I'm not that stupid. I won't tell her, will I?" I replied.

"You can't keep a thing like that secret. Be realistic. Get the divorce and marry Alice. She's bright and extremely attractive. What more do you want?"

"I'm not ready to marry again. I've made one terrible mistake; I don't want to make another."

"What about the child that's on the way?"

"I'll support her financially of course, but I'm not ready to settle down just yet and definitely not ready to change nappies and all that stuff. It's just not me."

"You think it's a good idea for a child to be brought up without a father, then?"

"No, but better that than living with parents who are perpetually at war."

"Why do you assume that? Once you stop panicking I'm sure you two will be fine."

"I very much doubt it. The fact is Alice and I have almost nothing in common."

"You do now. You can't turn your back on her. It's your responsibility."

"I won't be able afford it anyway. My wife will take me for every penny she can get. You remember what she was like."

"Look," he said, sounding exasperated. "Let me spell it out. In a few short months you will be holding your baby. Imagine that. Your child who will grow, go to school, to university and embark on a career. Do you really want to miss all that? Do you want it all to happen without you? What about the effect on the child?"

"I don't know. He'll cope."

"No he won't, that's just the point. I see kids all the time dumped in schools like this just to clear them out of the way. A couple of years ago a very talented young pianist tried to set light to the music room here. It was a protest about being abandoned as she saw it. These kids can't really understand what's going on. You met young Tristram. On the surface he's fine but dig a little deeper and he's not. You saw that yourself. You can't let that happen to your child."

"OK, OK, I take the point."

"Another thing; in some ways I envy you. You don't know how lucky you are that you're able to have children. Many people can't and I can tell you it becomes quite difficult in those circumstances."

"You sound as if that's very personal," I said.

"It is, actually. Mary and I have been trying for a baby for a couple of years now and just it does not happen for us."

"Oh I see. Is there a problem?"

"We've no idea. The doctors say there is nothing wrong with either of us but it doesn't work. You wave your dick around and hey presto, some girl is pregnant. We would give a lot for that to happen for us."

"You put it so elegantly."

"It's frustrating," he replied with some bitterness.

For the first time I was beginning to get some inkling of the real importance of children and their place in people's lives. It was not something I had ever thought about. Was I ready for a family of my own? I was not sure.

"What do you think I should do?" I asked.

"Well first of all, you need to persuade Alice to quit her course before too long. You have to find her some accommodation well away from the college and at least try and do the decent thing. If you can't marry her why not live with her? At least give it a go."

"And how do I pay for all this? I've got no bloody money."

"It so happens I can help you," he said, "at least with accommodation for a short while."

He explained that he had a cottage in Wiltshire we could use. He was due to go away on a year's sabbatical soon and he would like someone to house-sit, anyway. He just wanted a nominal rent and the bills paid. I could use the time to find something more permanent. I agreed to think about it.

As I drove back, much as I did not want to, I began to think perhaps he was right. I must face the reality of the situation that I was in. I had created a child and I had to make the best of it. I thought about the problems Mark and his wife were having. They could not have children and I was being handed one on a plate. I thought about the likeable Tristram and wondered if my son would be like him. Perhaps having a child might not be so bad. We could do all that father and son stuff. I could teach him football, cricket and things like that. Would he look like me? I hoped not. Would he follow in my footsteps? He would certainly be growing up in the computer age, which I could teach him about. Or would he would be like Alice, artistic and driven? Mark had at least shown me a way forward. It was extremely decent of him to offer the cottage and I had been extremely lucky. Would I get away with it as far as the college authorities were concerned? Probably not, but if I did the decent thing I might. May be it was time to move on anyway. There should be plenty of jobs for people with my skills in industry and I would probably make a lot more money.

I arranged to see Alice the next evening, apologised for my ill-considered comments explaining that it was just the shock. I suggested that when she felt the time was right we should live together and told her about the cottage in Wiltshire. She was thrilled about that. Next day I wrote to my wife and arranged to meet her for lunch. I obviously needed to get divorced rather smartly now, although I am afraid I had still put off telling Alice about her - it would be cleaner to wait until the divorce had all gone through.

The Old Mill is a pleasant restaurant in the village of Tatsfield in Kent. It was near Jackie's family home but she wanted to meet on neutral ground. I have to admit to being surprised when I saw her come in. She looked as attractive as when I first saw her, perhaps a little slimmer than I remembered. She was smartly dressed in a red suit and even the waiter looked at her with admiration. Nevertheless, seeing her again after eight years was a curious experience. The anger, the bitterness, the suspicion between us was oddly suspended in a sort of truce. It was as if we were picking up from a pleasant discussion we had had the previous day, with easy conversation about what I was doing now and where she had been. When we originally parted, she told me, she had taken a job with a film production company in Ireland and spent much of the time in Dublin. Curiously, she did not mention divorce. This puzzled me but I assumed she would get round to it sooner or later. She did not. So after the coffee I thought I might delicately mention the subject.

"We have to talk, "I said.

She guessed what I meant at once and looked pained. "Don't spoil it," she said, "I really enjoyed our lunch after all these years. I didn't expect to."

"I enjoyed it too," I said. "But we have to sort things out."

"There's no great hurry," she replied. "Look, I simply wanted to see you and say I was really sorry about the way I behaved when we split up. It was unforgiveable."

"We were both young," I murmured.

"No, it was my fault. I don't know why but at that time I just could not cope with a close relationship like that."

'You couldn't deal with sex, you mean,' I thought, though I heard myself say gallantly: "I'm sure it must have been as much my fault as yours."

"I've thought about it a lot over the years. I felt extremely guilty. I let you down." She was truly convincing and I began to wonder whether I was being too cynical about her motives for seeing me. Maybe she was truly contrite and wanted us to try again. Surely not. That would be disastrous!

"It doesn't matter," I muttered, "it was all a long time ago."

"I suppose so," she replied. Then, to my surprise, she abruptly ended the lunch.

"I'm sorry but I have to go," she said.

"We do need to sort things out," I repeated.

"Is there a particular reason?" she asked.

"Not really, it's just that......" I tailed off thinking 'just tell her about Alice for God's sake. What's the problem?' I had left it too late. That was the problem. She asked for her coat.

"We'll talk in a few days, somewhere private," she said. "I'll call you soon. Just for now, let's just remember the good things we had."

I could not think of many. She disappeared through the restaurant door leaving me none the wiser about what she really wanted. She did not call me in a few days as she had promised and I soon became involved in making arrangements with Alice. I had reservations about the wisdom of it but felt I had no alternative as Alice's condition became obvious. Nothing had yet been said to me by the college authorities and we moved in to Mark's cottage. Alice absolutely loved it there and seemed very happy. It was several months before I heard from Jackie again, not until after the baby was born.

THREE

Seb was with me in the hospital when my baby arrived. The pain had been almost unbearable. Never again, I thought, but when I felt the warmth of his tiny body seep into me and the pain hardly mattered. His head rested lightly on my shoulder as I cuddled him gratefully. My first born child, my son, was exquisite, his tiny hands, wrinkled but which would soon develop a smooth and perfect skin, waved helplessly about. His screwed up little face, still smeared with traces of blood, lifted my soul with its beauty. I was ecstatic. A new being had come into the world and he was uniquely mine.

"He needs a wash now," said the nurse and sponged him down. Seb held my hand and told me how wonderful I was and how guilty he had felt as he watched me endure the pain. I told him not to worry. It was natural. My little baby started crying as the nurse returned him to me, although he stopped for a moment when I cradled him. His eyes opened wide for the first time and I saw they were the colour of the higher summer sky with a translucent quality that seemed miraculous. Then his tiny lids closed, his mouth turned down, his forehead puckered and he started to cry again.

"He's got a powerful pair of lungs. He's going to be an opera singer I'm quite sure!" laughed the nurse as she helped me make him comfortable on my breast. His hand grasped my finger tightly as he fed. He had a surprisingly strong grip. I looked at his crinkled face once more and wondered what he would be when he grew up. Opera singer? More likely he would be a doctor like my grandfather or something quite different, a concert pianist or a famous painter, perhaps. Seb was sitting by the bed now and I noticed how tired he looked. It was not surprising since it was gone two in the morning.

"What shall we call him?" he asked. If it had been a girl he wanted to name her Rosemary, after his Granny. But since it was a boy we had agreed the choice was mine.

"I'm not sure. Perhaps Piers but only if you like it," I replied. He smiled at me in the way that had first attracted me, like a boy and full of warmth.

"That's a new one," he said and leaned forward to kiss me softly on the cheek. "I haven't heard you mention that name before."

"After Piers Plowman, you know the medieval poem. I read it last week and it's set in the English countryside. Somehow it seems appropriate for where we're living. It's just a feeling I have. It's so idyllic and close to nature there."

"The cottage isn't in the Malverns," he objected.

"Don't be so literal," I chided. He grinned.

"OK, that's fine by me, what about James as well?" James was his grandfather's name.

Next day I carried Piers James up the path of our cottage just outside the tiny hamlet of Clyffe St Mary. A gentle early summer breeze made the pink flowers of the clematis growing over the porch move a little. In the distance I could hear the cooing of pigeons from deep in the woods. Inside the cottage, Seb had created a spectacular greeting with flowers cut from the garden. Vases of daffodils, tulips and primroses stood on the floor, tables and window ledges. In the smaller alcoves there were jam jars with buttercups, Queen Anne's lace and a myriad of other wild flowers. I thought it was quite wonderful and I loved him for it.

It became my habit to take Piers for a walk through a small wood on the edge of the village. I would put him in a baby carrier and, as I made my way through the trees, I showed him the flowers by the side of the path. It was a way of teaching him. I liked to point out their colours like blue speedwell, purple cranesbill, yellow melilot, white stitchwort and columbine. The wood covered the side of an escarpment and at the end, a path led up a steep incline to the top of the Marlborough Downs. I sometimes took Piers up there to show him the view across the plain. Normally we went no further than the top but this time I decided to walk along a bridle path towards a white horse cut into the hillside. The bridleway snaked along and after about twenty minutes I came to a little track that led to the horse. I made my way down a stony, perilously steep path and stood on the hill carving. I had read that it was not Stone Age but was probably dug out in the nineteenth century but nobody was certain. I liked to imagine it was much older as Stone Age remains were often found in that area. Nearby I came across some flints and picked one up. It seemed to have been shaped into what could be an ancient arrow head. It was a reminder that people had lived in these hills for thousands of years. I loved that sense of being part of this culture, of something deeply rooted in an ancient past.

    The weather was hot for May and it had not rained for several weeks. The fields were turning a browny-yellow colour and the hills in the distance were shimmering in a stormy heat haze that blurred the edges of the earth and sky. I could hear the rumble of thunder not too far away and the air became still. On the other side of the wide valley an RAF transport aircraft rose into the sky and turned in a wide curve above us.

    "Look at the aeroplane Piers," I said. "You could be a pilot when you grow up, and fly one just like that one up there in the great big blue sky." He gurgled and stared vaguely in the direction of the aircraft.

    A storm was imminent so I decided to return along a track at the bottom of the valley before we were caught in a downpour. I continued down the path and into a small wood. A few yards into the trees I was surprised to find the remains of several tumble-down cottages, one of which still had the walls and roof timbers standing. I pushed my way through the weeds that obstructed the door, went inside and found myself in what must have been a tiny kitchen. In the corner was a rusting hand pump. I tried pushing the handle several times and, to my surprise, a stream of water immediately gushed out. It smelt quite clean and fresh. I went through a doorway into another room. It had a stone floor through which weeds were growing and threatening to take over completely. On the far wall a fire place was still blackened with soot. I wondered who had sat by it and why the cottages had fallen into disuse. The ceiling was down and I could see the sky through a web of rafters and over-hanging branches.

"What do you think of this place?" I asked Piers. "Shall we get your Daddy to buy it and live here?"

The distant sound of a cuckoo seemed to echo through the air and then, much closer, a rat-a-tat came from just outside the cottage. I moved to a window. A spotted woodpecker, its black and white feathers and red marking quite distinctive, was drilling at a tree trunk only five or six yards away.

"Look, at the pretty bird darling," I said, and held Piers up. It was as I put him down again that through the window I saw the woman. Small with greyish hair, probably in her sixties and wearing a flowered cotton dress, she stood on the path that ran in front of the cottage looking at us. For a moment I was unnerved. I felt like an intruder. But she smiled pleasantly and when we emerged she made a big fuss of Piers.

"I love babies," she said, tickling him under the chin. "He's lovely - such fantastic eyes."

It was something everyone remarked on and I smiled and murmured modest pleasantries. Piers was indeed a beautiful baby and I could not help the swathe of grateful emotion that engulfed me whenever I looked at him.

"My mother used to be the midwife around here," the woman said, as we walked together down the path. "She delivered most of the children in this district for a long time. Of course they're grown up now and gone away. Not much work for young people around here nowadays, you know."

"That must be very sad," I ventured. "You must know who used to live in the cottages then?"

She did not appear to hear me or perhaps did not want answer so did not reply. We soon came out of the trees and made our way down a rough track towards a farmhouse. The woman was easy to talk to and I told her about Seb and the cottage we had borrowed.

"We can't live there permanently," I explained, "It belongs to a friend of Seb's who's away. But he comes back in September next year. It's a shame because this is such a wonderful place to bring him up."

"Yes," she said stroking his hair. "What's the baby's name?"

I told her and she smiled.

"Piers was my great grandfather's name," she said. "He lived in the old cottage you were in. It's nice to hear the name being used again. When was he born?"

"At Easter," I said.

"What day?" she asked.

"The twenty-third."

"I meant what day of the week?"

"In the early hours of Easter Saturday - at ten past one in the morning!"

She leaned forward and touched my arm. "He's a Chime Child, then," she said.

I stared at her, completely bemused. "What does that mean?" I asked.

"A Chime Child is one born after the midnight chimes on Good Friday," she said. "The child is said to have special gifts." She smiled at him and added: "It's just an old country saying," as if that was all the explanation necessary. We had stopped outside the gate of the farm.

"What sort of gifts?" I asked.

"You'll have to wait and see," she replied. "I'm Ellen, by the way. This is where I live."

"I'm Alice," I replied and held out my hand. She took it and smiled at Piers, who did not appear to notice her.

"It was nice to meet you, Alice," she said. "Pop in for a cup of tea, whenever you're over this way,"

Bidding me farewell, she turned down the garden path and disappeared round the side of the building. The oppressive heat of the day intensified as I came out of the lane into Clyffe St Mary and it started to spot with large, heavy rain drops. I cut through a farm at the back of the village and ran through the fields to our cottage, arriving breathless, wet through and elated.

"He's a Chime Child," I told Seb as he came in that evening. I explained about the old lady I had met and what she said about Piers being special. He laughed.

"Of course he is," he said. "I didn't need the local witch to tell me that!"

"Don't be nasty," I snapped at his silly remark. "She was a very charming. Her mother used to be the local midwife."

"There we are," he replied. "I was right. The name midwife comes from the Anglo Saxon med-wyf. It means wise woman and also witch."

"Huh!" I snorted. "Male hang-ups about childbirth, that's what calling them witches shows. It frightens the life out of men, always has done - far too unpleasant all that screaming and blood and worse all over the place."

"I was there for the great event, my sweet." He could be such a smoothie.

"Yes, and I was pleased you were. Anyway, as you pointed out, it also means wise woman - and that's something else that men resent. Women with brains frighten the poor little things. No doubt that was another reason for calling them witches and burning them at the stake."

"Take it easy, darling. It was only a joke."

"Anyway I like the idea of him being a Chime Child," I went on. "It might an old fashioned country myth, I know, but it makes me feel I belong here."

"Well, if it makes you happy then I'm happy," he replied.

"I must show you this old cottage I found," I said. "I'd love to live there. It was so beautiful, so peaceful. It badly needs doing up but we could buy it and restore it ourselves."

"Love to," replied Seb. "We'll have to walk over there one day."

She was taken up with the baby and thought of little else and I was beginning to mull over about our relationship. Although we were getting on well most of the time, was that sufficient? The doubts I initially had about setting up home with her still lingered. We had little in common and in truth my initial wild obsession with her had faded and been replaced by a feeling of tenderness towards her. Is that what love is? I wanted to love her, perhaps even thought I loved her at times, but all the same I now often felt rather detached and only remotely involved. I had assumed that when I set up home with her real love between us would grow especially when the baby arrived. But as time passed I remained unsure of my real feelings about him and where we were going. She appeared to be quite happy for the moment, I was not unhappy so that would have to do. I even wondered whether I had ever really felt love for anyone other than my Granny. I hardly remembered what I felt about my mother. Yes I was fond of the women I had had close relationships with and was occasionally deeply upset when they did not work out but that was more likely to be my bruised ego than anything else. Perhaps I was incapable of real love, if I ever found out what that actually meant.

The baby dominated our lives and I definitely had a back seat. Everything was Piers needs this and Piers needs that. He did not respond a great deal to me but I imagined this was because he was so young and food from his mother's breast was his priority. I would hold him but he always wanted to go back to her. He seemed little to do with me and I found being woken up in the middle of the night every few hours by a crying infant demanding food very wearing, particularly as it was making me extremely tired at work. I began to wonder exactly how I fitted into their lives, apart from providing the money. She seemed to be creating her dream world but what about my needs? I like the country like most people but I did not want to spend my life in the back of beyond growing vegetables and weeding flower beds. It might seem idyllic in the height of summer but I knew that when the cold draughts of winter came it would be a different matter. It was pleasant enough here now but I knew it would not suit me long-term.

Of course Alice and I had our good and bad moments like any other couple. The good was that she was very affectionate, cooked me nice meals and seemed quite contented with life. She was cheerful now that she had started drawing and painting again. She had abandoned abstracts and begun making lovely pencil drawings of Piers that even an ignoramus like me could see were superb. She had now moved on to oil paintings of him and also the local landscapes, which her agent was sure she could sell. The bad were the annoyances that caused friction between us. Now that she had started painting again she was so obsessed by it she did not tidy up the house very often. She used to leave her discarded clothes lying round the bedroom, which really irritated me. All right she did pick them up when I mentioned it but far worse were the soiled nappies she occasionally left in a heap on the bathroom floor. I hated the smell and could not understand why she did not put them in the nappy bin straight away. When I complained about this she said the bin was full, she had been busy and asked me why couldn't I empty it and put them in the bin if I was so offended by the smell? I supposed when she lived at home her mummy used to rush round after her all the time. When I unwisely said this she flew into a rage and countered by saying that as I never did any clearing up she had to do it all. This was true. On the other hand she was at home all the time and I had to work all day so as far as I could see she had plenty of spare time. Of course I said I would help but her untidiness really began to irritate me. I liked things to be put back in their place once they were finished with. I mentioned to her my Granny told me that if you did that it took no time at all and the place stayed tidy with very little effort. Alice just sniffed and told me I was a control freak. It was very frustrating.

She liked to have classical music playing while she painted. Now I quite liked listening to classical pieces from time to time, especially if they were lively and exciting. The music teacher at my school used to play us short pieces in lessons so I did pick up some

knowledge of music. But what Alice liked to listen to was often rather dreary and went on forever. To make matters worse, when she discovered a new piece she played it over and over again. One particular day when I came in from work she was painting and playing yet another grim somewhat bleak piece. All right I was in a bad mood and wanted to hear something a bit less depressing.
   "What's this?" I asked.
   "Shostakovich," she replied. "Do you like it?"
   I did not see why I had to pretend to like it when I did not.
   "I suppose it's perfect if you enjoy feeling suicidal," I snapped.
   "Well I love it," she snapped. "It's immense music. He's one of the greatest composers of the twentieth century. I studied it at school. You have to make an effort to understand music like that not just dismiss it."
   I suppose I asked for it but that really annoyed me. I wished that sometimes she would give it a rest and not shove her superior, private school education in my face. I did not really want a silly argument but somehow words came out of my mouth that I knew perfectly well were certain to make her really angry.
   "Give me the Rolling Stones any day," I said. "'I Can't get No Satisfaction' says far more to me than that dreary stuff."
   She looked furious. "What's that supposed to mean?" she demanded.
   "That's for you to decide."
   She turned away. "I give up," she said, throwing her paint brushes down and rushing into the kitchen. I let her go but I could hear her crying. I was angry too so I let her stew for a few minutes before following her. Tears were streaming down her face and, ludicrously, she was peeling potatoes. I felt a real heel. What I had said was quite unnecessary. We had different tastes, that's all.
   "I'm really sorry," I said.
   "It's not working is it?" she replied, sniffing.
   "It's just a little tiff," I said and put my arm round her.
   "You meant I can't give you any satisfaction. It was nothing to do with what music I like."

"What rubbish," I said. "I'd just like to hear something else from time to time. Anyway I adore you, you know that."

She pushed me away. "Leave me alone, I'm trying to cook supper," she said.

Fortunately, Piers woke up and started crying. This was something I usually found rather trying these days but on this occasion it was a welcome diversion. I picked him up and attempted to cuddle him but, as usual, he just reached out to go to her. Of course I apologised again later and put my ill temper down to an awful day at the college, the summer heat, sleepless nights and anything else I could think of. If required I can grovel with the best of them.

Seb seemed in a better mood next day so we decided to go to the Goddard Arms in the village for a pub lunch. It was very hot again. We sat down outside and Seb went to order the meal. When he came back from the bar he was accompanied by a burly, weathered man in his forties.

"This is George Dale," Seb said. "He knows your old lady."

"That's right," said George. "She's a herbalist, you know and makes and sells natural medicines and I'll tell you one thing - she knows more about children than any doctor. If your little one's sick go and see her, she'll know a remedy for sure. She has a cure for almost everything. They've had the knowledge in her family for hundreds of years. One of them was supposed to have been burned as a witch in the fifteenth century."

"That's terrible," I said.

"It was a long time ago," he went on. "They thought disease was the result of God's anger. It was punishment for sin. Healing was His forgiveness. Perhaps she tried to cure somebody, they died and she was blamed. The church liked to keep its hands on such matters and wasn't too keen on competition. How did you meet her?"

I told him about walking by the ruined cottages.

"Ellen Cooper was born and brought up there," George said. "At one time the cottages were used by farm workers but they had no electricity or gas so after the First World War they gradually fell into disuse. Ellen married Albert Cooper, who owned the farm as well as the land nearby and the cottages. He died ten years ago. But she's a remarkable woman, you know, she's known locally as the Wise Woman of Clyffe."

"Really?"

"In country areas like this, there's often been such a person - a wise man or a wise woman - it's traditional. She's often sought out when things go wrong in people's personal lives. She's a sort of alternative to the vicar or the social services. Ellen's a clever woman, intelligent and sensible. She also teaches the piano and singing."

"Perhaps she can teach Piers, one day," I said. "She told me he was a Chime Child."

George said he had never heard the term. "So I can't tell you anything about it," he went on, "but there's one thing you should understand about all these country sayings, though. People think they're just jolly little stories to frighten the children. But they've been around for centuries and there's a deep rooted basis of truth in most them. They wouldn't have persisted that long if there wasn't more to them than just simple stories."

With that George drained his glass and took his leave.

"I've got to get back to my boys," he said. He tickled Piers under the chin. "What a lovely baby, Alice. Incredible eyes! It's nice to see you again after all this time, Seb."

He left and Seb went to the bar to order lunch. When he returned I asked him how he knew George.

"I knew him a little at university. He was a mature student. After he left he joined the police on the fast track scheme."

"He's a policeman?"

"That's what I said. Although if he was fast tracked what he's doing out in the sticks I've no idea. He's just a police sergeant. I would have thought he should have made Inspector by now."

"Perhaps something went wrong."

"Probably."

After lunch we took Piers for a walk across the fields at the back of the village. A pair of skylarks rose into the sky and a kestrel circled overhead before dropping like a stone into the long grass. It was thrilling. We stopped at a stile and Seb climbed over taking Piers from me.

"Look at that, Piers," he said pointing out a V-shaped skein of geese crossing the pale blue late summer sky, honking as they went. Piers moved his wobbly head about. "He's watching them, Alice," Seb called out.

"I don't think so." I said. "He can probably hear them but he can't see anything that far away. He's too young to focus his eyes on anything at that distance,"

We walked on through the field and reached the track that led towards the White Horse. I suggested we went to look at the ruined cottages.

"I'd rather not today, darling," said Seb. "It's too hot and I'm feeling bushed - next time, eh?"

"I'm sure we could buy one of the old cottages very cheaply," I said. "It would be wonderful if we bought it soon. It could be ready for us by the time we have to move." Seb did not seem receptive to the idea.

"It's bound to need a lot doing to it," he objected. "It would be expensive. You'd probably need to have electricity, drains and all that sort of thing run out there, not to mention the expense of all the building work. It would cost a fortune."

"We could do a lot of it ourselves," I said. "That would save a great deal."

"DIY is not my strong point," he replied. "Somehow I can't see myself doing roofing and bricklaying. I'm sure the builders round here charge the earth but hey, there's an answer. We could always ask the little people, to help us."

"Very funny, I'm serious about this."

"I'm sorry," he said, "but the whole idea is bonkers. It's quite impractical. Another thing, I need to be on-line, you know that.

And I very much doubt I could get broadband out here without paying some exorbitant charge."

We walked along in silence for a short time. I was rather annoyed with him. I looked around at the glorious landscape, the early wheat ripening in the fields and the wild flowers growing in the hedgerows. All this he had dismissed because it lacked some electronic, man-made device he thought he could not live without. He had dismissed the whole idea without any real thought for me. Of course I always knew at heart he was an urban creature, only really comfortable in towns and cities, and yet I thought I could convince him if I only I could find the right place. How foolish of me! It was clear that when Mark returned Seb would want to move back into a town.

In spite of this, I persisted with my dream of living somewhere like this and during the next couple of months I started to look in estate agents windows in Wootton Bassett to get some idea of the price of local property. The type of house or cottage I wanted was rare and many were rather expensive. Disappointed, I went into a book shop and started looking at the remaindered books. Among them was a dictionary of ancient superstitions. I quickly looked up the entry for Chime Child. It confirmed what Ellen Cooper had said about the time of birth and added that such a child would love and control all animals, have knowledge of herbs and a way of healing others, have immunity from ill-wishers and the power to see spirits. I told Seb when I returned to the cottage. His rationale was not able to cope with it. He just used it to rubbish Ellen.

"I kept telling you she's a witch," he said triumphantly. "You don't believe in that nonsense, do you?"

"Of course not," I replied, "but I think the idea is charming."

I made several trips to the ruined cottage and each time I went the more I could see the possibilities. It had its own water and electricity could be run up from the farm which was only a couple of hundred yards away. Access for cars might be a problem but there was a concrete track along the foot of the valley to the farm and just before the gate you could drive up the side of a field and park close by the cottage. It was in a better state than I first thought and I decided it might not cost too much to repair. If Seb really was useless at building work then I reckoned that I could do much of it myself. The view from the cottage was partly hidden by saplings and bushes, but when they were cleared I saw that we would have the magnificent sight of the Marlborough Plain. I called in on Ellen Cooper several times and found I liked her more and more. She told me she owned the cottage and might consider selling it to the right person. I decided to redouble my efforts to convince Seb. I was sure he would come round in the end.

FOUR

Alice seemed to become less moody as Piers started to grow and put on weight. I suppose the whole business of feeding and caring for a baby puts an enormous strain on the female body and she must have been exhausted much of the time. Her painting was going well although how she found the time and energy I have no idea.

Her parents came down to visit in September. I had to work that day and even though I was late back they were still there when I returned. I rather liked her mother who, unsurprisingly, looked like a care-worn version of Alice. I say unsurprising because Alice was quite unlike her father. He was a domineering, powerfully built man in his fifties with big shoulders who looked like a former test match fast bowler specialising in bouncers. He monopolised the conversation and I almost felt obliged to call him 'sir'. I first met him when I went to see them with Alice so that she could tell them she was pregnant. Her mother was nice about it and said she knew these things happened and that she was happy for us. He looked terrifyingly angry, hardly said a word to either of us and when we left I thought I was lucky to escape without a ball crashing in to my ribs.

They first came to see Piers just after he was born and her father hardly addressed a word to me. He took little notice of the baby, as if he was embarrassed by the whole thing, but he was very tender with Alice. She was obviously his little princess and I was the common working-class swine who had taken advantage of her. On this latest visit, however, he seemed delighted with his new grandchild even gingerly holding him for a minute before giving him back. Finally, he took me into the garden saying he would like to have a chat. It did not take a genius to work out what he wanted.

"We are a respectable family," he informed me, "and I do not approve of living in sin."

"Living in sin?" I replied in astonishment. I wondered what century he was living in.

"Alice has told her mother that she wants to marry you," he went on. You could see he was thinking 'God knows why!' I was clearly not what he had in mind for his son-in-law. "Are you two going to get married or not?" he asked.

"Not at the moment," I replied, equally direct.

"Why not?"

I muttered something about it being my business, and he shook his head.

"I am delighted to have a grandson," he said. "That said, I won't pretend I'm pleased by the way it's happened. In my days you got married before having a child. The boy will need a proper family set up."

"We are a proper family," I protested. "Not being married makes no difference to that."

"In my book it does. Where's your commitment? You could walk out tomorrow. There's nothing to stop you. What guarantee does Alice have about that? You've taken no marriage vows. How can she be sure that you won't take up with some other woman in a few years?"

It was a very offensive thing to say but I kept my cool. He was the product of his class and he could not help his perception that it was the natural order for him to pronounce on everything and be unarguably right. But I was not going to let it pass.

"Do you seriously think a piece of paper and a few easily spoken words in a church would make any difference to that?" I asked. "Thousands of couples live like we do."

"Call me old fashioned if you like," he replied, "but I don't approve of it. Can you give me your word that you'll never be unfaithful?"

"Can anyone say never?" I countered.

"This isn't a student debate. You know exactly what I mean."

"What do you take me for?" I replied. "It's my business."

"Of course it is," he replied. "But it's mine as well. She's my only daughter and I don't want to see her hurt."

"I quite understand that but you needn't worry," I replied. "She'll be well cared for by me."

"So why not get married?"

"I don't see the point. We're happy as we are."

"You would do better with allowances and tax, if you were married," he said.

Alice had told me he was an expert on tax avoidance, net asset values, returns on investments and all that sort of thing.

"We get by," I said.

"May be," he replied. "How much do you earn?"

"We get by," I repeated.

"Fair enough," he said. "None of my business, I understand. It's nice here, and Alice tells me that you have it for a year. I don't wish to intrude on the idyllic existence you both have, but it will come to an end before you know it and after that what then? You won't want to rent some grubby little house in Swindon, will you?"

"I'm not sure what you're getting at."

"I'm sorry, young man, but I'm going to cut to the chase. You obviously don't have two beans to rub together. You need thousands these days to even get on the property ladder. Now Alice's mother and I have discussed this and we will help you with a deposit if you wish. But we'd like to see you married. Naturally it is your decision."

"I'm not sure what you are driving at?"

"It's simple enough. I'll give you the money if you two get married."

I knew he was trying to help but I was angry at his overbearing and condescending attitude.

"And if I don't want your money?"

"Well, it's up to you," he said. "For Alice's sake I will ignore what you just said. I think I've made you a generous offer."

"I'm sorry I didn't mean to be rude and it's very kind of you," I replied through clenched teeth. "I really appreciate it and I'll discuss it with Alice later."

"You do that," he said coldly and strode back into the house. What a cheek! He clearly thought I was a loser and that he could push me into agreeing to anything he wanted just by throwing money at me. I sat down on the garden bench. Yes the deposit he was offering would solve a lot of problems but I objected to being forced into a second marriage. I suppose I could tell him that I was terribly sorry but unfortunately I was not available to walk down the aisle. It would amuse me to cause him a few apoplectic moments in the perfectly ordered pattern of his life. Pressure, why was there always pressure on me? I knew perfectly well Alice wanted us to get married and now here was her obnoxious father sticking his oar in. I had managed to survive at the college so far by persuading the few colleagues whom I had told, that it was in no one's interest for the authorities to know about Alice and I living together. I knew this situation would not last forever and once news reached the college management about why Alice had suddenly quit her course, I was certain to be told to look for another job. What then? A year ago I was in control of my life but now I was everyone's puppet to jerk around. I felt like getting into my car right then, driving away and leaving them all to it.

"They're going," Alice called out. I went to the gate with them and observed the conventions, kissing Alice's mother goodbye and coldly shaking her father's hand. Their large new Mercedes was parked alongside my ancient, rusting Beetle. No wonder he obviously thought I was a waste of space. As they left he wound down the window and, looking at my old heap, said with a superior smile: "I used to have one of those when we first married. Great little cars!" He obviously thought mine was the same age. It probably was.

However, it was clear I had to get on with divorce proceedings and a few days later, I rang Jackie. She had agreed we should talk. I was not teaching that afternoon, so I made some excuse to Alice about working late and met Jackie at her parents' house. They had gone on holiday and so Jackie was alone. She greeted me warmly with a surprisingly lingering kiss that was quite different from the way she used to embrace me. She had obviously learned something in the intervening years. Mind you, I did not mind. But why do such a thing? There was nothing between us anymore. It must be one of her little games, I thought, not a little wearily. She made me some tea and we sat down in a pleasant conservatory which overlooked the garden. It was time to get down to business.

"It's been over eight years since we split," I said.

"I suppose it has."

"We both need to move on, don't you think? We should get a divorce and sort things out."

"I suppose so."

"Well, surely, in all that time you must have met someone else."

"True, but there's no one at the moment. I don't suppose you've been a saint either."

"I can't deny it," I said.

"Have you met someone special, then?" she asked with an innocent smile.

It might have been simpler to tell her the truth right then but I did not. I just shook my head.

"Well, what's the hurry?" she asked.

"No hurry, but I should have thought that anyone as attractive as you would have no problems snaring some unsuspecting victim?"

She laughed and made some non-committal remark. Though an open window I heard children's voices coming from the garden. I could see two boys playing cricket. They were laughing, shouting and really enjoying themselves. I assumed they must belong to the neighbour.

"You were saying?"

"Yes, I met a few guys over there but I suppose in Ireland being married was a bit of a hindrance."

"So you would be happy if I contacted a solicitor and start the ball rolling?"

"Sure," she said. "Excuse me." She got up and went to the conservatory door and called out to the boys. "Mind Granddad's Dahlias, he'll be cross if you break them down."

I almost fell out of my seat. "Did I hear you say granddad?" I asked.

"You did. That's just what they call my father."

"I'm sorry," I replied, a little embarrassed.

"You were good at cricket weren't you?" she asked. "Go and show them how to bat or bowl or something and I'll make us some more tea."

I wandered out through the patio door and across to the boys. They stopped and stared at me so I introduced myself, telling them that I used to be a good cricketer when I was young.

"I'm Henry," said the bigger one, a neat, fair-haired boy who must have been ten or eleven.

"And you are?" I asked the other boy, who was smaller with untidy, brown curly hair.

"Sam," he replied shyly with a nervous smile.

"OK, Henry," I said. "Let's start with you and basic batting technique." I took the bat, showed him how to hold it correctly and play a defensive stroke. I lobbed the ball under arm at him but he made a real mess of it.

"No," I said, "not like that. Keep your left elbow up, the bat straight, step towards the line of the ball keeping your head over it and watch it carefully."

He soon got the idea and so I turned to Sam. He was also slow to grasp the idea so I seized the bat and by bending over him showed him exactly how to hold the bat, play a forward defensive stroke and extend it into a drive. To my surprise, the next ball I lobbed at him he drove into the shrubbery like a seasoned professional and looked really pleased. I rather liked him with his diffident smile. He seemed to be an unconfident child and lacked the self-assurance of Henry. He had a slight accent that I was unable to pin point. I thought it might be Canadian. I then showed them both how to bowl an off-break. My time at the Catholic boarding school was not entirely wasted. I thought how great it was going to be to do this with Piers in a few years' time. If I started to teach him the correct way to bat young enough he might even play for a county. I loved the idea of sitting on the boundary at Canterbury on a hot summer's day and watching him as he elegantly drove and cut his way to his first century. Of course it was a dream but doesn't every significant achievement start with a dream?

Eventually, the neighbour called to the boys and they both disappeared next door. I had enjoyed teaching them and for that matter simply chatting to them as well. As I watched them go I made a decision. I would put my doubts aside, get a divorce quickly, definitely marry Alice as soon as I could and accept her father's offer. I would have a son or a daughter and the family of my own that I used to dream about when I was a child. I returned to the house feeling really buoyed up about coming to the right decision at last. Jackie was sitting down in front of a tray with a fresh pot of tea on it. She had been watching me. She found it amusing, for some reason. I never could work her out.

"Enjoy yourself?" she asked.

"Nice boys," I said.

"They are," she replied. "But what they get up to around here, the pair of them, well...." She laughed and we chatted pleasantly and inconsequentially for a few minutes while I drank another cup of tea. However, she seemed a little distracted, as if her mind was on other things, so I decided it was time to go.

"You'll be hearing from my solicitor," I joked as I stood up.

She looked at me in a rather odd way and asked me what I thought of Sam.

"He seems a nice kid," I replied, wondering why she had asked. She looked straight at me and calmly spoke the four words that were to utterly change my life.

"Sam is your son," she said.

My first reaction was complete shock and disbelief. I did not want it to be true, ergo it could not be.

"What are you talking about?" I snapped. "You said they were the neighbour's children."

"No, I don't think I did say that. Henry lives next door but Sam is your son. He lives here with me. I was waiting for the right moment to tell you. I just decided there wasn't one."

"You really expect me to believe you?" I snapped. "I wondered why you were being so nice to me. You've gone and had a kid by some damned Irishman. He's chucked you and you want me to be a meal ticket."

"Don't be absurd," she replied. "Whether you like it or not he's your son. In any case I'm sure I earn far more than you."

"I'm not listening to any more of this rubbish. I'm going." I stood up but she grabbed my arm so I sat down again.

"Seb! Just take it easy," she said. "You've got it completely wrong. When I wrote to you originally it's true I was thinking about a divorce, but when we met up I actually enjoyed seeing you again. You were very charming, as you always were, so afterwards because Sam is your son I wondered whether you might like to give it another try."

"You've got to be kidding! Have you gone mad? You must live in some sort of dream world."

"Seb," she replied. "Just take a deep breath, calm down and listen to me. I will tell you exactly what happened. To begin with, I didn't know I was pregnant when I left you."

I snorted: "But we hardly had sex, just some rather unsatisfactory, hardly earth moving attempts which didn't really work. If you remember that was the problem."

"Yes it was - it frightened me. It hurt and I didn't like the sweaty closeness of it. I was young and very inexperienced. I just couldn't relax and dreaded it. Can't you understand that?"

"Why didn't you say something?"

"You were my first and I couldn't talk about things like that to anybody."

"It was not the experience of a life time for me either."

"Nevertheless, I must have been pregnant when I walked out but I had no idea. I didn't even understand what was happening when I started to miss my periods."

My world was making less and less sense. Maybe I was in some a crazy nightmare and I would wake up any minute. At one point I even had to suppress a laugh as I recalled Mark's comment that all I had to do was wave my dick around for a girl to become pregnant. I turned my head away so Jackie could not see. Fortunately she did not realise as she went relentlessly on:

"As you know, I went to Ireland soon after I left you and I was not sure about it until I'd been there for a few weeks. I was unable to bring myself to contact you and decided I would go ahead on my own."

"I'm sorry I just don't believe you," I hissed.

"Seb just listen to me," she pleaded. "How old do you think Sam is?"

"I haven't the faintest idea."

She pointed towards the sideboard. On it were some cards with large eights written on them.

"Sam was eight in May," she said.

"That does not prove anything,"

"You work it out. Just look at the dates."

I did not bother. "So this rubbish about the boy is the real reason you contacted me again, then?"

"Not at first. I wanted to see you."

"Oh come on!"

"Look I know this must have come as a shock to you. It was my fault we split up and I am truly sorry for that. But it's not rubbish. Sam's grown up over there but he has no idea who his father is. Think about it. You're his Dad. He really needs you to guide him, to be someone he can look up to, someone who'll help him. I've been ringing you because I thought it was time for him to meet you."

"Why?"

She stared at me in amazement. "Why do you think?" She sounded exasperated. "I told you. He really needs his father."

"Why isn't Sam here to meet me right now? Why has he gone next door?"

"It's too soon to tell him and he was invited for a sleepover. Sam's been so looking forward to it. I didn't want to disappoint him. He's made friends with Henry who goes to a different school and hasn't been around. It was all arranged a couple of weeks ago. Be reasonable, I didn't know you were coming here till this morning."

"And a sleepover is more important than meeting his supposed father?"

"Of course not. Don't you see meeting him must be very carefully handled? I didn't know how you would react. I thought it better to take things slowly. Sam's a lovely boy, but he can be a bit difficult."

I really was incredulous and could not think what to say.

"Doesn't having a son mean something to you?" she asked. I was amazed at her nerve.

"You vanish for nine years," I said. "I do not hear a whisper from you. You keep me out of his life all that time and now you blithely tell me he needs a father. What do you expect me to do?"

"I don't know," she replied. "You liked him didn't you? You seem to get on well with him out there in the garden. I suppose the least I want is for you to see him from time to time, nothing else. Is that too much to ask?"

"I'm not sure. I think it is, probably."

"Why? What's the problem?"

The problem was not a question I could or even wanted to answer at that moment was it?

"I just need to think," I replied.

It would hardly help to say to her 'oh, by the way, I already have a son and a family of my own now.' I could just imagine what she would say. I might tell her eventually but I was not going to let Jackie and this boy ruin my life. It was time to go. I vaguely heard her wittering on about knowing that it had been a shock and how she quite understood, but all I felt was that I wanted to escape fast. I agreed to ring her in a few days but had no intention of doing so. As for obtaining a divorce, if what she said was true, the situation was becoming rather complicated.

To make matters worse, at the college next day I received a summons from the Rector. "Your private life was your own business, of course," he told me, and he congratulated me on my new baby and proceeded to spell out my future as he saw it.

"The mother of your child was a student here, I've been told," he said. "I know these things happen from time to time. That's human nature and I understand you're doing the decent thing and all that, but it's not good for the reputation of the college is it? You had a duty of care and you failed in that respect. As it happens, we feel it is time to freshen up the college with some new blood. Consequently I will be making some departmental changes next year and, in view of everything, it might be a good idea if you started looking for another job elsewhere fairly soon. You need to move on, perhaps into industry. You're a brilliant man in your own field and I would have no hesitation in recommending you for a research post in a private company. If you do get something and wish to leave quickly, we can negotiate an end to your contract and naturally I will give you good references for that but I'm afraid because of your situation I could not do so for another teaching post. You do understand, don't you?"

I knew exactly what he meant. This way there would be no fuss and it could all be swept under the carpet. No scandal and good for the college. What on earth would I tell Alice?

FIVE

Seb was grumpy and pre-occupied in the days following my parents' visit but when I reproached him for being irritable he quickly apologised and was very nice to me. He was clearly making a real effort to improve our relationship and often brought me little presents when he came back from work. I was reasonably happy but it was at this time that I first became a little concerned about Piers' sight. By this age he should have been following things with his eyes. He would look at me when I spoke to him but he seemed to switch off when I pointed at things around us and said their name. I also began to worry that he might have learning difficulties. I would wave at him across the room but he took no notice until I spoke. Then he would laugh and chortle away. I tried to discuss it with Seb but he told me not to worry so much. He was sure Piers was fine. I mentioned it to our elderly GP, Dr Jacobs, and he was also rather dismissive.

"He'll be fine," he said. "He's quite normal. Children's vision is always blurred to start with. They do not see properly, that is like we do, until roughly the age of two. You have nothing to worry about."

That evening I discussed it with Seb. "I think I might take him to see Ellen Cooper," I said. I knew it was risky to tell him but I wanted him to understand that Ellen was a worthwhile person who knew a lot about children and who could help us.

"Of course I can't stop you," he replied. "But I shall be very upset if you do."

"Why? It can't do any harm."

"She just peddles a lot of mumbo jumbo. She'll probably want to bleed him with leeches or something. I don't want her anywhere near my child."

I was surprised he was so adamant and as a result I put off going to see her. A few weeks later I again took him to see Dr Jacobs. He seemed less sure that Piers was normal and decided it would do no harm for Piers to see an eye specialist. The Consultant, Mr Franklin, was a charming man and after the tests he told us he would talk to his colleagues and send the results to our doctor. Seb was working in Manchester when Dr Jacobs called me in to his surgery to hear the Consultant's report.

"Isn't the baby's father with you?" he asked.

"No, I'm sorry; he's away giving a lecture." I replied. "Is it that serious?"

"Well, yes, it could be. Mr Franklin thinks Piers does have a serious problem with his eyesight."

"What sort of problem? Will he have to wear glasses?"

"There's no easy way to put this. I'm sorry to have to tell you, and Mr Franklin is not yet entirely certain, but your baby may have a condition called Leber's Disease."

I stared uncomprehendingly at him. "What's that?" I asked. "I've never heard of it."

"Well, I've never come across it before in forty years of practice. It's a condition that affects the eyes, the retina to be precise. It's very difficult to diagnose with any certainty exactly what's wrong at this age as there are thirteen types of Leber's Disease. We'll have to do more tests as he grows. Essentially the light receptors in his retina have not developed normally. If the Consultant is correct, as he develops, he will have a little, rather poor eyesight to begin with but I'm afraid that in a few years, difficult to say how many, possibly his early teens or later, he will become totally blind."

"Oh no!" I felt sick and numb. "Are you sure?" I gasped.
"I'm afraid so."
"What's the cause? Is it a virus or something?" I asked.

"No, I'm afraid it's hereditary," he replied. He did not seem to notice how shocked I was and just carried on with what he must have thought was the good news.

"I'm pleased to say our tests show there is no problem with Piers apart from the Leber's. Consequently, with regard to him possibly being a little slow you should have no fear. In that respect he's developing quite normally."

"What do you mean exactly?"

"Many visually impaired children also have multiple handicaps these days such as deafness, learning difficulties, spasticity and problems like that. In some ways you're quite lucky."

Lucky! I could not grasp what I had just heard and I was horrified. At the same time, ludicrously, in a way it was a relief. At least he was not brain damaged. His behaviour made a sort of sense now. In a daze I heard the doctor telling me about all the wonderful provisions there were available now, good social workers who would help me and special schools and colleges where he can be trained in all sorts of skills. It's not just basket making and piano tuning these days.

I wept as I pushed the buggy all the way back to the cottage and when I went inside I locked and bolted the door, took him in my arms and held him very tightly. For once he slept quietly. At about four George Dale knocked on the door. He often popped in for a cup of tea and a chat about music or literature. He was very well read and I usually enjoyed talking to him but the idea of discussing the novel he was currently reading was the last thing I wanted to do. Seb had asked him to keep an eye on us while he was away but I sat there without moving until he went away. I cuddled Piers for at least two hours when I had to feed him. I did not bother to turn the lights on as darkness set in and about half seven there was another knock on the door and this time I unbolted it. George was standing there.

"I called in earlier," he said, "I thought you were in but you didn't answer so I was concerned."

"I must have fallen asleep," I told him. "He's been keeping me awake at night."

"Just making sure everything is OK," he said.

"That's very nice of you but I'm fine."

"You don't look as if you are."

I just managed a weak smile. I suppose I must have looked rather bedraggled. "I'm just a little tired," I said by way of explanation.

"How's your lovely little baby?" he asked. I just burst into tears.

"Hey, take it easy. There is something the matter, isn't there?" he murmured. I had to tell him.

"I've just been told he's going to go blind," I said.

"No! I don't believe it."

"I don't either," I said and explained what the doctor had told me.

"Poor little chap," he said, "how awful. Does Seb know?" I shook my head. "Is there anything I can do? Can I make you a cup of tea or something?" he asked.

"No thanks, I just need some time to work things out and get my head straight. It's been a bit of a shock."

"I'm sure it has."

I watched him go and regretted saying anything at all to him. He seemed a little embarrassed and it had not really helped. I closed the door and bolted it again. Not long afterwards the telephone rang. It was Seb. He seemed to have completely forgotten about the Consultant's report being due that day. He was full of enthusiasm about the course, his new friends and lectures he had given.

"I gave them a talk about cracking the Enigma code," he said. "It went down a bomb. They loved it. It is amazing how little this generation really knows about what went on in the Second World War."

"That's wonderful, I'm very happy for you," I said, but something in the tone of my voice warned him that his course and his new friends was not something I wanted to discuss right then.

"Look," he said, "I've been thinking about your idea about the cottage. It might not cost too much. I'd like to go and look at it when I get back."

I dumbly agreed.

"How's our baby?" he asked.

I had to tell him, I tried to tell him, but I could not. The words were still jammed in my throat so I told him about George calling instead.

"I reckon he fancies you," he said, laughing. "I'll have to watch him."

"Don't be ridiculous," I snapped.

"I'm not. I heard that he lives on his own with his two children. Apparently his wife left him several years ago. You're a very attractive woman. So why wouldn't he?"

"I wish you wouldn't say things like that. I don't like it."

"Just kidding," he replied. "I like him too and it was very nice of him. He was probably after a cuppa."

"I didn't offer him one. He was here for hardly more than a couple of minutes. He had to get back to feed his boys."

"I'm much more interested in my son," he replied. "How's Piers?"

'Tell him now!' I thought but the words were trapped in my pain and would not come out. "He's much the same," was all I could utter.

"Wonderful," he said and after a few inconsequential remarks rang off.

I spent the next few days trying to work out just how I would tell him and imagined what he would say. But when he finally returned I had not thought of any way that would not really upset him. He picked up Piers.

"Here's something to play with in the bath," he said, putting into his hand a yellow duck he had bought. Piers gurgled and laughed. Lunch was rather tense but he put this down to my lack of sleep while he was away. 'I could tell him now,' I thought, tell him the real reason why I had not slept. It was the perfect opportunity. It was simple enough - be straight forward. 'Piers is going blind you know. He's not mentally defective, though, the doctor told me, isn't that a relief? Like some coffee?' But not a word came out. I just nodded and started clearing the plates away. When I finished he suggested we go for a walk. We made our way up through the trees onto the top of the hill. I would tell him as we went along, it would be easy. The track had become narrow. Seb carried Piers on his back in a baby carrier and so they moved ahead. I could see his little head bobbing around. It was a glorious late autumn afternoon with the whole valley drenched in a warm soft light. The woods and fields glowed with muted colours and I was torn to pieces by the knowledge that my little boy would never see it. I wept silently and hung further behind. I could hear Seb talking to him about the birds and animals. We reached the white horse and Seb waited for me to catch up. He did not seem to notice my swollen eyes.

"Where's the cottage?" he asked.

"Down there, in that grove of trees."

"Hey," he said, finally looking at me. "What's the matter? Have you been crying?"

"Yes," I replied.

"What's the matter?"

I could only mutter incoherent excuses and say I was sorry to be such a misery.

"It's probably just a touch of the post natal depression," he said. Sensitivity was not his greatest attribute. "We had a discussion about it one evening. It's very common."

"You discussed me!"

"No, not really, just PND in general."

"Who with?"

"Just some colleagues,"

"Yes."

"Who exactly?"

"Peter Williams, you know, from Exeter. His wife suffered from it. Scott Collins, you've never met him, and Rachel Reed - she'd been through it herself after she unfortunately lost a child."

"Who's she? You haven't mentioned her before."

"No one special, she was another lecturer on the course. She once wrote an article about it for the Guardian women's page."

"You discussed me with her?"

"I told you, it was just a general discussion."

"Well if you thought that was the problem I don't see how you could have discussed it without bringing me into it."

"Well, all right I did talk to her in private, but what's wrong with that. It helped me understand."

"You understand nothing!" I snapped and started to walk on down the path to the woods. My anger began to subside and when we came to the ruined cottage I caught his arm.

"I'm sorry," I said.

He looked depressed. "It doesn't matter," he replied. I thought he would ask me what the problem was but he just stared at the cottage. "Is this it?" he asked. I nodded.

He told me it was crazy, hopelessly impractical, needed too much doing to it and we could not afford it. But it would be a wonderful place to make a home and we should seriously consider having a go.

"I want you to be happy," he said, putting Piers down on the ground and pulling me to him. I loved him deeply at that moment. I felt so secure in his arms. I was sure the moment to tell him had come. I glanced down at Piers. He seemed to be listening to something. A robin was only a foot or so way from the carrier. It was hopping around pecking at grubs.

"Look," I whispered.

The tiny bird flew on to a low branch close to Piers and let out a torrent of song. Piers laughed, started making cooing noises and tried to turn his head in the direction of the bird. To my astonishment it flew down and perched on the frame of the carrier just by his arm. It sang out noisily and Piers gurgled with pleasure.

"Amazing!" Seb whispered and pulled me closer. "It would be marvellous to bring up a child so close to nature."

The robin took off and flew high into the trees.

"You don't understand," I replied.

"Yes I do, it would be wonderful to bring him up here. I agree."

"Yes, it's essential but you don't understand why." Seb began to look rather irritated.

"Try me," he said.

"He can't see any of this."

"What do you mean?"

"He's going blind."

"Blind? Rubbish! Who told you that?"

"The doctor."

Seb looked at me as if I had gone mad. "That quack! He doesn't know what he's talking about." He bent down flicking his hand in front of the baby's face. Piers blinked. "Look, he's reacting. He must see something."

"Yes he has some sight now but he will eventually go blind."

"I don't believe it." Seb and waved his hand in front of Piers again and once more he blinked. "See, there you are. And he certainly saw that robin a few minutes ago."

I was suddenly filled with hope. I picked my baby up and stared into his eyes. They were still as beautiful as everyone said - clear, translucent and a dazzling blue. Perhaps the doctor was wrong after all. I felt completely confused.

"Come on, let's go," I said, unable to think.

"It's nonsense," said Seb. "I'm going to have a word with that damned doctor. How dare he upset you so much?"

When we got home he made me tell him again what the doctor and Consultant had said.

"Well I don't believe it. They must be wrong," he said.

"But his eyes don't follow anything. They should by this time."

"He's probably just thinking about something else. He looks at you when you feed him."

"Yes but by this age he should be following things further away."

"Perhaps he's just short sighted."

"I don't think so. The doctor was quite adamant."

Piers started crying loudly and flew into a rage. To say the least it was not helpful.

"I still do not believe it," replied Seb looking rather morosely at Piers. "But if he is going to go blind it's something we have to deal with."

Did he imagine I had not already thought about this for days?

Poor Alice. She was really distressed. Of course I soon realised that the doctors were right about Pier's blindness even if I did not want to admit it. I had been grasping at straws because it was a colossal shock to me as well. My first reaction was pity for him but then, quite unexpectedly and with an insidious insistence, feelings of revulsion slowly began to seep into my thoughts. At first I tried to suppress these appalling thoughts but once they were in my mind I could neither un-think them, deny them nor escape from them. What had this constantly crying almost sightless baby to do with me? I walked down the High Street in Waterbridge and all I could see were normal kids everywhere, with normal mums and normal dads. Why was Piers not like that? They would do the ordinary things with their children as they grew up, just as I had imagined I would. For me this would never be. Piers would have to be looked after all his life. I would have to live with the terrible burden, and deep within me I knew I did not want to do it. But I must whether I liked it or not. I tried desperately hard to put such negativity out of my mind and think positively and practically. How did one bring up a child who was going blind? What was it like to be blind? I had no idea. At college I tried shutting my eyes, taking some cautious steps and trying to imagine what it must be like but it was fairly useless. As soon as I moved I blundered into a chair. God help the little mite! I thought, and immediately felt overwhelming guilt about my unforgiveable thoughts. Added to this were the complicated feelings I had about Jackie's son. I did and I did not want to believe Sam was mine. I had liked him and he seemed intelligent and friendly and I was secretly very pleased about this. But the difficulties it made in my life did not bear thinking about. I wondered about asking for a DNA test but it did not require much thought to dismiss that idea. It would almost certainly confirm what she had said. The truth was not what I wanted to believe. The more I thought about it the more problematic the questions it raised. For a start, assuming Sam was my son, unlike Piers he was exactly what I thought my son would be like. How would I deal with that? Realistically, the best I could ever offer him was to be a visiting father, hardly satisfactory for either of us. Secondly, how would it affect my relationship with Piers and Alice? Clearly it would definitely not be helpful. Would it not be much better to keep my distance? What a mess!

Gradually a half acceptance of the situation, at least with Piers, seeped through me. His blindness was not his fault. How could I not feel sympathy and compassion for him? I tried very hard to do so but I did not. No matter how much I wanted to I was unable to escape from my darker thoughts about him. Of course I hid it all from Alice and outwardly maintained at least a semblance of resolve to deal with whatever problems would arise. I said nothing to my colleagues at work and maintained the happy daddy image. When we told her parents about Piers, her father became quite irrational and asked if my side of the family had a history of blindness. I suspected he was trying to prove that it could have nothing to do with his own pristine lineage.

I heard nothing from Jackie for a few weeks but one day she rang and said she had seen a solicitor and wanted to meet and discuss the divorce. She wanted to have lunch and asked could we meet somewhere near the college. Frankly, she was the last person I wanted anywhere near there, too many prying eyes, so I agreed to meet her in a pub I knew just outside East Grinstead. As I walked from my car I saw her sitting at a table in the garden. Next to her was Sam. Why was he here when we were supposed to be discussing divorce? She was up to something again. I was just about to make a rapid exit when she saw me and waved. So I had to join them and we ordered lunch. Sam remembered me from my visit and chatted to me in a friendly way. He was a likeable child who reminded me of the chorister Tristram. Neither Jackie nor I mentioned divorce in front of him but after the main meal was finished he went to the toilet and we were on our own.

"You two seem to get on very well," she observed.

"What have you told him about me?" I asked.

"Nothing as yet," she replied. "I said you were a friend. But I think he has to know the truth fairly soon, don't you?"

"I don't know. He must have asked you where his father was at some point?"

"I simply told him that his father and I had not got on and we both decided it was better if we split. He seemed to accept that. But he's going to ask me again before long and this time I will have to tell him about you."

"What about our divorce?" I asked.

"I have some papers in the car you need to take with you, look over and sign. I'll give you them when you go," she replied.

Sam returned and Jackie suggested he go and play in the children's area.

"I don't like playing by myself," he complained.

"I expect if you ask Seb nicely, he'll come with you," she said.

"Please Seb," he said tugging at my arm and fixing me with his large dark brown eyes which I noticed were just like mine. How could I say no?

First of all, he wanted me to push him on the swing. I said he could make it go perfectly well by himself but he insisted, saying I would make him go higher. Next he wanted me to watch him on a climbing frame. Once on it, he claimed he was stuck and needed help. I was fairly sure he wasn't but did not mind playing his game and lifting him down. He was indeed a friendly child and kept giving me big smiles. He asked me whether he could have an ice cream so I took him across to the bar and ordered one. Much as I was loath to admit it, I enjoyed being with him. He was a breath of normality in comparison with the highly tense atmosphere I was living in at home. When it was time to go he gave me a big hug and I agreed to meet them again in a few weeks. She gave me the envelope and I drove straight to the college and locked it in my desk draw without bothering to open it. It was certain to be full of legal stuff and probably demands for money. I was late and would read it tomorrow. Back at the cottage I tried to be as nice as I could to Alice and even cooked supper that evening. She was much more cheerful and was clearly feeling able to cope.

Next day I unlocked my drawer and took the envelope out. There were no divorce papers in it, just several childish drawings of cricket on which were written 'For Seb by Sam'. I stared at it initially in surprise then felt quite pleased. At least someone liked me. Would Piers grow up like that? I hoped so. If not, perhaps we could have another child, a daughter would be nice. Mark told me daughters always love their dads. Suddenly it dawned on me. Piers was likely to be the only child I could sensibly have with Alice. I had done some research on Leber's disease and, assuming Leber's disease was definitely the cause of his blindness, in all probability she was carrying a faulty gene. Consequently, the chances of having a normal baby with her were just twenty-five per cent. Could we take the very high risk of having another child who would go blind? It was out of the question. We could never have another child. Feeling shocked and saddened at this thought, I quickly put the drawing back in the envelope and locked it away again. Just why had Jackie sent it? I doubted it was accidental. Was she reminding me of what she claimed was my responsibility? I rang her at once and she apologised saying she had picked up the wrong envelope. She would post the legal papers to the college.

"No," I said. "I will collect them in a few days." I did not want to risk anyone here coming across them.

SIX

Seb's attitude seemed to be changing. In the months immediately after Piers was diagnosed as visually impaired he was very concerned and said he was determined to get the best possible treatment. I was pleased at his support then but now I was beginning to sense a kind of remoteness. More tests turned out to be inconclusive and the Consultant told us that for the moment he could not be a hundred per cent sure of his diagnosis. On the plus side he thought Piers could see something of what was close to him but his distant vision was almost non-existent. He told us that normal child development uses all the senses to understand and make sense of the world and what a child can see plays an enormous part in this. Consequently Piers needed to learn as much as he could before he completely lost his sight. So I took him out for long walks and, for example, even though he was just a few months old I pointed out trees and flowers, telling him what colours they were and making him smell and feel them. Seb showed little interest helping me do this and seemed to be lost in his own thoughts for much of the time. When I complained he apologised and put it down to worrying about his job situation.

    The support worker told me that blind people could tell a great deal about the world from their other senses, particularly hearing. It wasn't any better than the rest of us, it was just that they listened much more acutely. They could tell a lot about a person by the qualities in
the voice, whether you were friendly, whether you didn't like them, what sort of mood you were in and things like that. They could also tell a lot about their environment by the sounds they could hear, even from their own footsteps. We could all do it if we listened carefully. I was a little sceptical about this and tried walking along the road,

shutting my eyes and listening to the sounds made by my own shoes. I was surprised to discover I could tell when I was passing a brick wall, or a hedge, or a shop window just by the different sounds my footsteps made. A wall made a hard crisp sound from the slight echo, a hedge a rather dead and muffled sound and a plate glass window a kind of boing sound. Piers would soon learn this and I felt his future might not be so bleak after all. I told Seb when he came home but his one-time optimism was fast diminishing.

"Yes," he said, "but his life can never be normal whatever we do."

This negative attitude made me rather impatient and angry with him.

"Obviously, he will have to adapt," I said, "but I don't see why he shouldn't be able to do what everyone else does."

"But he won't be able to! His blindness will stop him. You must accept the fact that some things will not be possible."

"Obviously it will be more difficult for him, I agree, but I see no reason why he should just give up. Human beings can do amazing things. Why not Piers? I think he'll be able to do almost anything if he puts his mind to it. Other people have."

"Like who?"

"Homer."

"Homer?"

"You know – wrote The Iliad."

"Huh, of course I know that. That's typical of you. Anyone else would have said Stevie Wonder or Ray Charles but not you. You just come out with high-brow rubbish like that to show off your superior education."

I'm afraid I just laughed at that. "Don't be childish," I said. "I just remember how amazed we all were when our Classics teacher told us."

"You're living in a fantasy world," he snorted. "I very much doubt anyone knows for certain that Homer was blind in any case."

"It just shows what's possible. Don't you understand that?"

"No I don't. Homer was a genius. It's much more likely Piers will just be ordinary. We must accept that."

"Well I don't. What about Andrea Bocelli, then? He's a wonderful singer," I countered. "And George Shearing, the jazz pianist, was born totally blind. He went to a school for the blind and learned the piano there."

"You're being ridiculous, now."

"No I'm not. There have been plenty of successful musicians, composers even. Rodrigo, went blind when he was three. You would never believe it when you listen to his wonderfully evocative Guitar Concerto. It conjures up such extraordinarily atmospheric images of the Spanish landscape you would think he could see the snow-capped of the Sierra Nevada. Anything is possible. Piers doesn't have to end up in some menial job."

"All right," he replied. "There may be a few gifted blind people but, as in the rest of the population, they're extremely rare. The reality is that most blind people struggle to earn anything more than a bare living at whatever they do."

"But for all we know he might be also be a gifted child," I said.

"That junk the old witch told you? You really believe that? I can't imagine how an intelligent woman like you falls for such irrational rubbish."

"But being gifted does not have a rational explanation. Why can one child in a family be brilliant and another just average? Ellen is just as likely to be right as you are."

"That may be so but I hope he's not. I don't want my son to be a freak," he replied. "It's bad enough already."

"What do you mean?" I was horrified.

"Gifted children are nearly always freaks," he said. "Musical prodigies, mathematicians and chess prodigies, most of them usually grow up into real weirdos."

"That's just rubbish. Are you telling me that Shearing and Rodrigo were weirdos?" I snapped, determined not to be put down. "Well if he was to grow up like them, I'd love Piers to be a weirdo."

"We should come to terms with the reality not your fantasies. For a start, he's likely to have the utmost difficulty at an ordinary school. He'll almost certainly have to go to a special one."

"But things are changing fast these days. You know that better than me," I said. "Technology will be immensely different by the time he grows up. Who knows what advances will be made?"

"Human nature doesn't change though. He'll meet prejudice and ignorance whatever he does. I'm more worried about how he'll cope on his own. We won't be able to look after him for ever."

Although some of what he said was undoubtedly true I felt shocked and angry at his negative attitude.

"We are not sure what the cause is," I protested. "We don't know for absolute certainty it is Leber's disease. It might have been a virus."

"Nonsense!" he said. "Whatever the cause it's probably hereditary. The doctor told you that. Where did it come from? There's no blindness on my side of the family! Can you say the same for yours?"

"I don't know. How can you be so damned certain?" I retorted.

"Because I've looked into my family history, there's never been any blindness. I'm certain of that. It can only have come from you! Leber's disease is always passed on from the mother."

"So it's my fault, then."

"It certainly isn't mine."

The remark opened a chasm between us. I swung between guilt, rage, and hope that it would all come right in the end. We hardly spoke and when we did he bit my head off.

A few weeks later my parents came down to see me and dropped their little bombshell.

"Seb's not around is he?" my father said, almost as soon as they had walked through the door.

"No he's at work," I replied.

"Good, I'll take Piers for a little walk then, if you like." I stared at him in astonishment. It was most unlike him.

"Why don't we all go?" I suggested.

"Your mother's got something she wants to tell you," he said, looking cautiously at her. She nodded in agreement.

As I put Piers in the buggy and my father said they would be back in half an hour. I sat my mother down and made her a cup of tea. She looked a little uncomfortable and I could not imagine what it might be about.

"What's so delicate that he has to leave you to it?" I asked.

"You know your father. He never can face talking about personal things."

"So what is it then? Have you or has he got cancer or some other dreadful disease?"

"No, nothing like that," she replied. "I've never told you much about your grandmother, have I?"

"I do know she came to England in the twenties."

"That's right. She was actually a folk singer who fled from the Ukraine to escape communist persecution."

"I knew that."

"But what I haven't told you is that her brother was a member of the Kobzari."

"The what?"

"The Kobzari. They were travelling folk singers and musicians. They have made a living singing and playing musical instruments in the street for hundreds of years. It was part of a tradition in the Ukraine going back centuries. They formed guilds, had their own language and culture. The communists did not like that. Stalin had many of them arrested and shot for just being Kobzari."

"Really? How awful. What's this got to do with me?"

"The Kobzari were all blind."

"How extraordinary!"

"You had to be to belong to their street singers' guild. The point is your grandmother's brother was a member and he was blind. Blindness runs in the family."

"Oh my God! But Granny wasn't blind."

"No, that's right. She wasn't. But her mother was. I'm very sorry but I must have inherited the condition and passed it on to you.

I had no idea. I thought it was all right because I wasn't blind and you're not. I never dreamt your child would be blind. I'm so sorry. I feel responsible for Piers' blindness."

I felt quite sick. No wonder my father had left her to it. She was crying silently so I leant over and took hold of her hands.

"Don't worry, it's not that bad. None of us could have known," I said. "Even if I had I would have had him anyway. We all love Piers and he'll learn to cope."

"But I feel so terrible about it."

"Look Mum, you shouldn't. It can't be helped. Whatever we might wish it makes no difference to the way I feel about him. He's still my lovely little baby."

We were still holding hands when my father returned. He made no reference to it. I was not surprised. He simply could not cope with anything like that. I fed Piers and gave them some tea and sandwiches. Afterwards my father took me to one side.

"I thought we would have heard from you two about getting married by now," he said, as if he thought what my mother had just told me was nothing to do with him.

"What do you mean?" I asked.

He told me about his talk in the garden with Seb and his offer to give us the deposit on a house.

"Oh yes, that," I hastily said, making up some rubbish about not being able to decide where we wanted to live. Seb had never said a word about it.

"Have you made a decision?"

"We're still mulling it over," I replied.

"The offer will not be there for ever, and, while we are on the subject of where you will move to, it would be nice if you came and lived near us, so we can see more of Piers. You do still want to get married, I take it?"

"Of course."

I was furious with Seb. Not surprisingly, when he came back from college I really shouted at him. His reaction was to say that he did not want my father's damned money and he objected to my father thinking he could use it to force him to marry me.

"I've had enough of your interfering parents. I certainly don't want to live near them. If they lived at Land's End I'd move to John O'Groats. "I'm going to the pub," he snarled and stormed out of the house. I had not told him about my grandmother's family history and after that outburst I was not going to until we could talk about it rationally and that seemed a long way off. I knew exactly what he would say. The atmosphere between us was going from bad to worse.

Once I was in the snug bar of the Goddard Arms and sitting down with a pint, I calmed down a little and started to think things over. Of course I should have told Alice about her father's offer but his insistence that we should get married annoyed me and put me in a difficult situation. It meant that I would have to tell Alice about my first wife at the same time, and once she had got over the shock if she did not murder me at once, she would certainly be very angry. Not only that, it would enormously increase the pressure on me to get divorced and marry her, and I had begun to seriously have grave doubts about the wisdom of that. If I was honest with myself, I had always wondered whether we had too little in common in the first place to last the distance, let alone cope with the enormous stress caused by bringing up a handicapped child. I thought it was much more likely that it would end in going through another marriage breakdown and, joy, oh joy, a second divorce. She loved me, at least I think she did, but I was very unsure of my own feelings. We got on fairly well some of the time it is true, but would that always be enough? After this evening's contretemps I was even less sure. I sipped my pint gloomily and considered the whole picture. The tension between us was clearly becoming quite difficult. Worst of all, I still did not seem really to relate to the baby. I had imagined that would come with time but as yet there was little sign. He barely seemed to recognise me when I came in and constantly demanded all her attention. He was marginally better after he was fed although he usually fell asleep quickly. What sort of future did he really have I wondered? Alice's dreams of him being a great performer were sheer fantasy, and I thought the outlook for another career was not good. Even if he managed to get work when he grew up it was likely to be low paid. As well as that, my own prospects at the moment were nothing to look forward to. I could hang on at the college for a few more months but I would have to leave by the end of the summer term. I could not apply for a job in teaching and I had as yet made no attempt to find work in industry. I knew that was likely to be difficult as I had no experience outside university teaching. My future seemed to stretch out like infinite, dark space in front of me and I could see no answers, nothing but hopeless, insoluble problems. I heard the pub door open and glanced up. George Dale came in. He nodded, bought himself a pint and joined me.

"You must be in the doghouse," he said, "sitting alone staring into your beer."

"You're right about that. We just had a big argument."

"Well, I hope you didn't make the mistake of winning. You'll have to go to the chip shop for the rest of the week if you did."

"I'm not that silly."

"Your Alice is an attractive woman," he said. "But I bet she can certainly pin your ears back if she's provoked."

"You're not wrong about that."

"Just pick some wild flowers on the way back from here and give her a bunch. I used to do that. It never fails."

"You're a genius!"

"How's the baby?" he asked.

""Fine," I said. "He's growing fast. He has his moments."

He laughed. "They're OK at that age," he said. "But you wait till he starts growing up; you've really got something to look forward to then."

"What do you mean?"

"Mine are teenagers now, and that's bad enough," he said, "but I've never forgotten the terrible twos. The tantrums they had beggared belief. You would not believe a toddler could have such an iron will. I remember once we went to a department store in Swindon with my eldest son when he was that age and he refused to get out of the car. I tried to persuade him to no avail and he just dodged around the seats to try to stop me grabbing him. I got fed up with his messing around, picked him up and carried him into the store. He didn't stop screaming and crying so I sat down on a couch with him still howling, while my wife went and looked at furniture. He just lay rigid beside me for half an hour giving the whole store the full treatment. You'd have thought I'd beaten the living daylights out of him. Other parents with kids went by and stared at us. What's the matter? I was asked by a passing mother. It's the terrible twos, I explained. Terrible twos, the woman said. Mine is eight and she still lies down on the floor kicking and screaming if she can't get her own way!"

"You make bringing up kids sound so enticing."

"Don't worry," said George, "it gets even worse as they get older. Both of mine are little, well not so little, monsters now. They're either playing computer games all the time or they're outside quarrelling, causing ructions and annoying the neighbours. At least they would be if they didn't know I would come down on them like a ton of bricks. Actually, they're not bad lads, just got too much to say for themselves. They're hard to live with at the moment. They argue, argue, argue but I wouldn't be without them."

"You really know how to cheer somebody up," I said.

"Don't worry, it'll be great when they leave home, Seb. I can't wait." He roared with laughter at my expression of horror.

"You don't mean it, surely?" I asked.

"Of course not, I love 'em to bits - some of the time. By the way. I was so sorry to hear about the baby's sight problems, poor little mite."

I stared at him. I thought nobody in the village knew about Pier's blindness except the doctors. How did he know? Alice and I had decided to keep quiet about it for the moment but she must have told him. I would have to have a word with her when I got back.

"Thanks," I replied. "It's something we have to deal with."

"Sure. Like another?" he asked.

While he was at the bar my mobile rang. It was Rachel, whom I had met on the course. She now worked at the college and said she wanted to meet me next day for lunch in Waterbridge. When I asked was there any particular reason, she would not say, except that there was someone she wanted me to meet.

As I walked back to the cottage I went over the evening. It had started badly but somehow George Dale's account of the awfulness of bringing up children had, paradoxically, cheered me up. He wasn't such a bad bloke. However, it also made me ask myself what I really wanted from Alice and once again I felt I was not at all sure. I began to think of Sam and the straightforward relationship I seem to have begun with him. I could no longer pretend that he was not my son. All I had to do was go and see him from time to time. That was what Jackie wanted. No strings, nothing, just be a father to him. He would like it. I would like it and it would probably restore my sanity. The problem was how to juggle the ensuing complications. Perhaps I had to start with Alice, find the right moment and tell her. Yes, that was the way forward. So once more I resolved to put things right with her. And I would make sure we did the best we could for Piers. The poor little chap had a real struggle ahead of him in life and I would help him as much as I could. As I made my way out of Clyffe St Mary I did what George had suggested, picked a bunch of wild, and some not so wild, flowers from the hedgerows and gardens that I passed and presented Alice with them when I reached the cottage. She burst into tears and clung to me like a limpet.

"I'm sorry," she said. "I don't know what's the matter with me. It's just so hard when you're not here."

It was clearly not the moment to tell her about Sam and Jackie. As for Rachel's phone call, it would probably be wiser not to mention that either. She would only be jealous. I decided I might tell her before I left for work next morning. Then I remembered that George had asked me about Piers blindness and I stupidly mentioned it.

"I met George Dale in the pub," I said. "He knew about Piers being blind."

"Oh yes, I told him," she replied.

"I thought we'd agreed not to tell anyone just yet."

"Yes but he called in on the day I was told about it. I'd just seen the doctor and he could see I was very upset. He was very sympathetic. I'm sorry I couldn't keep it to myself."

"So he knew before me?"

"Yes but that's hardly my fault is it? You weren't here."

That remark annoyed me. "I should have been the first person you discussed it with."

"You were away in Manchester," she replied. "You didn't even remember the doctor's appointment when you rang up. I was terribly upset and I had to tell someone."

I had become irrationally angry – the effect of the alcohol I had consumed, I suppose - and I just blundered on: "You did not bother to mention it to me for days," I shouted. "How do you think that makes me feel?"

"You should have been here. Don't try and put it on me! I didn't mean to tell him then, it just slipped out. What does it matter after all this time? Why are you so angry? I hate it when you shout."

"I'm not angry with you, just disappointed."

"Don't be so silly. Anyone would think you're jealous."

"Jealous? Huh! He's always sniffing around, you've got to admit it – all those cosy chats you two have when he pops in. What's that about?"

"Don't be ridiculous. You asked him to keep an eye on us."

"Yes, well so long as that's all it is…."

I had begun to feel a total idiot. I knew perfectly well there was nothing in what I was saying yet I could not retreat without losing face. I must have looked a bit foolish or something for she burst out laughing and I found myself smiling sheepishly in response.

"Sorry," I muttered, looking at the floor.

"You're just like a child," she said. "Come on let's put today behind us. You still love me don't you?"

She grabbed me by the hand, kissed me with some passion and dragged me up stairs to the bed. Perhaps it was the strain of the whole evening or the effect of three pints of special but it was a mistake. Our attempts at love making ended in dismal failure. I lay there for an hour feeling quite depressed as she told me it did not matter, that it happened to everyone from time to time. But I knew it was my fault. The terrible truth was that deep down I suspected that I no longer wanted to make love to her. The magic had gone. Next morning neither of us mentioned it and she just gave me a chaste peck on the cheek when I left for work.

When I arrived at the restaurant Rachel was sitting with a tanned, extremely good looking man in his late thirties.

"This is Carl Neumann," she said. "He's from the University of San Jose in California."

"Sebastian Winter, pleased to meet you," I said, formally shaking his hand.

After we had ordered, he said he had to use the bathroom and left the table.

"Who's he?" I quickly asked.

"He's recruiting new staff for a research project at San Jose University. He came into the college yesterday and I was asked to show him around. He said he was particularly interested in new technology and I mentioned your brilliant lecture on the course about the work done at Bletchley Park during the war so he said he would like to meet you."

"With what in mind?"

"I'm not sure. I think he might offer you a job. He's looking for visiting lecturers."

"I see. But I couldn't go over there just at the moment, could I?"

"Why not?"

"You know why."

"You could take them both with you."

"I don't think so. Alice wouldn't go anyway."

The waiter arrived with the first course and Carl returned to the table.

"Has Rachel told you why I'm here?" he asked.

I nodded. "She mentioned something about you recruiting for the University of San Jose."

"That's right. Did she tell you what the job description was, exactly?"

"No."

"As you probably know, San Jose is right in the middle of Silicon Valley in California. I work for a software company called Gemina and at the University we have something called the Zuckerman Foundation that funds international appointments. I happen to know that Professor Zuckerman is fascinated by the breaking of German wartime codes by British mathematicians. In fact he named his software company Gemina, which you have probably already worked out, is an anagram of enigma. Rachel tells me you gave a brilliant and fascinating lecture about it recently."

"It's been a hobby of mine for a long time."

"I would like to sit in on one of your lectures and talk to your students. Would you have any objections?"

"With what in mind?"

"Well the Zuckerman Foundation wants to fund a visiting lecturer at the University of San Jose in the Department of Computer Science. I understand you're an expert in computer operating systems."

"I did my thesis on Windows and Apple operating systems."

"Great. You could be just the person I am looking for. Mr Zuckerman wants to start a project to develop a new one. The visiting lecturer post is part time, consequently he would also like whoever we appoint to be part of the research team in Gemina. Rachel told me you got a First at London University so your record and your qualifications sound ideal. Frankly, on that alone I would put you top of my list at the moment, but it would be nice to see you in action."

"That's fine by me. Come into the college tomorrow morning. I'm talking about the work done by Alan Turing and how it's still relevant."

"I'll be there."

Carl appeared at the appointed time and I spoke for an hour about Turing's work. As I had given the lecture before I knew both how to make the students laugh and also understand the importance of the great man's work.

"That was superb," Carl told me afterwards. "The job is yours if you want it."

"I'm bowled over."

"And your pay will be commensurate with the post."

"How much?"

"I like that," he said with a smile, "direct and to the point. You would work for Gemina and be paid by them both for the research and the lectures. You would be required to deliver a couple of lectures a week and the rest of the time would be spent on research. Let's say that the salary is negotiable but likely to be at least twice what you must get here."

"It sounds fantastic," I replied. "Of course I would have to talk it over with my partner."

"Naturally, just let me know fairly soon. I can add one more carrot. You would also be appointed Assistant Professor in the Faculty and the initial contract would be for a year. After that it would be down to you."

His phone rang so he stepped away from us to answer it and I took the opportunity to ask Rachel what she thought.

"Changing your mind now?" she asked, mocking me.

"Well Alice might not like the idea to begin with but it does seem too good to turn down and the work sounds fascinating."

"Nothing to do with doubling your money, then?"

"Of course it is. But Assistant Professor as well? How could I say no?"

Carl came back and told me that he had spoken to the Zuckerman Foundation and they were interested but I would have to let them know before too long. Life is strange. Not long ago I was told I was a naughty boy and not wanted. Now I was being offered a highly-paid job. There was a mirthful irony about it.

That evening when I got home I was feeling very excited about the job offer and the prospect of going to America. However, Alice appeared to be rather depressed again so I did not tell her at once. She hardly said a word at supper.

"What's the matter, darling?" I asked, as tenderly as I could.

"It's my painting. I haven't been able to paint at all today."

"Why?"

"Because it's almost impossible to think at the moment. Piers gets into terrible paddies and cries and cries and I don't know what to do. He only shuts up when I feed him and when he falls asleep. And when he does, I'm so tired I fall asleep as well."

I tried to be sympathetic. "I am sure it's normal," I said. "It will pass in time."

"I don't sleep at night," she went on, "and even if I do drop off, he starts crying again and wakes me up five minutes later."

"It will pass," I insisted. "It won't be long before he gets past this stage."

"Will it really?" she snapped. "How do you know? You're hardly here. You won't understand. I can't talk about it."

"I'm sure I will but you have to tell me."

"You won't."

"Try me. I'm a good listener."

She thought for a good minute and then raised her tearful eyes. "When I look at him I just feel so guilty," she said. "He's going to go blind and it's my fault and it always will be. I created a child who was flawed. And because of that he will suffer a great deal. I'm to blame. Try living with that!"

I tried to comfort her but her mood lasted for a couple of hours. Later she seemed to brighten up, told me I was so kind to her and apologised for her bad moods. It seemed the right time to tell her my good news but as usual my timing was execrable.

"Well perhaps this will cheer you up," I said. "We're going to America. I've been offered a brilliant job in a software company in California."

She looked unimpressed. "It's out of the question," she said tersely.

"It's the answer," I urged. "With the money I'll earn we can buy the best treatment for him over there and maybe get enough together to buy a house. Property is much cheaper in the States."

"Yes but medical treatment is horrendously expensive over there," she replied. "Unless you have costly insurance you don't get any treatment unless you pay for it and you won't be able to insure Piers with a condition like his."

We argued for some time before she stomped off to bed claiming she had a headache and nothing resolved. At breakfast next day we barely spoke and when I came home in the evening the argument was repeated but this time she added that she simply had no desire to go to America. It was not where she wanted to live.

Her mood persisted for the whole of Sunday and even when we took Piers for a walk it did not help. He cried and screamed with rage at God knows what. His dreadful tantrums were really getting me down. I started to wonder what sort of monster we had brought into the world. He was ruining her life and my life for that matter. I could see that it would be impossible for me to take the job and cope with all this over there and it made me extremely fed up. I thought about the family life I had always yearned for and once imagined might be possible with Alice and Piers. It was clearly never going to be. I felt very bitter. It was obvious we were drifting apart and I seemed unable to prevent it.

That night was particularly difficult. I had hardly been in the bed a few minutes when just as I was drifting off to sleep he started crying.

"I'll go and see him," Alice muttered. She seemed to quieten him down quickly and soon returned to the bed, which of course also disturbed me. I lay awake in silence for a while and then went back to sleep only to be woken once more by his bawling. I hardly came to at all this time and I felt the bed shift and creak as she got up. It did not seem to last long before I became aware of his crying yet again. I tried to shut it out but this time I felt Alice shake me.

"It's your turn," she said.

"You don't have to be so rough," I snapped.

"Well you wouldn't wake up. I must get some sleep. I've got up to him four times already tonight while you've been snoring your head off."

"What's the time then?"

"Half past three."

"Hell, is it? I've got to give a lecture tomorrow. How am I supposed to do that if I'm half asleep? Can't you do it?"

"Well I haven't had any sleep at all yet. I can't cope. You have to take your turn."

"He's only trying it on. He just wants you to cuddle him. All babies do this. We have to ignore him or he'll do this every night. He'll soon drop off."

"No he's not, he's just hungry. Babies demand food when they need it even if it's inconvenient."

"OK, OK I'll put some gin in his milk. That should keep him quiet for the rest of the night!"

"No you bloody well won't," she screamed.

"It was just a joke. What's the matter with you? Have you lost your sense of humour? Of course I wouldn't do that. What do you take me for?"

"Just get up and go and feed him. There's a bottle by the cot."

I staggered sleepily into the other bedroom. Piers was laying there, his tiny face bright red and screwed up with rage. I picked him up and gave him the bottle which he noisily sucked. After a short time he seemed satisfied so I put him back and returned to the bed. Alice was sleeping heavily so I carefully got back in, trying not to disturb her. I had scarcely settled down when he started crying again. I ignored it and tried to get to sleep. I heard Alice get up and I pulled the duvet over my head. Ten minutes later he was silent and she returned. I was nearly asleep but she shook me and told me off.

"You didn't wind him," she snapped. "Of course he won't sleep if you don't do that."

"How am I supposed to know that?" I demanded.

"It's basic child care," she retorted.

"Well it's your job to do things like that not mine. I have to work hard all day to earn the money we need. You just swan around at home playing at being a great artist and bringing up the baby."

"Bringing up a child is just as hard. It's not my fault. Don't shout at me."

Piers must have been disturbed by the noise and he started crying again. I looked at her expectantly but she did not move. Cursing I got up, went into his room, picked him up and, I'm not proud of this, but I really shouted at him.

"Just shut up, you little bugger! Just shut up!"

Of course he cried all the more and Alice came rushing in.

"Give him to me!" she screamed and pulled him out of my hands. "You can't treat a baby like that!"

"I can't stand this," I said. "You're spoiling him."

"Don't be absurd. If you don't want to help, for God's sake go back to bed and leave him to me."

After Piers quietened down I heard her go down stairs and when I awoke in the morning she was not lying next to me.

I dozed in the arm chair until dawn cuddling Piers. When Seb saw us he repeated his accusation that I was spoiling the baby and we had another row. He went off to work in a sulk, and I spent a long time going over what had happened in my life since I had met him. I oscillated between thinking what a terrible mistake I had made and feeling appalled that I should have such dreadful thoughts about the man I fell in love with. Last night had been difficult for both of us and in the cold light of day it seemed ludicrous that we shouted at each other over the baby crying. I was upset at what he had said about me playing at being an artist, but he had apologised for that and said it was due to his lack of sleep. That was rich considering I was the one who had to get up at least eight times while he just slept on mostly oblivious of the crying. In spite of the quarrels I still loved him. If we could only get through this difficult patch, I told myself, it would be all right. In between I felt a confused anger and guilt about everything from my baby's future to stopping Seb going to America. He clearly wanted to take the job and probably needed to do so. I understood that but I was convinced taking a blind child over there would be crazy.

Later, when he came back from work he returned to the subject of his job offer and in the end I told him he could go on his own if he wanted to but I was staying here. Of course he said he would not dream of doing such a thing. The atmosphere, nevertheless, was tense and not helped by Piers once again crying a great deal. He was seven months old and it suddenly occurred to me he might be teething. I peered into his little mouth but I could see no sign of tiny teeth. I ran my fingers round his gums and could feel hard little lumps. His teeth were definitely starting to develop. I told Seb this but he was not interested. He suggested I talk to the health visitor about it and went back to watching a gruesome Scandinavian crime serial on television that featured the usual lunatic policewoman. It was late so I went to bed and left him to it. Next morning he seemed much more relaxed and told me he was going to tell them he would not be taking the job and would start to look for something in this country. He thought it was best for everyone if it was settled as soon as possible.

As I drove to work next day I reflected on the very difficult time we were going through and began to feel bitter about the cards fate dealt to me. Why did I go to the college art exhibition with Mark and meet her? I normally avoided such things. It was a chance decision with unforeseeable consequences that had damaged everyone. As for her pregnancy, I had welcomed it, OK may be not immediately, but I had begun to think that my life was about to change for the better. I started to look forward to having a proper family life. I even found myself gazing at other people's babies in the street and thinking that having one of my own would be fantastic. Up to then I had never considered children as being anything but a burden to be avoided at all costs. But, again, a chance encounter with that boy at the cathedral school had changed my thinking and I had begun to really look forward to having a son like that. I had done the decent thing and set up home with Alice, but look at us now. Our relationship was becoming increasingly fractious and I wondered where it was all going. Worse still I had begun to feel I could not cope with it. Alice seemed to be getting more neurotic by the day and it was not easy to see any sort of normal life ahead of us.

    I knew that she and Piers needed my support. Could I give it wholeheartedly over a long period? Well it was obvious I had little choice. Yet I viewed the prospect of bringing up our blind child with considerable qualms. I tried to think positively. It would be tough but it was something I must face head on. I resolved to put my doubts aside and deal with it. This thought made me feel a lot better for a short while yet my misgivings stubbornly remained. The most personally challenging problem was the knowledge that I had such angry feelings about Piers. I wanted to love him but I could not and I hated myself for it. It was not how I imagined having a baby son would be. I thought he would laugh and smile at me and look really pleased to see me when I came in but most of the time he did not seem to notice I was even there.

    I wondered if I should change my mind about the job, go to America by myself and put all this pain behind me, except that I knew I could not do such a thing. I had told Alice we would not go and was glad I had come to that decision. If she would not go, I could not. It was as simple as that. Or was it? I was acutely aware it was an opportunity only a fool would turn down and would secure our future financially. Perhaps I should try to stall Carl for a few more days and work on her. If I talked to her more about the benefits there might be for Piers, and how much better the extra income I could earn would be for all of us, she might come round.

As soon as I reached the college car park I tried to ring Carl on my mobile. However, he was not picking up his phone. I tried a number of times throughout the day without success and left a message for him to call me back. At about five o'clock my phone rang. But it was not Carl but Jackie.

"You have Tuesday afternoons free, don't you?" she asked.

I told her that was so and she asked me if I could come along to her parents' house tomorrow and sign the divorce papers. I agreed to go, thinking it would solve one of my problems. When I went home that evening Alice was very happy and excited about a new picture she had started. That she had started painting again was good but there was something oddly obsessive about her manner. It was as if she was using it to avoid facing all the difficulties we had. It worried me a little and so I said nothing to her about Jackie. I did not want to spoil her mood. I simply told her I had been unable to talk to Carl. She shrugged her shoulders indifferently. It was not the time to try and persuade her otherwise. Next day I had to give a lecture in the morning so postponed ringing Carl again till lunchtime and again I could not get hold of him.

I arrived at Jackie's house at three o'clock and she suggested that as she had to pick Sam up from the local school I should go with her. I could sign the papers later. We went in my ancient Beetle, "Sam would love it," she said. She was right. He took one look at it and told me it was really cool. He seemed pleased to see me and on the way back asked me all sorts of questions about how it worked. We had tea together and it was all very civilised. Afterwards, when Jackie took the cups out to the kitchen Sam cross-questioned me about what I did. Not surprisingly, he was interested in my computer knowledge.

"Uncle Seb, could I do animation?" he asked. He had started to call me uncle, which amused me.

"Yes," I replied.

"Could you show me how to do some?" he asked.

"I'm really sorry, but I haven't really got time now," I replied.

"Please, please," he said sidling round the table and pulling at my hand.

"I really have not got time," I repeated.

"Will you come and help me with my homework instead?" he asked, holding my hand even tighter and giving me a huge toothy smile. He looked so warm and friendly with his flashing eyes and his cheeky grin it was impossible to refuse. So we went to his bedroom and I sat down next to him. I soon saw that he was bright and responsive, and once again to my surprise I found that I really enjoyed it. He was very bright and easy to teach, and had picked up what I told him without difficulty.

When we finished, I stood up to go back down stairs and he caught my arm.

"Uncle Seb," he said. "I wish you were my Dad,"

It was completely disarming and quite unexpected. I did not know what to say to him. He was looking at me in such an appealing way I felt quite flustered. To make matters worse he added: "I really like you."

"I like you too, Sam," I muttered and retreated back down stairs in confusion.

"Catch you later," he called out.

Jackie was sitting at a table with the papers spread out in front of her. I told her what Sam had just said.

"It made me feel terrible. I wanted to tell him the truth but it's just too difficult."

"You should have done. It's not easy for any of us," she replied. "What's to stop you at least coming and seeing him a bit more often anyway?"

"Things have changed," I told her. "I may not be here much longer. I've been offered a job in America, in California."

"Wow, fantastic. You are lucky. I'd love to go there."

"I'm not sure I want to take the job though."

"Why ever not?"

"I'm not sure I want to live in the States."

"You must. It's more money isn't it?"

"Yes."

"Well, then. You'd be crazy not to go."

"I suppose so."

"If you're going away, this changes everything," she said, "particularly with Sam. You can't just disappear out of his life. It's not fair on him."

"I realise that. But I'm not sure I can be what he wants," I replied.

"Look Seb. Since our lunch the other week, he's talked about you the whole time. He senses something I'm sure. He keeps asking when you're coming to see us again. I really think it's time for you to tell him. He has to know sooner or later."

"I'm not sure."

"Seb!" she exclaimed in exasperation.

"OK," I said, nodding in reluctant agreement. If I was truthful I was quite excited about the idea. Deep down I wanted to tell him.

"I'll call him," she said.

I noticed the relief in her voice but I felt a little apprehensive about how Sam might respond. He came down the stairs and asked what she wanted.

"Come over here," she said. "Seb has something to tell you."

I had no choice now. "You know you just said you wished I was your Dad?" He nodded and grinned. "Well I am."

As soon as the words were out I felt a huge sense of relief as if a burden had been lifted.

"Great!" he cried. "I thought you might be. Are you going to come and live with us?" he asked, smiling broadly.

"Well that's not possible," I said, "but I'm certainly going to try to see you more often."

"Will you show me how to do animation, next time?" he asked.

"I certainly will."

Yes, there were huge problems ahead but I could deal with them later. I had a bright intelligent son whom I really liked and who appeared to like me. As to his reaction, I need not have worried. He looked delighted and came over, took my hands and gripped them tightly and looked closely at me. It was as if he needed physical confirmation of my existence.

"Come here," I said. "Let me give you a hug," and I put my arms round him. It was a big moment in my life. I knew there was no going back and I was really pleased.

"I thought you two were going to tell me you were going to get married," he said.

"We already are," Jackie said.

He looked a little confused. "I'm really pleased you're my Dad," he said and then went back to his bedroom saying he had to finish his homework.

Jackie looked at me sternly. "You'd better make sure you do come more often or you will have one very upset child."

"No I really do want to see more of him. I won't let you down. Look I must get back now."

"You'd better sign the papers," she said showing me where to do it. I stared at them.

"I think I'd like to read them carefully, first," I said. "I'll take them with me and post them back to you."

I put them back in the envelope and rose to go.

"You don't have to go," she said. "Why don't you stay the night? Sam would like it. That's obvious. You could borrow his bed and he could sleep with me."

I suspected what she really had in mind was somewhat different and shook my head. It sounded dangerously tempting. I might have done a few questionable things in my time but Alice would be extremely hurt if she ever found out, and she certainly would. Women always do.

"I won't tell if you don't," she said, as if reading my thoughts. "My parents won't be back tonight, we could sleep in their bed."

I stood firm. "No, it's not a good idea. I'll let you have these in a couple of days," I replied.

"You don't have to sign them, at all," she said.

"What do you mean?"

"We could come with you to America."

"Hang on a minute. Just slow down a little," I said, and opened the front door.

"Why not? Is there something you're not telling me?" she asked.

"About what?"

"I don't know, you tell me."

"Look this has all come as a bit of a shock, to put it mildly. I need a little time right now to get my head round it."

"Of course," she murmured. "Well, come and see us again soon, before you go."

"If I go," I said.

As I got into the car I saw Sam watching me from his bedroom window. I waved and he responded with a grin and a little flick of his hand. As I drove back, I was unable to stop thinking about him. He had set off feelings in me that I scarcely knew I had. I tried to put him to the back of my mind but I could not stifle the memory of his warmth. It was simple enough. All he wanted was for me to be a father to him. He might eventually grow to love me simply for whom I was and not care about my short comings. For the first time in my life someone wanted a straightforward relationship with me and it made me feel fantastic.

I knew there would be a price to pay because there always is, and I tried to work out what it would be. To begin with I would have to tell Alice as soon as I got home. 'By the way, darling, I've got a wife and son I never told you about, and he's such a nice kid.' I laughed inwardly, probably out of fear. It was not impossible to guess how she would react. And I would also have to tell Jackie before long that I already had a family. She would just say she guessed as much, which was almost certainly true. No, the sensible thing would be to sign the divorce papers and stay away from them. But no sooner had I come to that conclusion than I thought about Sam again. The image of his slightly anxious face and his warm smile were in my mind's eye and refused to go away. The feeling of my being genuinely needed by someone who had no other reason than to be loved for his own sake was extremely powerful and something I had never expected or for that matter ever experienced. The prospect both excited me, alarmed me and made me feel that I was not completely worthless.

Reality again reasserted itself. It was out of the question. As for Jackie's suggestion that we should all go to America, it was completely barmy. Panic swept through me. I just wanted to escape from everything and everyone, to put back the clock and start again. It did occur to me that going to America on my own would solve all my problems. But if I did that I stood to lose them all, Alice, Piers and now Sam. I just had to find a way to deal with it.

It was about ten when I walked up the garden path and let myself in. Alice looked sourly at me. The reception she gave me completely scotched any idea that it was a good time to tell her.

"Where have you been?" she demanded.

"Sorry," I said. "I had a long and boring faculty meeting going over course work."

"Why didn't you ring me and let me know?"

"It went on much longer than I expected. What's the problem? It's not that late is it? How's Piers?"

"Fine - for a child who cries all day long."

"I'm sorry, darling," I said, "I know it's tough at the moment but it will get better."

"What do you know about it? You just swan around all day with your chums having meetings, nice lunchies in between talking to pretty students. It's a hard life."

"Give it a rest," I said.

"That is exactly what I can't do," she said. "I'm exhausted and tired and worn out. I'm going to bed."

She rushed up the stairs. I could hear her moving about then silence. It was a relief. She could be so unreasonable. I lay on the couch and thought about the day. At Jackie's house it was an oasis of calm. In contrast, every time I walked in here there was some drama or other. I thought about my lovely son Sam again and our need for each other and felt quite emotional. I hardly knew Piers and all I got from him at best was the odd smile. He doted on his mother. As far as I could see he did not need me at all. What about Alice? Did

Alice really need me either? Did I need her? It was not a question I wanted to answer. I decided falling asleep was the best thing I could do, and that is what I did.

There was a tense truce between us for the next couple of days and things gradually began to resume a sort of normality. Alice went to see the old witch who gave her some herbal ointment to rub on Pier's gums. It worked wonders and his crying almost stopped. She became much less stressed and even resumed the painting. She had moved on from listening to Shostakovich all the time to her latest obsession, Renaissance Church Music. I'm afraid I found it rather tedious and made me think of death, cold empty stone vaults, skeletons and hooded faceless monks. Her current favourite, I saw from the CD case, was Allegri's Miserere, which, she informed me, was quite wonderful. She played it and I agreed it had stunning boy soprano sections but the bits in between were rather dreary. I had heard enough of that sort of stuff to last me a lifetime when I was at that dreadful boarding school. Fortunately, she knew what I would say and did not play it again while I was there.

On Thursday Carl rang me. He apologised for not returning my calls but was in Berlin and had been tied up in meetings. I played for time asked whether I could have another week to think about it. He agreed but said not to take too long as opportunities like this tended to fly away quite quickly. I had decided to give it one more try with Alice over the next weekend.

SEVEN

It was obvious things were not going well between us. Perhaps the most difficult part of our lives was in bed. Seb seemed to have lost interest in sex and when I tried to make love to him he just turned over and said he was too tired. He had not been in the right mood for some time but I was not unduly worried as I knew that many couples go through patches like this for all sorts of reasons. In the end they usually work things out and I hoped that it would not be too long for us. I put it down to his anxiety about work and hoped that once he found a new job things would return to normal.

But when Seb told me he had been given another week to decide about going to the States, I realised he still wanted to accept the offer.

"I thought you were going to tell them you wouldn't take it," I said.

"Yes, I did but they gave me a little more time. They really want me."

"But you promised you were going to say no. That's what we agreed."

"Yes but don't you listen to me? They wouldn't take no for an answer and asked me to think again. It's not just a matter of the job over there. There are practical considerations."

"I see. What?"

"To begin with, even if we stay here, there's the small matter of finding somewhere else to live. How are we going to do that if I haven't got a job? The best I am likely to be able to do is try to find freelance work. That means an uncertain income and building societies don't like that."

"But my parents said they would help," I interrupted.

"I know but without regular work, I won't get a mortgage and that would put paid to your parents lending us anything."

"They would probably lend us more than the deposit," I said, trying to reassure him.

"If we went to America I would not bloody well need their cash. I'd earn enough to buy a house without them," he replied. "I really don't want to damn well sponge off them."

"Don't get so angry with me all the time," I said. "It doesn't help. Can't we discuss things in a civilised way?"

"I'm sorry," he replied. "But it's so obviously what we should do. Why can't you see that?"

"Because I don't think you're right," I said. He glared at me, shook his head and sighed. "We'll find a way, you see," I added.

"How?" he snapped.

"I'm quite sure you'll get another job before long. The computer industry is crying out for people like you. I can sell my paintings. We'll manage somehow.

"And how many pictures do you think you can sell in a year?" he retorted. "It takes you months just to paint one."

"That's not fair. Most of my time is taken up looking after the baby. You know that. When he gets older it'll be different. He's so exhausting at the moment."

"Be realistic, however many you manage to sell, you'll be lucky if you make more than a couple of thousand pounds in a year."

"We'll get by."

"That's easy for you to say. You're not the one who'll have to earn the real money. I've told them I'll make a decision about the job in the next couple of days so I'm asking you for the last time to reconsider."

"And for the last time the answer is no. If you want to go, then just go."

He stared at me looking quite shocked. "I believe you mean that," he said.

"I do, I'm happy here. I love this place and what I want to paint is here not in California."

"I can't believe what you're saying. You want to split up, is that it?"

"Of course not, but you have to understand I really love it here, I belong here, it is in my soul, it is in my culture. I just could not live in America and I want Piers brought up here so that he will also understand what it is to be English."

"Why? He's hardly going to understand Hardy and Shakespeare is he?"

"Why not? He's not mentally handicapped just because he can't see."

"I didn't say he was."

"It's obviously what you think."

"Rubbish! You're just living in the past. That world has gone and we need to look to the future and I'm convinced for us that's in America. We'll both have much greater opportunities over there. You'd love it if we went there. Can't you see that?"

"No I can't. Life isn't all about having a swimming pool at the house and owning a new car every year. In any case I doubt that a handicapped child would be exactly welcome over there."

"You don't know that. There is wonderful help over there and a huge number of charities that are much far more generously endowed than here."

"Charity! I don't want charitable hand-outs for my son. I want him to be someone in his own right when he grows up, be independent and make something of his life."

"I do as well but we have to be realistic. I know that old witch has convinced you he's going to be highly gifted but that's extremely unlikely. What sort of future do you think he'll have here? His route is blind school and training for some sort of job which he might get if he's very lucky."

"Not if I have anything to do with it."

"Get real! What do you imagine you can do?"

"Educate him at home."

He laughed. "I give up," he said. "You seem to think the good fairy sprinkled him with golden dust when he was born and that magically everything will be all right. You just live in a dream world."

This sarcastic remark really exasperated me. He simply would not listen.

"I'm not going and that's final," I said. "I don't want to discuss it anymore."

"I'm going to the pub," he replied, and strode angrily out of the cottage. Frankly, it was a relief to have some peace for a couple of hours. I realised the strain it was putting on both of us but I never sensed just how much danger our relationship was in.

For the next couple of days Seb seemed rather depressed. He repeated rather gloomily that he had no idea where he was going to get work. The following Saturday we went for a walk in the local recreation ground. It had been very dry and warm and the balmy weather had extended into the early part of November. Seb still seemed in a particularly uncommunicative mood. I assumed he was preoccupied by his job problems and by my decision not to go to the States. I thought he would come to terms with it in the end. But I was wrong and it came out a quite unexpected way. We had stopped for a few moments to watch some boys playing football. Seb stared morosely at the youngsters. A boy trapped the ball and passed it to another whose shot beat the goalie. The scorer celebrated wildly, running to his mates and waving both arms in the air.

Seb looked bleakly at him. "Piers will never be able to do that," he said. Simple words that gave no indication of the real depths of what he meant.

"I don't see why," I replied. "They have balls with bells in. They play football with those perfectly well."

Seb looked angry and shook his head in contempt. "Football with bells!" he snapped. "You've no idea how I feel have you?"

"About what?" I asked.

"What do you think?" he asked with bitterness in his voice.

"How do I know, Seb, if you don't tell me? Just talk to me." I touched his arm but he pushed me away, shrugged and stared at the ground scowling.

"Seb!" I said. "Don't do this."

"Just leave it," he replied.

We returned to the cottage in silence and hardly had we stepped inside when he turned and faced me.

"There is something I have to tell you," he said.

It seemed like a cliché from a bad novelette. He was going to leave me. He had found another woman - probably that girl on the course. I felt sick with apprehension. But it was not that at all. It was the beginning of a slow and unstoppable slide to something far more difficult to comprehend.

"I'm not sure I can cope with all this," he said. "I thought I could but it's not working is it?"

"I admit I've been a bit difficult to live with," I replied, "but all couples go through difficult times like this. We'll survive."

"I doubt it."

"Yes, we will, of course we will. It's normal when the baby is young. Ask anyone!"

I moved close to him and took hold of his arm. He looked down at my hand and gently removed it.

"I'm sorry, but it's not you. It's Piers," he murmured.

"What do you mean?"

He took a deep breath and said nothing for a good minute as if he was trying to find some inner resolution. Finally, his searing words came out.

"Piers is not the son I thought we would have." I stared stupidly at him as he went on: "I want a son I can relate to like other men, do the normal things fathers and sons do, like kick a football in the park or play cricket. I want a son who'll go to college, bring home a pretty girl, perhaps marry and have children, be a success, or at least have that possibility. There is no chance of this with Piers. I just cannot go on pretending any more. He is not the son I wanted."

"Oh, I'll just take him back to the hospital," I snapped. "I'll ask if they'll change him for a baby that works properly, you know, under the guarantee."

"Sarcasm doesn't help," he said. "I'm sorry, I want a normal family, not a child who will grow up to spend his days dressed in shabby clothes living in some grubby hostel and poking around the street with a white stick."

"How could you say such a dreadful thing!" I shouted. I was so angry. But it was if a dam had broken in Seb's mind and his pent up feelings poured out.

"What's more it's quite clear he doesn't need me," he continued.

"Rubbish! Of course he does."

"No he does not. Who does he want to go to all the time? Not me, you! I am not even on his horizon."

Tears started to stream down my face.

"For god's sake turn the tap off," he shouted.

"I'm sorry I can't help it," I sobbed. I was shocked and barely heard what he said next.

"I'm not even sure it's my baby," he snapped.

For a second I was speechless. "How could you say such a dreadful thing!" I screamed.

He looked coldly at me. "Well we are both dark haired and he's blond. How do you account for that?"

"Don't be absurd," I snapped back. "It is just baby hair. You were probably like that. Many fair-haired children become dark as they grow up. How could you say such a thing?"

For the first time the realisation that the gulf between us might completely wreck our life hit me like an arctic blast. I was scared, confused and dazed. I picked up Piers, rushed into the garden and walked aimlessly to and fro. After a while I sat down on the bench and became aware of the warm late autumn sunshine and the sound of crows cawing in the woods. My Seb, the man I loved could not possibly have said such cruel things, could he? A few minutes later, he came out of the cottage and sat down next to me. He apologised saying that he was just finding it difficult to cope and that he did not mean it. But I knew he did. It was unbearable. To make matters worse, he burst into tears and I even felt sorry for him. We went back inside and I put Piers to bed. As I looked at him, chubby and sweet, the solution came to me. I returned to the living room.

"Why don't we try for another child?" I asked.

Seb looked at me with an expression of total distaste.

"What if it's blind as well?" he asked. The question was almost unanswerable.

"I'd love it just the same," I whispered. "I could have a normal sighted child anyway."

"The chances are remote. It's much more likely to be blind. You have to face that. You have inherited a faulty gene from somewhere."

"Do you think I don't know that already?" The words were out before I realised that I had never told him what my mother said about blindness in my family.

"What do you mean, exactly?" he demanded.

"Well, I'm sorry but I meant to tell you. My mother has been researching her Ukrainian roots."

"So?"

"The last time they came down she told me she had discovered that there was inherited blindness in that side of the family."

"What!"

"Just calm down. She had no idea of this and it came as a terrible shock to her."

Far from placating Seb it made matters worse.

"I don't believe she knew nothing about this. She must have done," he shouted. "You've kept this to yourself all this time. That's unforgivable. Why didn't you tell me straight away?"

"I knew how you'd react. We'd already had a row because you kept my father's offer of a deposit for a house very quiet. I didn't want another argument. "

"This is much more important than a deposit on a house. I had every right to be told."

I was extremely shocked at his reaction but it was difficult to deny that I should have told him. I did not answer for some minutes.

I suppose I should have apologised but I did not. I was too angry with him.

"So where does this leave us?" I asked, eventually, trying to remain calm.

"It's simple. Trying for another child is far too risky."

"Are you saying we can never have another child?"

"Yes, that's exactly what I'm saying."

"You're so cruel! You've no idea how hurtful that is."

"It's the truth and you can't face it."

At that moment I really hated him but he merely stared sullenly into space for a long time refusing to talk. Then he stood up and walked out of the house. I heard the car driving off and as the sound of the engine died away, I heard the pealing bells of the medieval church in Clyffe St Mary start up, floating through the transparent atmosphere. They must be practicing for a wedding – how ironic! It felt extraordinarily peaceful as if I was in another century. The evening light was exquisitely beautiful, almost unreal, and I had an almost overwhelming urge to try to paint it. In the circumstance this was so ridiculous that I began to think I must be having some sort of nervous breakdown and that I had been imagining this whole ghastly scenario. But I was not. I had no idea where Seb had gone. I assumed it was to the pub again and that he would be back later but he failed to return that night. Although this made me very anxious after the row, I was not too unhappy to be given a little time to think. I imagined he had gone to see Mark or some other friend to talk things over and he would come back before long, hopefully in a better frame of mind. I was still extremely angry at what he had said about Piers and my family. Even if it was true that my grandmother had passed the gene on to me, how could he say Piers was not the son he wanted? Not being able to play football or cricket seemed so superficial. I picked up Piers and cuddled him. He was so warm, so chunky, so real and so loveable how could Seb not feel this?

The following day I took Piers out for a long walk over the downs in the hope it might help me decide what to do. It did little good and I returned in the early afternoon feeling very miserable and hoping Seb had returned while I was out. As I came up the path I heard my mobile ringing from inside the cottage. I rushed in and stood staring at it. It was Seb. After letting it ring for a minute or so I decided I should answer it but as I picked it up he rang off. This made me absurdly angry and instead of calling him back I just wanted to punish him. He could damn well wait. I gave Piers something to eat, put him down for a rest and sat down on the sofa. With all the stress I had not slept at all for two nights, so I suppose the exercise and then the warmth of the house made me feel very drowsy. I drifted off and it was late in the afternoon before I woke up. He had not come back. The cottage felt depressingly empty and I wondered if Seb had gone for good. The odd thing was that a part of me felt a great sense of relief. Yet when he did not return, for weeks afterwards I ached to hear him open the door, come in and hold me in his arms.

Walking out on Alice ripped me into pieces. I had not intended to leave her. I set out to go to the pub to have a few drinks and a laugh with George. But I had driven straight past it without having any idea of where I was heading. I knew that if I had gone in I would just have returned to the cottage at closing time and I did not want to do that. Deep down I really could not face dealing with the impossible baby who was tearing our lives apart and would do so for years. This had been staring me in the face for weeks and I had refused to accept it. It had been buried within me and I had been unable to admit it to myself. Now it had come out when I least expected it, triggered by kids playing football of all things. It seems so facile and so unexpected, but was it? Did it reflect something far more fundamental within me? It must do. Deep down I felt cheated by life. I felt cheated of my childhood by my father vanishing and my mother dying when I was so young. I felt cheated in marriage to a woman who had deprived me of years of happiness watching my first son grow up. I felt cheated by Alice's fragrant attraction that had ensnared me and delivered a flawed child.

She should have had the termination when I suggested it. I felt cheated by the dark inheritance that she had kept so quiet about. Instead, I was now expected to bring up a child that I had never wanted. What's more I could have no more children with her. That was a really appalling thing to face.

    I was confused. I knew I had provoked the blistering row we had. It would have been so easy for me to show some understanding but I did not want to. Had I therefore deliberately blown our relationship to bits? Perhaps it was simply inevitable. As I drove along I went over and over everything and gradually realised that my initial hope of a life with Alice turning out right in the end had been an unrealistic dream. It was never going to work and it was impossible go on with the pretence. I should never have set up home with her in the first place. It was obvious that Alice and I were quite incompatible. We thought in quite different ways. For all her intellect, she was at her core instinctive and aesthetic. I was practical and logical and we grated on each other. Her parents would have looked after her and the baby. At least her mother would have expected it. Had I subconsciously been considering leaving her for some time but lacked the courage to do it? It was a hard question I could not answer. Did I love her? Not now, I felt sure about that. Had I ever really loved her? I was not sure. I had been obsessed with her but is that the same thing? She had been a challenge but what happened had changed both our lives. Now here was the consequence writ large. A life together, looking after a child I would almost certainly be unable to love was inconceivable. Indeed I might grow, perhaps had already grown, to dislike him intensely for ruining both our lives. I could not face that prospect. I know walking out on her makes me sound dreadfully unfeeling but the alternative for her would be far worse. She would be shackled to a man who did not love her in a relationship bound together by a child who would always need the kind of support that I knew I was unable to give. I had tried to make it work but things had now changed.

    I drove like a lunatic and found myself in the college car park in Waterbridge. I went inside and stayed in my office that night. Not that I slept much, it was far too uncomfortable. Fortunately it was a Saturday so there was almost nobody around. By the next morning I was extremely worried about what I had done. Yesterday I had convinced myself it was the right thing to do for both our sakes. Now I did not know what to feel. In the grey morning light I felt little else but blame and anxiety. I did not want to return yet at the same time I knew she would be feeling deeply wounded and I wanted to rush back, hold her in my arms and comfort her. But if I no longer loved her what use would that be? It would only lead to more unhappiness for both of us. Yet if I did not go back, I would feel very guilty. Everyone would condemn me. It was an impossible situation. Only parents of a handicapped child, nobody else, can realise the immense stress of looking after a childlike Piers. It's not only the everyday things that are difficult to deal with but also the incredible burden of lifelong care that you know lies ahead. Of course it is a basic instinct for all of us to want to pass on to the next generation a perfect child. I might have been able to cope with Piers if I could have had a second normal baby with Alice. It would be fine if it was a boy but supposing it was a baby girl; even if it was sighted we would just be passing on blindness to future generations. I simply could not take the risk. Where should I go from here? I knew Sam and Jackie would welcome me with open arms but they were not the answer. I certainly did not want to try again with her even though Sam had shown me a glimpse of what my life could have been like. However, the price was too high. It all was very distressing. What a dreadful mess my life was in.

    I showered, ate some breakfast in a café and walked aimlessly round the town for a couple of hours, going over in my mind what had happened, oscillating between wanting to rush back to say how sorry I was and feeling very angry at the circumstances that had trapped me in a relationship with a child I did not want. What I felt about Piers was the worst part of it. It was not his fault but he had blighted my life and I felt considerable antipathy towards him for it. I know I should not but I did. I felt I was a monster for even having such thoughts.

At about midday I went into a pub near the college to have some lunch. I thought on a Sunday I would be safe there from meeting any of my colleagues. But as I tried to force myself to eat a toasted sandwich at the bar, Rachel Reed walked in with Carl Neumann. Of course they saw me and came straight over.

"What are you doing here?" she asked. "Shouldn't you be at your cottage with your lovely family?"

"I had a few things to do in the office," I said.

"Have you come to any decision, yet?" asked Carl.

"We're still discussing it," I replied.

"Well, Seb, I'm sorry but I need an answer. I'm going back at the end of the week. I wouldn't be happy about doing that without knowing your intentions. You know we'd very much like you to join us but of course there are other candidates. I think you've both had enough time."

"Right," I said, "I understand. If you two get a table I'll join you in a minute. I need to make a call."

It was obvious what I should do. I had to take the offer. What choice did I have? I went outside to ring Alice and give her one more chance to come with me. She would not like it and would probably say no. In that case I would go on my own. I rang her number but there was no answer. So I returned with the decision made and told Carl I would take the job. He seemed really pleased and told me he always knew I would join them. I sat with them while they ate, discussing the details of what my job would entail. At the end of their meal Carl departed somewhat abruptly saying he had another appointment to go to and leaving me with Rachel. I walked with her back to the college car park, preoccupied with my decision and saying very little. She noticed my unusual reticence.

"Is something wrong, Seb?" she asked.

"No, no, I'm fine," I replied.

"Oh come on," she said. "I can tell if someone's got something on their mind."

"It's nothing much. I had a really major bust up with Alice yesterday and I've just agreed to go to the States without telling her that's all."

"Well, if you want to talk," she said, "I'm going home now and I have the afternoon free."

It was just what I wanted to hear. She lived about ten miles away in a large old house in the village of Willow St Edith and rented out rooms to pay the mortgage. We talked for some time and I told her that Alice and I seemed to be incompatible and that we had probably split for good. She was sympathetic but, as I expected, she told me to go back and make it up. I said I could not do that right away. We talked well into the evening and in the end I asked if I could stay the night in one of her spare rooms.

"Well, my darling, I don't know about that," she mocked, laughing at me. "Can I trust you?"

"Of course you can," I said. "My life is in a big enough mess as it is. I just want a decent night's sleep and a little time to sort things out."

"You certainly do," she replied.

I rang Alice again that evening but her mobile was still switched off so I left a message. For the next couple of weeks I stayed at Rachel's house trying to deal with practical matters, handing in my resignation and sorting out my visa and application for a green card. I was surprised to find that I quickly got used to not living with Alice. I suppose being away from the emotional shambles of my life with her had given me breathing space. I no longer felt it would be a good idea to go back and see her. It would all flare up again when I told her I was going to America and we would just row.

On the day before my flight I went to see Jackie and told her. She said Sam would be upset and suggested I meet him from school and spend the rest of the day with them in order to break the news gently to him. Of course I could hardly say no, not that I wanted to. As soon as I saw him he gave me a fantastic smile and it was a wonderful feeling after the traumas of recent days. That evening was the closest thing to the family life I had always imagined. I played

French cricket with him and helped with his homework. Jackie made us a very nice supper and the time passed very pleasantly. I even read him a story before he went to sleep. As it was late I agreed to stay the night and slept in her parent's bed. I was rather surprised when after falling asleep I awoke to find she had slipped into bed with me. I suppose I should have told her that I was not interested but she was not there for the conversation was she?

Next morning Sam was delighted to see me at breakfast and looked on the verge of tears when I told him I was going to America that day. His reaction turned me inside out. He slipped round the table on to my lap, put his arms round me and just hugged me. I very much wanted to be the father he clearly needed but how could I with the mess my life was in? I took him to school and told him I would invite them out to California for a holiday. It left him looking a bit more cheerful. I went back to the house to say goodbye to Jackie and of course she asked me where she stood after last night.

"Do you want to give it another try?" she asked.

"I don't know," I replied. "I feel this is all happening too quickly. We made a mess of it before. I need to be completely sure this time."

"I doubt that's possible for anybody. There are no certainties in these things. Still, if it's what you think.....and what about Sam?"

"Of course I want to go on seeing him. When I've settled in perhaps you could both come across for a holiday. We could see how it goes and take it from there."

She reluctantly agreed. I promised I would write to him soon and left for the Airport, my mind in a whirl and wondering just how I had managed to make my already complicated life even more confusing. I made one last attempt that day to talk to Alice but her mobile was switched off once again and this time I did not leave a message. What was there to say?

EIGHT

Without Seb my life felt dreadfully empty, even more so because I was convinced the break-up was my fault. I felt humiliated and ashamed and constantly went over and over where it had gone wrong. When I had agreed to paint a portrait of him I knew perfectly well what his interest was and to be fair he behaved like a gentleman. But I grew to like him and I suppose I was flattered by the attention of an intelligent and experienced man. I suppose you could say I was naive. I had not expected to become pregnant, but when I did I refused to consider a termination. Not that I regretted having Piers, far from it. I thought that it would work out with Seb and I would be able to live in the country and we would have more beautiful children. I was in love with Seb and I had made him create what I wanted.

I could not work out the point at which things changed. Piers' blindness was obviously a factor but until recently Seb seemed to deal with that well enough once he got over the initial shock. Now he said he could not cope with it, and perhaps that was true, but I did wonder whether something else had changed his attitude. I could not think what it might be. He had lost his job because of me, which did not help and neither did my refusal to go to America. But I did not think he left me just because of that. Of course I should have agreed to go with him. It was me who had selfishly insisted we stayed living in the English countryside. It was a romantic dream that had now been shattered by the genetic time bomb inside me. Worst of all, I felt guilty because I was glad that he had gone and I could feel a sort of peace at last living with my little baby.

After he left, I dreaded meeting people and having to explain why Seb was not there. I told anyone who asked that he had been offered this fantastic job in California and had had to leave immediately. I would join him out there when he could arrange things. I meant it, because I thought he would come back soon to ask me to go again and I would have agreed at once. He did ring once but only left a message. He said he was definitely going to America, would pay the rent until Mark was due back and would naturally help us financially after that. But he would not come to see us. I suppose it was his weakness. I stared at my telephone for hours frozen with apathy and depression. My parents came to see me and I told them simply that we had split up. Of course my father said he had always thought Seb was a waste of space and I was better off without him. My mother wanted me to move back home but I sensed my father did not. In any case it was not what I wanted. He kindly offered to give me an allowance, which I gratefully accepted. I was angry with Seb but inside I ached for him, for his touch, for the warmth of his body next to mine.

The winter passed bitter, cold and bleak. The woods close to the cottage became a black lattice against the grey rain-filled sky. I tried to keep the place warm with logs from fallen branches and I can remember little about those long months except the sound of crows cawing, and feeling quite desperate most of the time. Spring came and the warm sunshine helped to raise my spirits. I slowly realised that I could piece my life together again if I was strong.

Gradually a sort of normality began to settle in. I started to paint again and also made myself draw Piers. He was such a beautiful child it was not difficult and I felt pleased with the results. At least it was something I could do. I made a decision. I had to try to become really independent. I would do some paintings and sell them. My agent was encouraging when I told her. Of course I thought I would never sell enough to make much of a living but I felt irrationally relieved at taking charge of my own future.

To celebrate, one warm Spring afternoon I packed a sketch book, some food for a picnic, put Piers in the carrier and walked on to the top of the downs. I made my way along the ridge, turned down the path past the White Horse and through the grove of trees to the ruined cottage. Once inside, I spread out a rug and sat down to have the picnic. I wanted us to eat at least once in what I had dreamed would one day be our home. Afterwards we both fell asleep in the sunshine. When I awoke Piers had crawled off the rug and was sitting by the window playing with some stones. I could hear small animals scuttling about in the undergrowth outside. Insects hummed and buzzed around the trees and bushes. In the distance doves cooed softly and further away the woodpecker's rat-a-tat echoed in the valley. Through the doorway I could see sun streaming through the trees making the long grass shine and picking out clouds of seeds drifting in the breeze. At the back of the cottage, in what must have once been the garden, a gnarled apple tree had scattered its blossom to form a carpet of pink petals over the grass. Everything was fresh with renewal.

A pair of wagtails flew down through the open rafters and settled on a window sill close to where Piers was playing. He must have heard them for he crawled to the window and pulled himself up. The birds did not move. Piers made some funny noises. They showed no sign of alarm but just twittered and hopped around. A vole ran along the floor by the wall and stopped no more than a foot away from him, sitting up, cleaning its whiskers and showing no fear. It even seemed to respond to his funny noises, stopping for a second and looking at him. It was quite extraordinary - almost as if it was trying to communicate. It was all too much and I could not prevent myself weeping, first of all because Piers could not see the vole or any of this and then with a burning rage that to live in this marvellous place was now out of my reach. As for my baby, what chance did he have? He would become totally blind, his father had walked out and his mother was clearly starting to go mad.

After some minutes I recovered, took out my book and drew little sketches of the inside of the cottage, of Piers playing on the rug, of the flowers growing through the window and of the overgrown garden outside. It was fascinating to see the way nature had just taken over the building with plants growing out of old pipes and up through the cracks in the flagstone floor. In a few more years the entire building would collapse and return to the ground from which everything used to build it had been taken. I packed up the picnic and, putting Piers back into the carrier, took the path that led down past the farm house. As we passed the gate Ellen Cooper called out to me from the garden and invited us in for some tea.

We sat down at a large wooden kitchen table that looked as if it had been scrubbed clean every day for the past hundred years. At one end of the room stood a Welsh dresser displaying a set of china plates, cups and saucers decorated with tiny blue flowers. The wall opposite was lined with wooden shelving on which were thirty or forty carefully labelled small brown earthenware jugs and glass jars. Next to them were small pots containing tinctures made from plants, like speedwell, nettle root and cranesbill, oils and ointments made from chamomile, marjoram and calendula. A little further along were herbal teas with names that you would not find on a supermarket shelf like horsetail, cowslip root and meadow sweet. Above them were several pestles and mortars of differing sizes. It was like stepping back a couple of centuries. Ellen put the kettle on an iron cooker and sat down.

"You seem to like it over there in the old village," she said.

For a moment I was unable to think what she meant and then remembered that the derelict cottage was part of the tiny group of farm cottages in which she had been brought up.

"I think there is something unusually atmospheric about that place," I said and told her about the way the animals seemed so tame and unafraid of Piers. She went across to Piers and looked at him. He woke up briefly, stared blankly, gave a little grunt, sighed and then resumed sleeping peacefully.

"He's gorgeous," she said. "He's got such lovely blue eyes."

It was what everybody said and I could not bear it. I told her about Piers blindness, Seb walking out and of my anger and despair.

"I'm afraid it's more common than you would think," she replied. "Some men find it difficult to accept handicapped children. I'm not sure why. Perhaps it's something to do with the desire to pass on a perfect evolutionary set to the next generation. Or maybe it's simply that they think it is a slur on their manhood and cannot see beyond the disability to the human being underneath. Give him time, he will come back when he's sorted himself out."

"I don't think so, he's gone to America."

"Has he? What are you going to do?"

"We're all right where we are at the moment. I suppose I'll look around for another cottage when the owners come back."

"I've got plenty of spare rooms in this place," she said. "The farmhouse has felt rather empty since my husband died. It would be nice to see them used again. You're a painter, aren't you? You could use one of the outbuildings as a studio."

"I couldn't possibly impose on you. I'll sort something out," I muttered.

"But it would be such a marvellous place for a little boy to grow up," she said. "He would learn so much about natural things, first hand."

"But he won't be able to see anything."

"That doesn't matter. He can use other senses to make up for it. I can tell any of my herbs just by the scent. He could do that. I could teach him the sounds of nature, animal cries, bird song as well. Anyway, you don't know yet how much he'll be able to see. He's not totally blind is he? Just a little sight can be very useful."

A car pulled in to the driveway. Ellen looked through the window and stood up. A girl of about twelve years of age emerged with her mother.

"That's one of my pupils," said Ellen. "I teach the piano. It helps pay the bills. Why not move in here when the time comes? It will help me and do you both good."

I felt overwhelming grateful for this nice woman's offer but did not know what to say. I knew I would love to live at this farmhouse but I was also aware how difficult Piers could be.

"I'm not sure what I'll do," I said. "My parents would like me to be nearer to them."

"Well, think about it anyway," she continued, "I think I could be of some help to you."

"It's kind of you," I said.

"When he grows up I could teach him to play the piano," she said. "It's something he could do and perhaps you could help me with my business. I need someone I can trust. Are you any good at book keeping?"

I nodded. "I am. My father's a bank manager," I replied. "When I was about eight he made me keep proper accounts of what I saved and spent from my pocket money. I really enjoyed it. I must have inherited a head for figures from him."

I looked through the kitchen door into the living room. In the middle I could see a large piano, black, beautiful, and gleaming. We had one like it at my school. She saw my gaze and explained that when her husband had died she had sold off the farm land and used some of the money to buy a Steinway grand.

"It had always been my dream to have one," she explained.

As I walked along the narrow road back to the cottage I mulled over what moving in might mean for us. I knew my dad considered that I had wasted my life becoming an artist but if I did accept her offer I was sure doing Ellen's accounts was something he would approve of. And I would feel that at least I could be of some use. As for Piers, learning the piano or some other instrument could change his life. I had heard a recording of Bernard d'Ascoli, a blind French pianist. He was brilliant. Why not Piers? I had to give him the opportunity. I knew I wanted to take up her offer even if, and I know this sounds silly, I felt I was being selfish. But I could be well organised and give Ellen the financial help she said she needed so why not take her offer? At least that way I would not be sponging from her.

Talking to Ellen about Piers blindness and Seb leaving me somehow released me and I started telling all my friends what had happened. They were very sympathetic about Seb going but strangest reaction came when I said Piers was blind. I had expected them to be very concerned, which they were for a while, but when they came to see us they were awkward with him and embarrassed somehow. Their visits became less frequent and eventually stopped. Even Gemma began to make excuses not to visit. George Dale called much less often and I became desperately lonely. It helped me make a decision about what I should do. In September Mark and his wife returned and I moved in with Ellen.

Piers was not an easy child to bring up. To begin with he did not understand that there was anything wrong with him. He thought the little vision he had was what everyone else had. But as he gradually began to realise that he did not see what I saw, he became quite difficult and began to have the most appalling temper tantrums. He was terrified of loud noises so, for example, taking him with me into a town to shop became almost impossible. He was frightened by the noise of cars, buses and lorries and hated the confused gabble of voices he heard in the street and in shops. Because he could not see it, unlike a normal child he did not understand what was going on. At the farmhouse he used to cry and scream in frustration at not being able to do the things he wanted to. The only way I could calm him down was to sing to him or put on the radio or a CD. He would stop crying very quickly and if it was rock music he would jig up and down in time. He liked me to dance with him, shrieking with delight as I whirled him around.

To begin with, he was very clingy and as he grew up I did everything I could think of to build his confidence and independence. For example, I used to take him to a nearby children's playground, make him climb the steps of the slide by himself, teaching him to feel and grip the protective side rails. In took a little time but he went from being terrified and crying to laughing with excitement as he hurtled down the slide.   I was determined he should learn to be as self-confident as possible.

At least the onset of his blindness was slow, and with his limited vision he was able to understand something of the world around him. I had to fill in the gaps by acting as his eyes and explain to him what he was unable to see. He used his hands instead of eyes and I taught him to feel the texture of things and use his other senses to learn what they were. He liked to feel my face and hair, my body and my clothing and he recognised mummy's smell. I even made sure I used the same soap and shampoo just so that he knew it was me. He hated me painting because he thought the oil paints and turpentine I used made a horrible smell so I had to make sure I had a bath afterwards or do watercolours. He was also very curious about other people who came to the house and was keen to touch their faces and their hair. When he was tiny, most people did not mind this, men even laughing when he reacted to feeling their prickly chins. He felt the face and bodies of other children as if to reassure himself but as he became older it was not a socially acceptable thing to do. I eventually had to dissuade him, particularly from touching other children who could not understand why he did it and did not like it.

Compared with most children he was a little late to start walking but once he did so he was into everything. He loved opening the refrigerator and helping himself to drinks or ice creams for example. Of course he was always hurting himself by banging into tables and chairs and, although we did our best to cover up sharp corners, inevitably he learned the hard way to hold out his hands to protect himself. I taught him go up and down stairs by himself and as he became more confident he went up and down much faster. A favourite and rather terrifying game of his was to rush down the stairs and jump the last few steps. I even taught him to run when he was about four by holding his hand and scampering along with him. He loved it and it was not long before he would scoot around outside and play by himself. He was very curious and used to investigate everything, digging up worms, feeling plant leaves and peering at them and always asking Ellen or I what they were. He learned to recognise thistles and brambles and even stinging nettles by bitter experience, and by their smell. Curiously, he had no fear of animals and I sometimes found him talking to horses or cows through the fence of the adjacent farm. He claimed they were telling him things. When I asked what, he would tell me it was a secret.

He was like any other child except that I had to spend an inordinate amount of time and patience explaining everything he could not see. Fortunately, far from being backward as I had once feared, he turned out to be very quick to learn. For example and to my amazement, quite spontaneously at about two and a half he started recognising letters and reading words. He used to look at the large letters on a cereal packet holding it close to his face and ask me what they were. Consequently, by using a magnifying glass I was able to teach him reading at a far younger age and far more easily than I had ever imagined would be possible. It was as if he already understood the importance of these things instinctively and by five he could read reasonably fluently. He had a phenomenal memory and once he had read or was told something he did not forget it. Ellen had a large library and, using the magnifying glass, as he grew up he absorbed information like a sponge from books. He even learned to play chess by the time he was eight. Ellen, who had played at school as a child, taught him the moves and some idea of strategy and tactics. At that age he had started to lose a little of his limited sight but he would visualise the moves in his head and call them out. By the age of nine he could beat most adults so I took him to chess tournaments from time to time, where he did reasonably well. He also proved to be musical and with Ellen's teaching and encouragement, he began to learn to play the piano. It helped that he had such a good brain. If he struggled with a piece Ellen would play it to him and he would listen and memorize both hands. He found it easy and, as well as the usual pieces from his primers, he used to play tunes he had heard on the radio, improvising the left hand chords.

    I had decided to educate him at home as I feared he would be lost in an ordinary school and that a special school would stunt his intellect. He was taught Braille by specialist teachers for the blind who came once a week. They also taught him to use a white stick but he was not keen on that. I suppose he felt that at least on the farm he did not need it. The local education inspector used to visit us from time to time but he was always able to do any test he set him. He was impressed. He said he was a child in a million, but then I always knew that.

Another pleasant surprise was that I managed to make a good living. Encouraged by Ellen and my agent, I painted a number of pictures of Piers as he grew, sometimes of him in long grass near the farm, sometimes deep in the countryside or playing by the ruined cottage. Fortunately, they sold well and fetched good prices. I did not think it was great art but I could call myself a professional artist, which made me feel much better. Eventually I bought the ruined cottage from Ellen to use as a studio and spent much of what I earned repairing it and building an extension. Seb also kept his word and paid an allowance into my bank account every month. It was the least he could do. He was not a mean man, not that I would ever forgive him. Ellen charged an absurdly low rent for our accommodation, saying she was happy with the way I did her accounts and helped her with her business. She was wonderful with Piers, saying it was like having a grandchild of her own. She used to sit with him in the garden or walk up to the old cottages and tell him about the plants, the wild flowers, the insects, the animals and birds. Above all, she taught him to listen and by the time he was nine he knew every bird in the area by its song as well as many animals from the noises they make. Although his sight was very poor, I felt that even if he did become totally blind at least he was able to have a picture in his mind and could remember roughly what the world around him looked like. Living in the country made him comfortable with nature and indeed at one with the wild life. This simply would not have happened if he had been brought up in a city.

Ellen also taught Piers to sing. He had a clear treble voice and when he was about ten, some of Ellen's pupils were asked to perform at the nearby Wootton Bassett Music Festival in aid of the troops. His eyes had become light sensitive and he had started to wear dark glasses. He accompanied himself and sang an arrangement of 'I Vow to thee my Country'. As you might imagine, it was received with great applause and the event was written up in the local paper. The reporter took a photograph and interviewed both of us. I was pleased that his talent had been recognised but felt some misgivings all the same. However, we were happy. The memory of Seb's betrayal gradually faded and I assumed I would never see him again.

PART TWO

NINE

The first few months in America were very difficult for me. I told Carl that Alice and Piers would join me later in the year and everything was fine. From time to time he would ask when they were coming over and I made up vague excuses. When I finally told him we had split up he said had guessed this was the case. I tried not to think about them and worked very long hours just to try to erase the terrible guilt of what I had done. Of course I could not occupy twenty four hours in every day like that and so I attempted to rationalise my actions by telling myself that it had been for the best for both of us without ever really believing it. Try as I might I could not escape from the mixture of relief and remorse I felt and the whole time I was over there these feelings never went away completely.

Jackie and Sam came across to California that summer for a holiday. I had rented a small house and I had begun to imagine that here in the States we had a much better chance of resuming our relationship. However, when I showed her my double bed room she said she had also decided that for the moment it would be better if we did not rush things. Although I was a little disappointed I said she could use it and I agreed to share the spare room with Sam. In a way I was actually quite pleased by this as Sam and I got on very well in a quite uncomplicated kind of way. I enjoyed talking to him and in the mornings he often liked to sit on my bed or get in with me and chat away. He was a lovely kid. I suppose he was the son I had always wanted. Jackie and I remained very friendly and she seemed to like entertaining my new colleagues when I invited them to supper. It was almost like having a proper family and social life. As time went on, however, the atmosphere started to change subtly and I began to sense that she was not really interested in a close relationship with me. I was not too worried by this. I liked to have both of them around the house and in a way it was simpler without the complications that might arise.

She seemed to get on particularly well with Carl who started to call round to see us more often. Of course I soon realised he really wanted to see her not me but I cannot say I was particularly bothered by this either. It was obvious that resuming my marriage was not going to happen. Eventually he asked me whether I minded if he asked her to accompany him to a business dinner for which he was expected to take a partner. I told him I did not and that although we had split up years ago we were still good friends.

Jackie certainly did more than her fair share of keeping the house straight when I was at work and busied herself about the place. As a result one day she came across Alice's portrait of me in a cupboard and asked who had painted it. Bizarrely in the circumstances, she seemed rather jealous, but I explained it by saying that I had commissioned the painting from a student at Waterbridge. She was not satisfied with that and cross questioned me with forensic accuracy.

"What was her name?"

"It's on the painting - Alice Watson."

"I suppose she was one of your conquests," she snapped.

"We were close for a while but it was all a long time ago, not that it is any of your business," I said, becoming a little irritated.

"Why was it hidden in a cupboard?" she demanded.

"It wasn't hidden. I just haven't got round to hanging it yet."

"I don't believe you. Did you live with her?"

"Why should you think that?"

"Oh come on Seb, I've known you were hiding something ever since we met last year. You were obviously in a relationship with someone."

"OK, so I was living with her for a short time but we've broken up now."

"Did you have any children?" she demanded.

I was quite taken aback by this completely unexpected question. Did she know?

"Other than Sam?" I prevaricated.

"Yes, of course. You made her pregnant, didn't you?" How could she have guessed?

"Well, it was an accident. These things happen."

"And you abandoned them?"

"I don't have to explain myself to you! It's none of your business!"

"Well I think it is my business," she retorted. "Why have you never told me?"

"Because it really is nothing to do with you."

"Do you still see them?"

"Hardly, they live fifteen thousand miles away."

"Is that why you came over here?"

"Partly. But I really have left all that behind. It was a mistake and I am the one who is paying the price." Of course she immediately misinterpreted that.

"Does that mean you're paying maintenance?" she asked.

"Of course I do. What's that to do with you? My life is here now. I have no intention of going back. It did not work out and that's all I am prepared to say."

Our relationship cooled somewhat after that. It was nevertheless a surprise when on the day before they were due to go back to England Jackie announced she would like to stay a little longer. Of course I knew why and I did not mind when Carl took her out again that evening. It was obvious he had become her target. Poor sucker, he would be trapped just like I once was. She probably thought he was a better bet than me and who could blame her. Eventually she told me they wanted to get married and that she would be moving in with Carl as soon as he bought a new house which had enough room for all of them. I wished her well.

We divorced, she married Carl, had another baby and Sam alternately lived with one of us then the other. He did well at school and I was able to help him a lot. I worked hard at the research centre, and in the end joined Gemina Software on a permanent basis. As well as the new operating system, I was responsible for developing a number of highly lucrative computer games and made an awful lot of money. Eventually, I was offered a seat on the Board, given substantial share holdings to keep me in the company, and made even more money. My private life meandered on without my meeting anyone I was really interested in. I had the odd girlfriend from time to time but when I thought it might become serious, I slid out from under. Sam grew from a charming little boy into a difficult, shy, bolshie teenager. Of course that was as it should be even if it made our relationship rather strained from time to time.

Living that far way most things in the Old Country seemed very distant and, after a little, unimportant. Well for me, everything that is except what I had done. I had acted unforgivably; I knew it and it remained vividly in my mind. But I justified it by telling myself that circumstances had made the decision for me. Yet I felt uneasy. Could I have stayed with Alice and made it work? I doubt it. Did I try hard enough? Probably not, but it was pointless dwelling on it. What I did could not be undone and that was something I had to live with. I thought time and distance would make it fade but it never did. I considered returning to England, meeting up with Alice and trying again. But there was always a work project that I simply could not leave and I knew that I would not be welcome anyway. My guess was that Alice would have met someone else anyway and forgotten about me. I thought Piers would probably be going to a special school and, like most blind children, learning something mundane that could help him eventually scrape a meagre living.

I had been in the States for almost ten years when I received a letter from my friend Mark. I had not heard from him for a long time. In it was a clipping from the Wootton Basset Echo that gave me quite a shock. There was a picture of a fair haired boy in dark glasses, described as totally blind and who the paper said had a wonderful voice. It was Piers. Ten years of guilt exploded in the pit of my stomach, spread into my body, into my arms and even into my fingertips. What had I done? I could hardly breathe, my heart was thumping and I wanted to cry. The newspaper article said Piers was the star of the music festival and that he was an intellectual genius with a photographic memory, who had learned chess at the age of seven and could play the game in his head. To say I was astounded would have been to understate my reaction by several magnitudes. I had never thought that he would be able to sing beautifully or play something so challenging as chess in a million years. How could he possibly have learned such a difficult game so young without his eyesight? I felt ludicrously proud and horrified at the same time. I had never once imagined that our wailing and crying sightless baby would grow into a boy who not only looked quite unlike what I had imagined but who was also clearly very clever, although I took the words intellectual genius in the article with a large pinch of salt.

What really surprised me was just how beautiful my son was. I suppose it was prejudice and stupidity on my part but I had always imagined him to be slightly overweight, puffy faced, looking rather scruffy and probably a bit dim. It never crossed my mind that he would be good looking, very talented and clever. How wrong I had been.

I stared at the picture of him and re-read the article with my nerves still jangling. This was my son and I had rejected him. I felt terrible and at the same time incredibly excited, and I wanted to jump on a plane and go back to see him immediately. But how could I? Alice would tear me to pieces after all this time. I had never written to her and certainly not to him. What would have been the point?

I had to talk to someone so I went to see Jackie. Of course I did not show her the picture. I could hardly say oh by the way this is a photo of the blind son I abandoned, could I? So I raised the subject with great caution.

"I had a letter from my friend Mark," I said.

"So?"

"Great news, he says he now has children of his own."

"That's nice". She looked quizzically at me. "And…..?" she asked.

"I suppose it made me think of my own child over there. He must be ten now. I suppose it made me wonder what he's like now and how he and his mother are getting on. A guilty conscience, I suppose."

"You did what you thought you had to at the time."

"I know and I've always felt terrible," I replied.

"It's a bit late now to start getting a conscience about it."

"It wasn't simple. Sam had come into my life."

"Your darling Sam; I knew you were never really interested in trying again with me so at least you don't have the pretence of caring about me now, do you?"

"I did care about you," I protested. "You left me, remember! Anyhow I don't want to go into all that. What do you think I should do?"

"What do you want to do?"

"I suppose I want to go back and see him."

"Why?"

That was an excellent question that I could not really answer truthfully – perhaps not even to myself and certainly not to her. He was clearly a very gifted child. Would I have been keen to rush back if the picture had just been of the unattractive child I had imagined and read that he was learning to be a piano tuner? I like to think it would have made no difference but could I honestly say that? He was what he was and he was my son.

"Perhaps I should try to get to know him."

"Why now, all of a sudden?"

"Mark's letter, I suppose. It made me feel terrible. I feel like shooting myself," I said.

She laughed. "Don't be melodramatic. There isn't the slightest chance of you doing that. You love yourself far too much!"

"Very funny, you can be very cruel. You've no idea how I've always felt about all this. It has haunted me ever since we came here."

"No wonder it never worked for us if all this baggage was there."

"I'm sorry about that. But I feel more and more torn apart by what I did."

"Well in that case, go back and face up to it."

"I don't know about that. Alice will kill me."

She grimaced and looked exasperated. "You always run away when things get difficult, Seb. For once in your life, do the right thing."

"That's just it. I don't know what the right thing is. Perhaps I should leave them well alone. Even if I returned Alice would just tell me to shove off and she would be right to do so."

"She may not. How old did you say he is, ten? Well, I agree he needs to know who his father is however inadequate, and he never will if you don't go back."

"There's no need to be so nasty. I've been a good father to Sam, haven't I?"

"Ah yes, you've been wonderful."

"I'm being serious. Don't you think he'll be upset if I go back to the UK?"

"I doubt it. Of course he'll miss you but he'll soon be going to university and want his independence. I don't think you have any choice. Go and see them. Who knows what will happen?"

After another week of dithering and rereading the press cutting many times, I decided she was right and that I must go to see them and try somehow to make amends. For a start I could help them by giving money towards his education. Alice would probably shoot me when she saw me but, what the hell - I could wear a bullet proof vest!

I had holiday due so I explained to Professor Zuckerman I needed to sort out some family matters back home, boarded the first flight to England and caught the train to Stowe Minster. I had seen Mark before I left all those years ago and had confided a little in him. At least at the time he understood the extremely difficult choice I had to make. Mark was now in charge of the choir at the Cathedral School. What I liked about Mark was that he criticised you but he did not judge. He saw life as a series of impossible challenges that most of us inevitably fail. He told me his two boys both had places in the Cathedral School.

"I thought having children would never happen for us," he told me after we had adjourned to the pub. "It took us years and I had just about given up when Peter, he's nine, and a year later, Thomas arrived. Now here I am with the two of them growing up fast. How's your son, the one in America?"

"Sam's a real American teenager now, and you know what that means - obsessed with computer games and softball. He's quite unlike me; I still love cricket and football. I'm an unrepentant Brit."

"And how have things gone with Jackie?" he asked.

"Brilliantly! We've divorced now."

"What is it with you, Seb? Why do none of your relationships ever last?"

"I prefer not to ask myself questions like that. It wasn't my fault, she left me."

"And that was nothing to do with you?"

"I didn't fool around with other women, if that's what you mean."

He laughed. "You're impossible," he said, "I give up. The only person you seem to have been able to relate to for any length of time is Sam."

"You're not the first person to say that," I agreed, and nervously brought up the reason for my visit.

"Talking of women in my life, do you ever see Alice?" I asked.

"No, why should I?"

"I assumed as they still live in that area you might still go down there from time to time."

"Not for years. I sold the cottage, didn't I tell you? Alice had moved in with Ellen Cooper at the farm. I did see her a few times after the sale, as you asked - just to make sure they were all right, but I rarely go down that way now. Frankly I'm too busy these days."

"Do you know if she's met anybody?"

"I thought you might ask that. I really have no idea."

"I see," I said, shaking my head. "I just thought you might have gone to see them, after the newspaper article you sent."

"When have I got time? I did speak to the reporter and he told me he thought the boy had a remarkable voice and that I ought to audition him for the Cathedral choir. But what would he really know about it? In any case however good his voice is, he's about ten isn't he? – he's a bit too old to start here really. We like them younger than that so they can be properly trained. In any case there would be too many problems coping with a blind boy in this place."

"That's a shame," I said. "It would have been lovely for him to come here."

"Alice wouldn't hear of it anyway, if I remember what she was like. Not the easiest lady I have ever come across. Did you know she was doing very well now with her paintings? I read in the Times that her work was selling for thousands now. My painting is probably worth at least ten times what I paid for it."

"Really? Lucky you! I wonder what my portrait is worth. Still I'm pleased for her. Did the reporter say anything more about Piers being a gifted child?"

"Well, you read what he said. He's obviously a clever boy. Shame he's blind."

"It certainly is."

"He also said that the story might be picked up by the nationals and when that happens he could be really big - articles in papers like the Guardian and Mirror, appearances on TV. But as far as I know it hasn't happened."

"I doubt Alice would agree to anything like that," I replied.

Mark grimaced. "She won't be able to prevent them printing the story, if they want to," he said. "Who knows what will happen after that? And before you get too excited don't forget questions might be asked about where you fit into all this. You do realise that."

This had not occurred to me and my first reaction was to think I should catch the next plane back.

"Go and see her," Mark said. "I assume you're here because you want to see Piers."

"Obviously, but I would be shown the door without any hesitation," I replied.

"You never, know," he said. "Women are strange creatures. I know I'd risk it. It's why you came all that way, isn't it? You had a good relationship with Sam. Perhaps in time you can do so with Piers."

"I was hoping you might come with me."

"No way! You have to sort this out yourself, chum."

I had little choice. I had to try at least. I formulated a plan and next day bought a country style coat, a flat cap and a pair of powerful binoculars. I had decided that a cautious approach was probably sensible and that I should first try and observe them from a distance. Dressed as I was, if she saw me I would be mistaken for a bird watcher. I hired a car, headed for Clyffe St Mary and parked just above the village in a lay-by on top of the Marlborough downs. It was close to the bridle path that runs along the top of the ridge above the farm. I started along it, reached the wood above the farm in about twenty minutes, sat down on a hillock close to the trees and focussed my binoculars on the farmhouse. I saw Mrs Cooper a couple of times walking to and from a large barn but no sign of Alice or Piers. I was a little surprised to hear the distant sound of wind chimes coming from the farm and wondered why they had been put up. It was probably one of Alice's batty ideas. After a while I saw a small car moving along a concrete track at the base of the hill and watched it drive into the farmyard. Alice got out followed by Piers. A large golden Labrador ran to greet them, barking and wagging its tail furiously until Mrs Cooper appeared at the door and quietened it down. They all went into the house but a few minutes later Piers came out wheeling a bicycle. He got on it and to my amazement rode off down the track at high speed. Surely he must be able to see to do that. Yet he was wearing dark glasses. Two minutes later he returned, dismounted and went back into the house carrying some letters. Not long afterwards he came out of the house again, this time with the dog, wandered through a gate at the back of the garden and along a path that led up to the woods. In one hand he held what looked like a thin tree branch that he pointed in front of him and in the other hand the dog's lead. The animal walked patiently ahead, looking round from time to time as if to make sure Piers was still there. The remarkable thing about him was that although he went slowly along he seemed to be moving quite easily. He did not stumble at all or trip on the uneven path. How could a blind boy do that? Saying he was totally blind must have been exaggerated by the newspaper just to sell a good story. They both vanished into the wood. I shifted my position to get a little closer and saw them again in what must have been the garden of the old cottage. To my surprise, the building had been repaired with a new slate roof and an extension added. I assumed someone must have bought it and was using it as a holiday cottage. I could also hear different wind chimes, this time much closer, louder and deeper in pitch. Piers sat down on an old garden seat. He was even better looking in person than in the newspaper photograph. His dark glasses and blond hair gave him almost a film star air. I wondered whether his eyes behind the dark lenses were still that lovely translucent blue. Little birds were hopping around him. He started singing what must have been a folk song, and the way his pure voice floated through the trees was magical. And this was the son I had rejected. What dreadful mistakes we all make in life. I felt terrible and all but turned round to go back. At the same time, and I knew I had no right, I felt overpoweringly emotional about him. I knew that I simply had to get to know him and be part of his future whatever the difficulties. I must have caused Piers and Alice great pain but I felt that I must somehow find a way to repair the damage and be of some use to them now. As I watched a small roe deer came down the hillside, meandered into the garden and went right up to him. It had no fear and Piers just stroked its head. It spotted me and snorted in my direction. Piers looked straight at me and I froze. He cannot have known I was there but his look was extremely disconcerting. The deer quickly moved away and Piers continued to stare in my direction. A crow circled above me and croaked a couple of times. A minute or so later, I heard his mother call out to him but he continued to stare hard and straight at me. He knew I was there and I was intruding into his world. It was very disconcerting. He stood up and followed the dog down the footpath. I had been there long enough. It was time to go.

I returned to my accommodation in a small inn near Avebury, some five or six miles away. After tea I sat in my room for an hour thinking about them and rehearsing in my mind what I would say to Alice when we met. I still did not know whether she had a new man in her life. It seemed unlikely – not many men would take on another man's blind child - then again, someone just might. I had not seen anyone else at the farm but I could not be sure. The doubts persisted and I decided I had to know right away. I drove over to the lay-by again. Fortunately, it was not quite dark so I was able to make my way along the ridge to the woods without difficulty. Through the trees I was able to just about make out the refurbished cottage. The windows were lit up but the curtains were half drawn and I could not see who was inside. I focussed on the farmhouse. I could see Ellen Cooper playing the piano in the living room but no sign of Alice and Piers. They could be in the kitchen. I watched for some time to no avail and, although I knew it was clearly madness, it was obvious that I had to get much closer. I decided to start by investigating the cottage. I made my way cautiously down to the garden and along the narrow path that led to it. The wind chimes I had heard earlier were hanging by the cottage door, silent in the still night air. Through the kitchen window I could see little else except mugs, plates and pots and pans. I moved slowly along the side of the cottage to the extension and pressed my face against the window. Piers sat on a couch and Alice stood a few yards away painting at her easel. She was listening to some classical music from a radio and there was no sign of anybody else. I felt partially reassured but the doubt still remained. If she did have a new man in her life the only other place he could be was in the farmhouse. I moved stealthily away and picked my way down the main path to the farmhouse. Mrs Cooper was still playing the piano. The other rooms were in darkness. It was obvious there was nobody else in the house. Feeling greatly relieved, I quietly returned to the cottage and resumed my position by the extension window. Alice was completely absorbed in what looked like a portrait of Piers lying on the couch. Then I shifted and must have made a slight noise for he suddenly sat up and looked straight at the window. God knows how, but he knew I was there! I panicked and ran, hitting my head on those damned wind chimes which clanged loudly. I cursed and fled back up the path towards the top of the downs.

As I reached the edge of the wood at the top of the hill I stumbled and turned my ankle over on a loose stone. A sharp pain shot through my leg as I flailed around trying to regain my balance. I grabbed hold of a branch but it broke and I fell, tumbling and rolling, over and over down a very steep incline, flinging my arms out and desperately trying to stop myself. It made no difference. Down and down I went, crashing though bushes, over bruising lumps in the ground and quite unable to halt my momentum. I must have hit my head on something hard for suddenly everything went into blackness. When I came to I was aware of a terrible pain in my right ankle and an appalling headache. Worse still nothing made sense. I could not understand why I was unable to move and why was I lying face down staring into blackness. I vaguely knew I had to get back to my feet and tried to move but it was as if something had my foot in an iron grip. I decided I must have broken my ankle and cursed, vaguely realising what a nuisance that was going to be. I called out for help as loud as I could but almost immediately I lost consciousness again.

I heard the chimes clatter, turned the radio down and carefully opened the door of the cottage a fraction. The chimes were moving slightly but there was no wind and nobody was there. Perhaps a bird flew into it. A strange, animal cry sounded in the distance. I strained my ears but there was nothing more.

"That sounded like a fox," I said.

"It wasn't a fox," Piers replied.

He was still staring at the window looking rather worried.

"What's the matter?" I asked.

"Someone was outside," he said. "They were near the window.

"Are you sure?"

"Yes, but they're gone now. I heard them run away."

I went to close the curtains and saw that on the window pane was a greasy smudge that I had not noticed before. Looking closer at the glass, I could just make out the image of a face staring back at me. Someone had come right up to the house and pressed against the window. I felt a pang of fear and picking up a walking stick cautiously returned to the door and opened it a little more. I could see nothing except the path and garden close to the studio illuminated by the window light. Beyond there was blackness. I strained my ears but all I could hear was the distant sound of Ellen playing Chopin on the piano in the farmhouse.

"Come on Piers," I said. "Let's go back down; I've done enough painting for this evening."

I told Ellen and she was reassuring as usual, telling me it was probably some tramp or an animal. I was tired so I went to bed early and quickly fell asleep. Sometimes when I dream it is as if I have not fallen asleep and what I am dreaming is real life and actually happening to me. On this occasion I was lost in woods looking for Piers. I could hear his voice quite close by crying out and calling for help, but just when I thought I had found him he was not there and I had no idea where he had gone. Then I could see him walking along the top of a hill smiling. Miraculously he could see. I called out but no sound emanated from my lips. Try as I might I could not make a sound and he would not look in my direction. I found myself sitting in a church and above me on one of the pillars were a group of hideous gargoyles. In the middle of them was Seb's face frozen in stone, his mouth curled in a cold smile, his blank eyes staring down at me. I heard a choir singing and turned to see a group of choristers dressed in red smocks moving in a procession along the nave. Behind them came an open coffin carried by a group of blind men. As it went by I stood up and strained to glimpse the face of the corpse inside. I was certain it must be Piers. But just as I was about to see into the coffin, the image vanished and I was standing in front of my easel in the garden of the cottage trying to paint a picture of Piers in which I wanted to put a large red sun. But when I tried to paint it the colours ran down the canvas like tears of blood, turning the painting into a terrible mess that upset and bewildered me because I was unable to stop it. Much to my relief, I woke up and blearily realised it had been a nightmare and I was still in my bedroom. Why should Seb's face be in my dream? Perhaps the image on the studio window reminded me of him. It was very scary.

Downstairs the living room clock chimed five and I was feeling grim. I had a headache and decided that some early morning fresh air might lift it. I went to the kitchen, picked up a basket, and quietly closing the farm house door made my way round the back and along the path to a field where I knew I could pick mushrooms. The Downs were silhouetted against the dawn sky and a silver-grey light was breaking through thin clouds. I thought I smelt rain in the cool air. The dawn chorus was in full throat and the birds were making a fantastic noise. As the sun rose I became a little warmer and began to feel better.

I had gathered a couple of dozen mushrooms when, at the far end of the field near the gate, I noticed a flock of crows cawing and wheeling round in circles above what might be a nearly dead animal. I took little notice and went on picking the mushrooms. After a few minutes I became aware that the crows were making far more noise than usual. The light was improving so I decided to go across and investigate. I must have been some twenty or thirty yards away when I realised that it was not a dead animal, it was a man's body. I shouted loudly and the crows that were starting to land close by took off in fright, whirring round making a truly horrendous sound with their cawing. The figure was ominously still. I went slowly over to it and nervously bent down. He was lying with his torso partly in the ditch and one leg caught by a tree root. I wondered whether he was alive and lifted his shoulder a little. Whoever it was looked in a bad way. The side of his face was caked in mud and blood and covered in scratches and cuts. I bent nearer to try to see for certain whether he was alive or not and put my hand on the back of his neck. It was warm but he did not move. I reached into his coat pocket to try to find out who he might be and found an envelope. It was an airline ticket and the name printed on it made me recoil with shock. My heart started racing away and thumping wildly. He was the last person I expected to see.

Then he moaned. It startled me and I sat back.

"I'll call for an ambulance," I said, getting out my phone.

"I can't move," he groaned.

"I'll get help," I said. I rang Ellen, asked her to bring across the lopper that we used for tree pruning, a blanket, and to ring for an ambulance.

"It won't be long," I told him. He had slipped into unconsciousness once more and did not respond. I began to get worried that he might have already died. Then he moved his head slightly and asked for some water.

"Soon," I said. I suppose I should have been angry but oddly, I just felt nothing.

Ellen came breathlessly over the field and I told her who it was.

"I thought we'd seen the last of that awful man," she said. "What's he doing here?"

"I've no idea but we've got to help him."

"Of course."

We concentrated on cutting through the root in which his ankle was trapped. It did not take more than few seconds. We pulled him up into a sitting position. He looked dreadful, his face yellowy- grey with dried blood on one side, his eyes sunken.

"I always knew you were my guardian angel," he whispered, making a painful attempt to smile at me.

I said nothing. Ellen wrapped the blanket round him and he muttered profuse thanks.

"I'm very tired," he said and lay back on the ground with his eyes shut. I was really worried he had a brain injury and tried to keep him talking but his eyes did not open. I began to doubt whether he would last much longer. After what seemed an interminable time, an ambulance came hurtling along the lane so I stood up and waved frantically to them. They stopped and two paramedics rushed across the field to us. As they examined him he woke up once more but just groaned. They put his head into a support and lifted him on to a stretcher.

"He should be alright," said one of them. "It looks worse than it is."

"I'm so grateful," he muttered.

They carried him back to the ambulance, which drove off at speed and I knew my life was about to change and almost certainly not for the better.

TEN

About two weeks later I was collecting wild flowers at far the end of the garden of my studio and failed to recognise the figure with a walking stick looking down at me from the top of the hill. I was used to being stared at by strangers. Unlike the usual hiker or birdwatcher, instead of continuing his walk along the ridge he came down the path and hobbled into the garden. Apart from the massive bruise on the side of his head and the grazes on his face, Seb looked little different from when he walked out - perhaps a little grey-haired on his temple and somewhat thinner. We both stood there, strangers but not strangers. It was almost as if he had just returned from the Goddard Arms somewhat worse for wear and had fallen over. It was a curious feeling. To my astonishment he produced a small bunch of freesias and offered them to me. I stared at these pretty flowers in astonishment. It was what he used to bring me when I painted his portrait. Did he think a small bunch of flowers would make up for everything he'd put me through? I wanted to throw them at him. Instead, I took a deep breath, coldly thanked him and rather formally asked him what he wanted.

"To thank you," he said. "I'm so grateful. If it hadn't been for you I could have easily died. It was incredibly kind of you to help me."

"I didn't realise who you were," I replied.

"You mean you'd have left me there if you had," he asked, with a cheeky grin.

"Of course," I said, coldly matching his smile.

He laughed. "I suppose I deserved that," he said.

I nodded. "You certainly did."

"Fortunately it was only concussion and a sprained ankle. They kept me in for a few days for observation. It's still a bit painful but, hey, I always used to enjoy rolling down a grassy bank when I was a kid." He laughed nervously but I did not change my expression.

"Why were you on the downs in the dark in the first place?" I asked

"I came along much earlier in the evening and stayed too long."

"Were you watching us?"

"I'm afraid so, but it was not deliberate, " he said. "I'm over here on holiday and I came for a walk on the downs for old times' sake. I was doing a little bird watching. I had just spotted a pair of kestrels hovering over the field down there when I saw you come out of the farmhouse and go up the path to the cottage."

Bird watching? Who did he think he was fooling? He had not changed a bit. He was still a consummate liar. "And you came right up to my studio looking through the window, didn't you?"

"Yes, I'm sorry about that. I knew I shouldn't but I couldn't stop myself."

"You left a face print on the glass. You've no idea how frightening that was."

"I'm really sorry. I didn't mean to do that."

"What do you want?"

"To talk to you about seeing my son, of course."

"You've got a nerve!" I said, fury seeping into my voice. "Just go away. You're not wanted here. There's no way I'm going to let you see Piers."

"I just want to get to know him a little," he said. "Is that so unreasonable?"

"After what you did? Don't be absurd."

"I know and I'm acutely aware of how wrong it was. I still feel very guilty about that.

"And so you should," I snapped back. "I don't want you anywhere near him."

It was too late. Piers had started to come up the path from the farm and Seb saw him.

"He's amazing," he said. "He moves around so easily. You'd never guess he can't see."

"Leave us alone," I hissed. "Just go back to America!'".

"Look," he responded, "I can understand how you felt when I left but you refused to come, remember. It wouldn't have happened if you'd come out there with me."

"No, no, you can't try and blame me. That's not fair. You left me, I didn't leave you."

"OK, OK, but blaming each other isn't getting us anywhere. It was a long time ago and these things happen. I've come back because I want to make up for it to you both."

"What do you think you can do?" I snarled. "I don't want anything from you. I've brought him up on my own. You have no place in his life."

"Don't you think he will want to know who I am sooner or later? He's coming up the path now. Just tell him who I am and see what he says."

"I don't think so. You must be insane! What do you expect me to say? Oh by the way this is your dad, he's an awfully nice chap really and he's terribly sorry he left us."

"Something like that would do nicely."

"Don't be sarcastic. You could have written, or sent him a birthday card. You've never shown any interest in him! Why now? You're contemptible!" I wanted to hit him.

"I sent you money all this time," he said. "You must give me some credit for that."

"I didn't need your money."

"I see, so your daddy came to the rescue, then?"

"That's very offensive, even for you! Yes my parents kindly helped me for a while but I wanted to survive on my own and I did. I'm proud of that."

"I know, I know, you're right. I apologise," he said. "It was a stupid thing to say. I was really pleased to hear that you've become so successful. I always thought you were amazingly talented. Let's calm things down or we'll get nowhere. How are your parents anyway?"

"They're fine but what do you care? You never liked them."

"They never liked me would be a more accurate way of putting it. Your father clearly thought I was a complete waste of space."

"Huh, well he wasn't too far out was he?"

"OK, OK this is getting us nowhere. We have to move on."

"That's rich!" I hissed. "You have to move on, you mean. I've already done so. Now just leave us alone. Go away and don't come back!"

Seb held both hands out palm up in a gesture of surrender. I heard the gate to the garden clink and saw that Piers was at the other end.

"I understand how you feel" he replied. "But I'm not going to go away. You must face the fact he'll have to meet me one day and it'll be better if we can at least be civil to each other."

I ignored this last remark and retreated down the garden quickly reaching Piers.

"Who were you talking to, Mum?" he asked.

"It's just a man I knew a long time ago," I said. "He's going now. We should go back to the house."

"It's lovely to see you again, Alice," Seb called out. I ignored it. Piers took my arm and I led him back down the path. I could feel Seb's angry eyes burning into my back as he watched us all the way.

"Why were you shouting at him?" Piers asked.

"Oh, he was not being very nice."

"Who was he?"

"Just someone I used to know. Come on."

I suppose I should have told him right then who Seb really was but I could not bear the idea. What was he doing spying on us? It was really creepy. I said nothing to Ellen until after Piers had gone to bed.

"I don't like it," I told her. "I feel so vulnerable. Why is he back all of a sudden?"

"Curiosity I should imagine. He must wonder what his son is like," she replied.

"But why should he suddenly come back after so many years?" I asked. "What does he want?"

"I don't think you need worry too much. He probably just feels remorse."

"Remorse is not in his vocabulary!" I replied.

I knew he must have another motive but what it was I could not imagine. If it was curiosity I hoped it was satisfied. Somehow I doubted it and I was sure he would reappear soon. Well, he would get the same answer.

Seeing Piers from just a few yards away in the cottage garden had unexpectedly set off strong feelings in me that I found hard to put into words. The baby I had abandoned was no longer simply the photograph of a blind boy I had seen in a newspaper. He had become a real person and I wanted to reach out to him. It was not just that I somehow needed to explain myself to him, to say I was deeply sorry about what I had done and that I would make it up to him. It was deeper than that. I suppose above all I wanted him to understand and accept me. Life is full of hard choices and sometimes whatever you choose to do is wrong. Ten years ago I had made the right one for Sam and the wrong one for Piers. Perhaps I could put it right now if Alice could be persuaded to be a little more reasonable. But why should she? She must see me as some sort of monster and I wondered if she would even tell him who I was. Somehow I doubted it and if she did, how he would react? More than likely he would hate me. Who could blame him, and suddenly it felt very painful. I wanted to meet him, talk to him and try and explain things. But explain what? The truth was that I abandoned him as a tiny baby and had never come back until now. What would he think of that? Very little, I should imagine. Like his mother he would probably just tell me to go away. If I had any sense I should do what she said, return to America right now and leave them alone. I could not. I had to know what he would say even if it was not what I wanted to hear. I suppose above all what I needed was him to forgive me, and as long as there was just a slim chance he might I had to go on. As for Alice, although I don't underestimate how hard it must have been for her to deal with at the time, in a curious way you could say that in some ways it had been good for her. It had made her face up to who she was and what she wanted out of life. She had become a successful artist, someone in her own right with a reputation. Would she have done that if I had stayed? Who knows? Was she now tough and independent because she had been forced to grow up by what had happened? Possibly, but of course she would not see it like that. She probably thought I was worthless then and now. She was probably right but whatever my imperfections, the decision I took undoubtedly did her, perhaps even both of us, a favour. It was just another of those absurd contradictions in my confusing existence.

As I drove back to my room in Avebury I thought about the ferocious ear roasting I had been given. True I had expected it, except that she was much more hostile than I anticipated. In my more unrealistic moments I had thought she might still have some feelings for me but obviously she did not. No, if I was to get access I clearly needed to think of a different way of meeting Piers other than by attempting to batter down the portcullis. That would only result in boiling oil being poured on my head.

I had a depressing supper at the Inn and retired to bed early to try to think about how to proceed. I recognised the expression in Alice's eyes that told me the shutters had come down. Fortunately I had a good night's sleep and awoke feeling surprisingly optimistic. My depressed mood had gone and I set about making a new plan. My original idea of offering her financial help was clearly the wrong strategy and I needed a more subtle approach. I left it for a few days and spent the time considering the matter whilst visiting the extraordinary Avebury stone circle, Silbury Hill and the other Neolithic remains in that area. I suppose if I had been a Stone Age man with a club I would have just gone and taken Piers. It was a nice primitive idea but obviously I did not want to do that. I just needed to get to know my son a little, not take over his life. What was the harm in that? To stand a chance of forming any sort of relationship I needed to talk to him on his own. But how could I do so without her finding out and preventing me?

A few days later I decided I should again make a circumspect return and observe them from the woods above the farm. I drove there and, as before, I parked in the lay-by on top of the downs. As I sat there wondering quite how to remain unobserved another car pulled in. A middle-aged couple with a dog got out and went towards the bridle path. They would be the perfect cover. I jumped out and followed them keeping just a few yards behind. If Alice saw me she would think I was with them. As we entered the cover of the wooded area I let the couple go ahead, sat down on a tree stump and trained my binoculars on the farm. There was little activity for a few minutes then I saw Alice come out of the house by herself, get in the car and drive off. There was no sign of Piers. I thought he might be in the garden of the cottage so I cautiously went down the path that led to it. He was not and I returned to the top of the hill. After waiting for a few more minutes I decided to go a little further along the ridge so that I could see the back of the farm. It was as I came out of the woods that I saw him a few yards away sitting on a bank. I froze. He slowly turned his head and looked straight at me through his dark glasses. Sometimes chance or fate takes a hand in one's life and as far as I was concerned this was it. He was by himself and this was my opportunity. I walked slowly towards him.

"Hello young man," I called out, my nerves jangling almost uncontrollably.

"Hi," he replied.

"I was just going for a walk over the Downs," I said, inanely.

"I know," he replied, "I heard you coming."

"You're Piers, aren't you?"

He nodded. "You're the man who was talking to my mum the other day? I recognise your voice."

She obviously had not told him who I was. Well perhaps I would but not yet. "That's right." I said. "Can I sit here?" He nodded so I sat down on the bank next to him, wondering quite what I would say. "It's lovely on top of the downs isn't it?" I muttered after an awkward pause.

"I like it," he replied.

"There's a wonderful view from here," I murmured and then realised the stupidity of what I had just said.

"It is," he replied. How did he know what sort of view it was? As I searched for something more sensible to say he continued: "Mum found a man lying on the ground down there. She thought he was dead."

I stiffened in surprise, wondering what he would say next. "That must have been a shock for her," I replied.

"I already knew he was there," he said. "The crows told me." This just sounded like childish fantasy.

"How?" I asked, humouring him.

"It was the way they were crowing," he said. "They were waiting for him to die so they could feed on him."

"Who was he?" I asked.

He shrugged. "I don't know. Mum said he was a probably a tramp."

"Do you really think they'd have eaten him?"

"Yes, if mum hadn't found him and he'd died. Crows eat dead animals. It's natural."

"Was he really dying?"

"I think so."

"These terrible things happen," I told him. "It's not very nice."

He thought for a few seconds. "There's life and death and decay all around us, I know that. I smell it and hear it all the time. What nature does sometimes seem harsh but it's not. It doesn't worry me. Death is part of life but we would not exist without it. The birds, the animals, plants, everything that grows will die in the end and will be replaced. I will, you will. It's the way nature works. Nothing is ever wasted and we're all part of it. It's just the way it is."

He was extraordinary. He appeared to be child-like but at the same time he clearly thought about and understood so much more than I had expected. I heard the wind chimes tinkling in the distance.

"I like the sound of those chimes blowing in the wind," I said.

"They're pretty," he replied.

"There seem to be two sets," I said, "one at the farm and one at the cottage."

"My mum put them up for me so I know where I am when I'm in the garden or up here. So I can always find my way back."

"That was clever of her," I said. He nodded in agreement. "You can't see very well can you?"

"No," he replied. "I'm blind." He glanced at me as if to say 'you know that perfectly well.'

"Well something has been puzzling me;" I said. "The first time I came along here I saw you riding a bicycle very fast down the track to the farm."

He nodded. "My mum asks me to get the post sometimes," he replied.

"How do you do that if you're blind?"

"I can see colours and shapes but not clearly. The concrete road is white and the grass is green so if I keep to the white bit I should be OK."

"But you ride so fast," I said.

"It's more fun. Mum tells me not to but it's much more exciting like that."

"Don't you ever crash and hurt yourself?"

"Sometimes, but it doesn't matter."

"That's astonishing!" I replied. What a gutsy boy my son was! He took his sunglasses off and looked in my direction, his startling blue eyes almost un-nerving me. He looked as if he was wearing contact lenses of the sort used by actors to glamourize them. At the same time they were oddly expressionless. It was quite disconcerting and then, even more unsettling, he asked me a question that was very much to the point.

"Why do you want to talk to me?"

I almost blurted out who I was but managed to prevaricate. "What do you mean?" I asked.

"You told my mum you just wanted to talk to me. I heard you. Why?"

I knew I should say that I was his father there and then but the words would not come out. How would he take it? What would he say? I could not bear the idea that he would just reject me, which seemed more than likely. I needed to get to know him a little better and the time was not right. In any case I had decided Alice should tell him. So I muttered incoherently:

"Well, um, I knew your mother a long time ago and….. I've been in America and…..err."

"Were you her boyfriend, then?" he cut in, much to my relief.

"Yes, I was, "

"Mum said you weren't very nice to her,"

"She's right, I wasn't," I replied. "I feel bad about it and I just came to say how sorry I was, nothing else."

"What did you do?" he asked.

"Nothing much. We just quarrelled a lot."

"What about?"

"All sorts of things."

"She was really angry, yesterday," he said.

"I know and I don't blame her."

"Why?" he asked.

"Because I deserved it."

"What did you do?"

"Oh, it's complicated," I said. I did not want to go too far down this penitential line.
"I had to take a job in America and go by myself. She was rather upset about that. I had no choice, though. These things happen in life."

He pursed his lips quizzically, as if he understood this and then sighed.

"America," he replied. "It must be a wonderful place."

"It is. I live there now and I'm just over here on holiday."

"I'd love to go there," he said.

"Perhaps you will one day." My brain raced ahead uncontrollably as I pictured him living with me in my house in San Jose. I could not stop myself adding: "You could come and stay with me if you like."

"That would be amazing," he said. "I've read a lot about America."

"How did you manage that?" I asked.

"What?" he asked.

"You said you read a lot about America."

"I can see a little, close up," he replied. "I use an old magnifying glass. It's easy."

"What are you interested in?"

"I love plants and animals and birds. The birds talk to me."

"The birds talk to you?"

"Yes, they tell me things. Lots of animals do as well."

"How?"

"They don't actually talk but I understand the noises they make. I always have. They are my friends." I looked at his face but he was quite serious. He clearly believed in this fantasy so I did not argue.

"What else do you like doing?" I asked.

He shrugged. "I like playing chess," he said.

"I used to play a bit when I was a boy," I replied.

"And I also like playing the piano and singing. Ellen teaches me."

"I heard you singing the other day in the garden," I said. "What was it?"

"I don't know - probably 'Down by the Sally Garden,' " he replied. "I've been learning it. I like folk songs. Some of them are very sad but when I sing them they make me feel better. It's funny that, isn't it?"

"Yes I suppose it is. Do you often feel sad?" I asked. His answer turned me inside out.

"I haven't got a Dad like other children," he replied. "He went away when I was very young. I don't know why. Maybe it was because I was blind."

"I can't believe that," I gasped, alarmed at the way the conversation was going. "I'm sure he would never have done such a thing."

"Why did he go then?"

"I expect he had his reasons. Have you got any friends?" I asked, desperate to change the subject.

"Well there are a couple of girls who come for piano lessons. I used to play with them last year but they always rush away these days. I haven't really got any friends, except the animals."

"Don't you go to school?"

"No, mum and Ellen teach me at home. I'd like to go to school but mum says there isn't a suitable one around her."

"What about when you go to the park? You meet other boys and girls there, don't you?"

"Yes, but they hardly ever speak to me, and when they do they often call me zombie or say I'm an alien and stuff like that."

"That's dreadful. Why?"

"I don't really know."

"Aren't you lonely?"

"No, not really. I'm used to it and I can talk to the animals."

A car horn tooted and Piers stood up picking up two long thin sticks from the ground next to where he had been sitting.

"That's my mum back from shopping."

"I see you have two sticks now," I said.

"Yes, I use two when Goldie doesn't come with me. It helps me know where I am. I must go down now."

"Fine," I replied. "Could I ask you to do something, or rather, not to do something for me? Don't tell your mother I've spoken to you."

"Why not?" he asked.

"Because she'll be even angrier with me than she was the other day."

"I could tell her I liked you."

As you can imagine, those simple words delighted me.

"No definitely don't do that," I replied.

"Will you come and see me again?"

"Of course I will," I replied. This simple request, so direct in its appeal, made me feel both deeply ashamed and ludicrously elated at the same time. I was being given a chance to make amends with him that I knew I did not deserve.

"I'll see you then," he said and departed, going more swiftly down the path than I thought was possible. I watched him all the way down using his sticks, one in either hand like probes. It was almost as if he could see. I returned to my car even more conscious of the damage I had done to him and wondering how I could repair it. On the positive side, I had been surprised to discover that I found him easy to talk to and I felt far more comfortable being with him than I thought I would. It was a good start. Alice would try to stop me, of course, but since he wanted to see me then I would have to find a way of circumventing her opposition.

Over the next few days I went back a couple more times but he did not come up to the top of the hill again. It was frustrating because I had decided to tell him exactly who I was, and I did not have much time left. I was due to return to California in a few days. I had to know how he would react when he knew who I was. If he rejected me I would go back to America and stay there. If he did not, and after what he had said to me on the hillside I thought this was more likely, I would negotiate a little more time off from Gemina so that I could come back and try to form a real relationship with him. However, not seeing Piers for a few days gave me a chance to think things through and I began to feel simply telling him I was his father right now was not the smartest thing to do. He would almost certainly ask Alice why she had not told him who I was, and this was likely to alienate her even more. She would put every obstacle she could think of in my way. No, I had to stick to my plan of persuading Alice that it would be better coming from her. That way she could hardly object to my seeing Piers, especially if he told her he wanted to see me. So I formulated a plan to get him on my side. What better way was there than taking him an expensive present? It would annoy Alice, but hey, it would be no worse than poking a stick into a wasp's nest. I could always beat a rapid retreat from the angry queen. I had to find Piers something he would be thrilled with but which she could hardly refuse to let him have. So next day I drove to Worcester to do some shopping.

Seb said he would be back and I had little doubt that he would. Consequently, I began to imagine he was watching us from somewhere in the trees or on the hillside. Every now and then I looked anxiously out from the kitchen window at the downs but saw no one. I told Piers not to go up there for the moment. I did not want to risk him meeting Seb. He was such a trusting boy and would believe the lies Seb was sure to tell him. He argued about it but in the end I stamped my foot and he reluctantly acquiesced. He went into a sulk for a couple of days, which worried me, but he would not tell me why. Ellen noticed me watching the hillside and told me to get a grip and not let my imagination make matters worse.

A week or so later I was inside my studio when I looked through the open door and thought I saw Seb's face deep in the shadows of nearby bushes. I rushed out and hunted round for some minutes but there was no sign of him. Then I heard voices and knew it was too late. He had not been skulking around the hillside but had driven right up to the farmhouse gate and was now talking to Piers. I rushed down the path and ran over to him, furious at his nerve.

"He's amazing," Seb said to me as I reached them. "He knows all the wild flowers and plants. It's incredible; he can tell them just by their feel and their smell."

"He can see what colour they are as well," I said, angrily.

"He's never wrong."

"How would you know?" I snapped at him and turned to Piers, who was holding a small bunch of herbs he had been collecting. "You'd better take those to Ellen, darling, she needs to prepare them as soon as possible."

"Look Mum," he said, holding up his wrist. "Seb has bought me this. It's a watch that speaks the time." He pressed it to show how it worked.

"Very nice, now just do as you're asked for once," I retorted. He stared at me, disappointment etched on his face, then slowly retreated into the barn.

"I told you to stay away from us," I said.

"And I said I was not going to," he replied.

"How dare you bring him presents?" I shouted.

"It's only a cheap watch," he replied, doing his best to look rather injured.

"It's a bit more than that. It must have cost a lot of money."

"Not really. It has very big numbers as well so he might be able to read them. I thought he might like it."

"I can get him things like that if he needs it," I said. "Do you think you can just buy your way in to his affection?"

"Don't be ridiculous. I just thought he would find it useful. Where's the harm in that?"

"Have you told him who you are?" I asked.

"Not yet. I thought it might upset you and I would rather not do that. In my view it would be better coming from you."

I told him that he should go back to America. He just smiled, said I should not be too hasty and as it happened he was returning to the States, but he would be back before long.

His visit made me extremely worried. It was obvious I could not prevent him seeing Piers indefinitely. It had also become clear that I should have been open with Piers about who Seb was in the first place. I went to find Piers right away and took him up to the cottage garden where we sat on the bench. Telling him that the stranger who had come into our lives was his father was not easy.

"You know I told you Seb was an old boyfriend," I said. He nodded. "Well that was true but there's something else I should tell you that may come as a bit of a surprise." He stiffened, looked at the ground but said nothing. I had no option but to go on.

"He is also your father." He just nodded but still did not utter a word. "Are you OK about that?" I asked. He just shrugged his shoulders.

"I don't know," he said.

"It won't change anything between us, if that's what you are worried about."

"I'm not," he replied.

"He went to America when you were very young," I told him.

"Why did he go?"

How could I tell him the horrible things Seb had said about him when he had left? I made up some nonsense to explain it but I'm not sure he believed me.

"Will he come back again?" he asked.

"He said he would but I don't know. What do you think about it?

"I don't know."

"If it upsets you I'll tell him he can't come and see us."

"No don't do that. He's nice to me."

"Ok I'll just say he can see you occasionally."

"If he's my father, why doesn't he come and live with us?"

"Because he lives in America."

"Do you want him to?"

"No, not really."

"Why not?"

"Because we've lived apart too long. What do you think about him?" I asked.

He took a deep breath. "I like him, he's nice to me," he said, looking rather anxiously at me. He told me about their conversation a few days earlier and explained that he had said nothing to me because Seb had told him it would make me angry. How could I be annoyed with him? His innocent face could melt my heart at any time, so I just smiled ruefully and told him to go and do some piano practice.

Back in San Jose I took stock. I had made a start but I now really wanted to play a much larger part in Piers' life. Yes Alice was more hostile than I had expected but I was confident she would not be able to hold out for ever. Piers clearly liked me and that was a huge unexpected bonus and made me confident that she would lower the drawbridge eventually.

One afternoon I had to deliver a lecture at the university and afterwards, quite by a chance, I met an English woman called Margaret Gower at one of the Department's social gatherings. She told me she had been invited by the Society for the Blind in California to talk to students about her experiences in England as a teacher specialising in the needs of blind children. She told me about a boy she visited in Wiltshire who was quite brilliant and could get to Oxford or Cambridge with the right help. It had to be Piers she was talking about and so I told her I was his father and we had split up many years ago.

"It was probably my fault," I said. "I'm afraid I was unable to deal with having a blind child."

"That's very honest of you," she replied. "Most people refuse to face up to the truth about themselves. It's not any easy thing to admit. I do understand."

"As it happens, I went over there to see them a couple of weeks ago," I said. "I wanted to see what I can do to make amends."

"Of course I'm not allowed to discuss them in any great detail with you," she replied. "But I can tell you that from my standpoint Alice is doing a brilliant job educating him at home, although he does have gaps in some areas and I do have concerns about his social development now that he's getting older."

"Is there any way I can help?"

"That's hard to say. You could try and persuade Alice that he needs to go to school now."

"If he's doing so well academically, why do you say that?" I asked.

"Yes, academically he's fine but his social development is sadly lacking," she replied. "He seems to have no friends and he finds it hard to relate to other children. He hardly meets any for a start."

"I suppose it's difficult to do that living at the farm."

"I'm sure it is but I'm concerned about him becoming a well-educated loner. That happens with too many blind people. In my opinion, home education is not enough for a blind child and will make things more difficult for him in future. I think he needs to go to school now and learn to make friends. And that is not easy for blind children."

"What do you mean?"

"Most of us learn to mix socially when we go to school. We frequently decide straight away if we like someone or not, and this might be because of something as apparently simple as whether we like the expression on their faces. The eyes play a huge part in this. Eye contact is very important in establishing all relationships and for a blind child this is not possible. He cannot see all those tiny signals that come from the face and subconsciously convey so much about what we feel. When a sighted child meets a blind child he will have difficulties as well because a blind child's eyes often look strange and expressionless to him, and he also cannot make normal eye contact. Consequently, for both blind and sighted children, meeting for the first time can be a difficult and sometimes worrying experience, particularly for the sighted child. Most blind children only make sighted a friend when another child gets to know them as a person. If Piers remains at home it's unlikely he'll be able to do this. Unless he learns to mix, and for most children this usually means at a school, I fear it may harm his development and he may not reach his potential. That would be a real tragedy for such a gifted child."

"He did say something to me about kids calling him names and being nasty."

"That's the reason. He looks normal but he can't make eye contact and that frightens other children."

"You say he should go to school. What do you suggest?"

"There are some specialist blind colleges with excellent teachers who do a fantastic job. There's one in Worcester. He could go there."

"It's a fair way from where they live, though."

"He could board. Many blind children do."

"I don't think Alice would ever agree to that."

"Probably not, so perhaps you could try to persuade her."

After this conversation, the more I thought about it the more I realised I had to return soon and do something. As Margaret had confirmed, Piers was clearly very gifted. It was obvious he required much wider social and educational horizons if he was ever to achieve anything. I had to find a way to persuade Alice of this, or failing that try to prise him away from her influence. One way for me to do this would be to go back to England to live. I could at least see him much more often and have some influence on his future. But I stood to lose an awful lot of money if I did that and anyway I liked my job and living in the good old US of A. And much more important was Sam. I could not just abandon my firstborn son, could I? Whatever I did I would have to stay living in America. Boarding schools for the blind would be a possibility but I was no keener on sending him to one than I thought Alice would be. He could go to a local comprehensive school but that would be a huge gamble. As for private education, I doubted whether many public schools would welcome a blind pupil however clever. I could see no real answers.

I needed to go back straight away and dear old Professor Zuckerman turned out to be very understanding. He agreed I could take as long as necessary to sort out my family matters but strictly on the understanding that I would return before the launch of the latest version of our operating system. This gave me about eight or nine weeks to play with so I immediately flew back to England.

T he gift Seb brought Piers next time he appeared must have cost hundreds of pounds. It was an electronic book magnifier specially made for partially sighted children. I was furious, but I could see it would be very useful to Piers. Of course Piers loved it and spent hours getting books down from the shelves, putting them on it and reading them. A week later, Seb appeared with another expensive gadget, a specially adapted computer with electronic braille and voice recognition, and I was forced to let him to show Piers how it all worked. Piers was delighted and with Seb's help he mastered the software with astonishing speed. Seb came more and more often to help him. It became obvious that Piers looked forward to his visits, particularly as he nearly always brought little bribes for him. I told Seb he was spoiling him but he brushed aside my protestations saying nothing was too good for his clever son. His attitude infuriated me. He was slowly worming his way into our lives.

Matters came to a head shortly after this when one of his visits coincided with the specialist teacher who kept Piers supplied with large type books and was teaching him Braille. The odd thing was that I saw Seb talking animatedly to her as she got out of her car. I assumed he was just being friendly. When she came in Seb went to help Piers with his computer and left me talking to her about Piers' development. She tried to persuade me once more that he should start at a Worcester College next year. I gave her my usual answer that he was better off here than going to a blind school. After she left I told him what she wanted and my response. Of course he did not agree with me.

"Margaret's right," he said. "Piers should go school. It can't be good for him never meeting kids of his own age. He's obviously lonely."

"He's not," I replied, "he's quite happy here."

"But he doesn't seem to have any friends and he talks to himself an awful lot. I've never seen any of the village children here. He talks more to the horses next door than other children."

"So what?"

"It's not normal."

"All children do that sort of thing," I replied. "It's just pretence."

"No, I've heard him. He thinks they can really understand him. It's a bit weird."

"What nonsense!" I said.

"Not at all. Anyway, it's not natural for a boy of his age to be on his own so much. He needs company, kids of his own age. He's too cut off here."

"He plays in chess tournaments and meets other boys there."

"That's all very well, but do the chess boys come here for a game?"

"Well no. He also plays with Ellen's pupils in the garden," I responded.

"It's not the same thing as learning to relate properly with other kids. He can only do that at school. On that subject he also needs better teaching. You've done well, I grant you, but Margaret told me he now needs to go to school."

"Margaret? Have you spoken to her before today?"

"Well, yes."

"When?"

"A few weeks ago in America as it happens. She was giving a lecture there. She told me about the brilliant blind boy she helped who lived in Wiltshire. I knew it could only be Piers."

"Is that why you came back in the first place?"

"No, I came back because I've always felt guilty and I was curious after all this time."

I really shouted at him: "Just idle curiosity was it? Idle curiosity about the son you said would never be able to play cricket or football with and who was not the son you'd always wanted."

"I knew you would throw that at me sooner or later," he replied. "But it doesn't get us anywhere. She thinks with the right teaching in a school he could get into Oxford or Cambridge. I agree."

"Don't be ridiculous," I snapped. "Where would he go to school? Worcester College? He'd hate it. Go to the local comprehensive? They wouldn't have a clue. It's out of the question. In any case, he would never survive away from here. He'd feel quite lost all the time. It works for him here because he knows every blade of grass. How would he cope?"

"I'm sure he'd get on perfectly well."

"What do you know about it?"

"He's a very clever child. That's obvious to anyone. Furthermore, he has a wonderful voice as well. I'd like Mark to hear him one day. I'd like to know what he thinks."

"What does it matter what Mark thinks?"

"They might offer him a place at the Cathedral School."

"Very likely! It's a crazy idea."

"But he won't get anywhere shut away out here in the back of beyond."

This last remark made me even angrier. How dare he talk to me like this? I really told him off and asked him to go. He stood there sullenly staring out of the window. Suddenly, I understood it all. He had discovered he had fathered a child he had been told was a genius. That was why he came back. It was every man's dream - a child who would demonstrate the quality of his father's genes. He could talk about his astonishingly clever son to all his university chums and bask in their admiration. He could smile and modestly applaud at the degree ceremony. He's the father, you know, of the blind boy with the double first at Oxford, amazing really. It was a good job he stepped in and organised things so he could go to university. His silly mother tried to hide him away. She would have been happy for him to be a country yokel! No matter that he had abandoned us he now wanted a vicarious glory. I wanted to kill him. I picked up the breadknife. Fortunately, before I could do anything really stupid, the door opened and Ellen came in.

Seb turned towards her. "Nice to see you again Ellen but I'm just leaving," he said.

"Not stopping for tea, then?" I asked. He smiled sourly and left.

Seb's next ploy was to ask that Piers be allowed to come out with him for a day. He said he was renting a house and would like to take Piers back there to sleepover one night so they could spend some time together and he could get to know him. I refused of course, but agreed he could take him out for an afternoon. They went to a local owl and small animal centre and Piers told me he had been able to stroke the heads of some of the owls, which he thought was fantastic.

The next time Seb asked if he could take him out for a whole day, perhaps to a wild life park. Piers overheard our conversation and was so excited about the idea it was impossible to say no. Seb took him to Longleat and brought him back on time. Not long after that he took Piers to the seaside for the day. It was a long drive. Seb rang to tell me they would be a little late so I did not mind. Of course Piers loved it and told me he thought splashing in the sea, building sandcastles, having a meal in a restaurant and arriving back at half past ten at night was superb.

A few days later Seb arrived after breakfast and said he would like Piers to come with him to get a professional photograph taken so that he could take a really nice picture of him back to the States. He knew of a photographer in Waterbridge and told me they ought to be back by late afternoon. It seemed harmless enough so why not?

ELEVEN

Of course I did not go to Waterbridge but drove straight to Stowe Minster. After my conversation with Margaret Gower I had decided to take Piers to see Mark and try to persuade him to accept my son as a pupil at the Cathedral School. True, I had to use a little harmless subterfuge to get him there but what alternative did I have? I would have preferred to have been open with her about seeing Mark but I was certain she would reject the idea out of hand. She would be livid, but hey, I got off lightly last time. I could understand why she felt the need to protect him, but in doing so she was wrapping him up in a cocoon of care and not really preparing him for the bumps and bruises of real life. After all he was not going to be her darling little boy for ever. He was growing up fast and needed to discover and explore the real world outside. Soon he must decide what he wanted to do with his life and the Cathedral School route to one of the big universities would enable this. Living deep in the country might be fulfilling her dream but what about his needs?

I telephoned the school who told me that Mark was tied up at a recording session in the cathedral but would be free mid-afternoon. So I took Piers to a photographic shop where I had the portrait of him taken. I arranged to have a couple of enlargements framed and then took him to a small restaurant for lunch. I had noticed over the past weeks that outside the familiar surroundings of the farm he became quite nervous and lacked his normal self-confidence. In the restaurant I had to guide him to the table, put his hand on the chair and help him sit down. He asked me to choose what he ate and show him where the glass of water was. He was clearly in need of reassurance.

After the meal we returned to the Cathedral. The route took us past the Cathedral School and we could hear the sounds of violins, a piano and other instruments coming through the open windows. Piers stopped me and we stood listening for a couple of minutes. He seemed transfixed and asked me where we were.

"It's outside a school where children with a lot of talent learn to play music and sing," I explained.

"It's so exciting," he said. "Can we go in and listen?"

"Not right now," I told him. "Perhaps later – I'll have to ask my friend Mark who works here and he's busy right now."

"Is that why we're here?" he asked.

"Yes," I said. "I'd like Mark to meet you."

I took him for a walk round the Cathedral grounds, and as we went round the Bishop's moated garden he held firmly on to my arm so that I could guide him. The way he clung on made me feel very protective and somehow worthwhile. When we reached the Cathedral he said wanted to go inside and so I took him to the main door. They were just taking a break from the recording and we were able to slip in. Inside he seemed to sense the enormous space of the building and it obviously intimidated him for he gripped my hand fiercely. The choristers were sitting in the choir stalls chatting quietly and Mark was talking to a slightly overweight, smartly dressed middle-aged man whose long, thinning hair was tied back in a straggly pony tail.   He was clearly the producer from the recording company. Mark saw us and waved a greeting.

"What a surprise," he said, "this must be Piers, of course. You've grown up a lot since I last saw you. You were a tiny baby then."

Piers grinned self-consciously.

"What are you both doing here?" he asked.

"We were just passing," I replied. "I popped in to ask whether you might have a chat with him sometime and hear him sing. He does have a wonderful voice."

Mark looked less than happy and took me to one side. "Look Seb," he said, "I'm sorry. I would love to hear Piers sing but you can see what we are up to at the moment. I really don't have time today."

"Sure," I replied. "I quite understand."

He introduced me to the record producer.

"This is Jonathan Goldman, from Augun Records," he said.

Jonathan smiled at us. "Wasn't he the boy who stole the show at the Wootton Basset Music Festival?" he asked. "Didn't I see a picture of him in the local paper a couple of months ago?"

"Yes, that's right."

"They said he had a wonderful voice. What do you think of it, Seb?"

"I think he does," I replied. "But I'm just his father so what do I know? I wanted to get Mark's opinion."

"Has he had any training?"

"Yes he's been having singing lessons for several years now."

"In that case, if it's all right with Mark, I would like to listen to him as well. Could you possibly wait until we've finished? We shouldn't be too long."

He retreated into the ante room he was using as a makeshift control studio and Mark took his conductor's place in the choir stalls where he clapped his hands and told the boys they needed to repeat the last section again. We sat down and listened to the boys, their fresh, pure voices echoing along the knave. I glanced down at Piers from time to time and he seemed absolutely transfixed by it. When the session ended Jonathan re-appeared and asked to hear Piers.

As I led him over to the piano he gripped my arm nervously. "Just sing like you do at home," I whispered. He looked so vulnerable, a tiny figure standing there in the enormous and imposing mediaeval architecture of the building. Mark asked him to sing a few scales which he did, gradually gaining confidence.

"Fine, very good, you do have a lovely voice Piers, " said Mark. "What would you like to sing for us?"

"I don't mind," he replied.

"What about that piece you sang at the music festival? 'I Vow to Thee My Country' wasn't it?" asked Jonathan.

"I don't have any music for it," said Mark. "I suppose I could improvise. Do you have anything else you'd like to sing?"

"I could play it and sing if you want," said Piers. "that's what I did at the Festival."

Mark shrugged. "OK, why not," he said, smiling, and helping Piers to the piano stool. He sat down and played a few notes before saying he was ready. "Off you go then," said Mark. Piers accompanied himself and sang it quite beautifully. I found it very moving and could see how it had been the highlight at the festival.

Mark nodded. "Good, and you play the piano well but I'd like to hear you sing standing up. I'll see if I have the music for something else." He started rummaging around in his music case.

"I do think Piers has a lovely voice," said Jonathan. "Can you find him something more demanding, Mark?"

"Do you know 'Linden Lea'?" asked Mark, holding up a sheet of music.

Piers said he did and Mark showed him to where he wanted him to stand. He played the introduction, Piers came in at exactly the right moment and sang it in a clear voice. As far as I could tell it was perfectly in tune. There were even a few claps from the boys in the choir and I could see Jonathan and Mark were both impressed. I wondered what had happened to the anxious child who held my arm so tightly only a minute ago.

"What about the 'Pie Jesu' from the Fauré Requiem? Do you know it Piers?" asked Jonathan.

"I don't think that's a good idea," interrupted Mark. "It's very demanding and he hasn't even warmed up properly. It's far too difficult. For a start, he won't know the words."

"Mum has it on a CD and I've sung along with it," replied Piers. "I know what the tune goes like and I think can I remember the words," said Piers.

"You know the words? But they're in Latin." Jonathan was clearly astonished.

"They're not very difficult to remember," replied Piers.

"Right, then, shall we give it a go, Mark?" asked Jonathan.

Mark again agreed rather reluctantly but first made Piers sing more exercises, Piers' voice gradually getting higher. When he was satisfied, Mark played the tune of the Fauré several times. Piers listened carefully and began to hum it.

"What do you think, Piers?" asked Jonathan.

"I'll try."

After a couple of abortive attempts Piers voice suddenly soared into the stratosphere and resonated around the Cathedral. It was not perfect but I thought he sounded like an angel. When he finished, this time the boys in the choir gave him a huge round of applause. Piers looked a little flustered but rather pleased. I walked over and put my arm around his shoulder.

"Brilliant!" I whispered to him.

Jonathan was clearly very impressed and turned to me. "I think we have star quality here."

"I'm no real judge," I said, "but he sounded very good to me."

"Listen, Seb," he said. "I own a recording studio in London. Could I try him out some time? Do you mind if I call you?"

I gave him my card. Alice would not like it but I could hardly say no, could I? Opportunities like this have to be seized.

"Ok boys, tea time," Mark called out to the choristers. "Would Piers like some? My son Peter could look after him."

Piers agreed he was hungry but asked me to go with him.

"You'll be fine," I said. "I need to talk to Mark. I'll come and get you later."

As the choristers filed out Mark called his son Peter across. I showed him the right way to lead Piers and explained that he would have to help him. Peter said he was sure they would be fine and I watched the two of them follow the others. I hoped Piers might make friends with Peter. That alone would justify the visit.

"What does Alice think about you bringing him here?" asked Mark as we headed for the staff room.

"Piers and I are spending a little bonding time together," I replied. "She agreed he could spend the day with me and it was a spur of the moment decision to come here."

"So she doesn't know you're here." Mark gave me an old fashioned look.

"Not exactly."

Mark shook his head in disbelief and then laughed.

"You certainly know how to make things easy for yourself don't you?"

The staff room was empty. Mark took some tea and buns from a trolley and we sat down in a corner of the room.

"Jonathan seems very interested in Piers," I said.

"If I know Jonathan he's got pound signs in his eyes. He knows that a good looking boy with a lovely voice will have the cash registers absolutely jingling."

"And I suppose being blind as well is nothing to do with it."

"Don't be so cynical."

"I'm just being realistic. Great that Jonathan might like to record him but it's not why I brought him here."

"You could all make a lot of money from this if it works out."

"I'm not interested in making money out of him," I said. "I wouldn't dream of taking a penny."

"Sure thing but Jonathan is brilliant at promoting his artists, which is why we allow him to record here. He makes money, and the school and cathedral make money. Of course Alice must agree to any record deals he may offer but let's not jump the gun. Why exactly did you bring him here?"

"I wanted you to hear him because I've been told by a teacher for the blind that he's bright enough to get to a top university, but only if he gets the right teaching. He would get that here."

Mark looked slightly pained and said we had been through all that before and he very much doubted whether the school would agree to it.

"Most of the boys come here at the age of seven or eight," he explained. "This is because they're expected to learn a wide repertoire of church music. He's a little old, and in any case I doubt if the music is available in Braille."

"He has a phenomenal mind," I said. "He can memorise anything. You saw how he picked up that difficult tune."

"I agree that was impressive but that's only half the problem," Mark objected. "The school is not equipped to cope with a child like that. He would have to have a specialist teacher of the blind with him all the time. I don't even know where you'd find one of those. And who would pay for it? Not only that, the school is a nightmare to move around even if you can see. There are narrow corridors and steep stone stairs everywhere."

"Well he has some residual sight," I said, "and he does have an astonishing facility to sense where he is once he gets to know the place. He moves around back at the farm without any problems."

"It's not the same thing. He's lived there all his life. I'm sorry but I just think it's not on."

"What about coming as a day pupil?" I asked.

"You'd have to live in Stowe Minster. Look Seb. It's just not practical; far better that he goes to one of the blind schools there are round the country. He simply wouldn't cope here."

I could not accept this. "At least talk to him and see what he's like for yourself."

He reluctantly agreed and after the tea we went to the boys' dining room and collected Piers. Mark insisted on talking to him alone and said I should come back in an hour. I went to the photographic shop where I collected the two framed enlargements. The photographer also supplied several tiny prints that he told me could be useful for passports, bus passes and similar documents. I wandered round the town to pass the time. Eventually Mark rang and I returned to the school. Piers was sitting outside Mark's office and I asked him to wait for a couple more minutes. Mark greeted me with a warm smile and I could see Piers had made a good impression.

"He's all you said and more," he said. "His general knowledge for a boy of ten is astounding but best of all he played the piano for me quite beautifully, far better than in the cathedral."

"I'm no judge," I replied. "Classical music is not my thing".

"He has remarkable dexterity and control and he's very musical. He's been well taught by Ellen Cooper but it's a God given natural talent that he has. And he's such a nice lad. I was rather taken with him."

"So what do you think?" I asked.

"Personally, I would love him to come here but I can't promise anything. Frankly, I still think it's unlikely the school will take him - just too many practical problems - but I will try. There are formidable obstacles to be overcome. I'll speak to the Head tomorrow and see what he thinks."

I said goodbye, collected Piers and asked him whether he had enjoyed himself. He said the Cathedral was so huge it scared him, but he liked the boys he had met.

"They were really friendly", he told me. He said he wanted to go home now because he missed his mother.

But returning to the farmhouse was not what I had in mind. Instead, I headed to where I was lodging, telling Piers it was too late to go back that day. When I arrived Rachel was very surprised to see him. I explained that he was with me for a sleep-over to give Alice a much needed break and I wanted to show him where I lived. She invited us to have a bite to eat with her and so I decided to call Alice later and tell her where we were. We had a very nice meal and afterwards he asked whether I had a chess set.

"How can you manage to play without a special board and pieces?" I asked.

"You call your moves out and I will tell you mine," he replied.

"How do you mean?"

"The board has a grid round the edges that shows where the pieces are. From White's side it's A to H across the board and 1-8 down the board. You make your move and then tell me what it is, like Pawn to e4, Bishop to c4. When I reply you move my pieces. It's simple."

"I don't know about that. How do you know what moves you need to play?"

"I see board and the pieces in my head and I can remember where they are," he replied. "When it's my turn to move I don't visualise the whole board, I see only the pieces on the part of the board I'm interested in. I work out what to do next and then I move."

We started the game and soon I was in deep trouble. He even corrected me when I became flustered and called out the moves incorrectly. I'm not much of a player but in the end he won with a Rook sacrifice that really astonished me. I was amazed he could see the move but he said it was obvious. Frankly, I had not believed the newspaper stories about his playing chess this way. I assumed he could simply see well enough.

Afterwards I lent him an old shirt to sleep in and helped him get into bed. As I leant forward to wish him good night, to my surprise he reached out.

"Can I touch your face?" he asked.

"Why?"

"I want to know what my Dad looks like." It was the first time he had called me Dad. As you might imagine, I felt quite wonderful. He put one hand round the back of my neck and with the other started very delicately to feel my face, slowly moving the tips of his fingers over my chin, then to my lips, then my nose, then my eyes, eyebrows and up to my hair which he fondled gently.

"You have nice soft hair," he said.

It was incredibly moving and I found it difficult to control my emotions. It said everything about my shameful neglect of this lovely child and his need to now discover exactly who I was. I felt a pang of fear that one day he might find out the truth about why I left them. I did not really understand myself and I hoped he would never ask. There were too many things I had said that now seemed shallow and cruel and which he must never know. Yet I knew that while this barrier was there I could never have a really deep relationship with him. It would always be an emotional barrier. He would ask me what happened one day for sure but I hoped that would not be too soon. For the moment I had to try be everything he wanted me to be.

I could only hope that I would be given the love I knew I did not deserve.

"What colour eyes have you got?" he asked.

"Brown," I replied.

"And your hair?"

"Black."

He moved his hand down onto my arm and squeezed my bicep.

"Are you strong?" he asked.

"Strong enough," I replied.

"I bet I'm stronger than you," he said. "Feel my arm." I put my fingers on his upper arm and he tensed the muscles into a surprisingly hard knot.

"You are a strong boy," I said. "We'll have an arm wrestling contest some time."

"Now," he replied. "Let's have an arm wrestle now. I bet I would win. Show me what it is."

"No," I said. "You've had a busy day and it's time for you to go to sleep."

"Ooh," he replied, sounding very disappointed. "How tall are you?" he asked.

"I don't know, about five feet ten, I suppose. Why do you ask?"

"I just wanted to know."

"Well now you know go to sleep," I said. But he would not release the grip he had on my hand. He told me he had really enjoyed the day and loved going to the school.

"I liked Peter," he said. "I think he could be my friend. Can I go there?"

"We'll see," I replied. "You seemed a bit nervous."

"Yes I was at first, because it seemed such a huge, cold place and I did not know anybody, but the teacher's voice made me feel confident and I'm sure I'd soon get used to it."

"We'll talk about it in the morning," I said, my hand finally slipping out of his grasp. He smiled, turned onto his side and closed his eyes. I did not move and just sat there watching him drift slowly into sleep. I had found the soft touch of his fingers exploring my face desperately moving and I cursed myself for the mess I had made of everything. It made me only too aware of what I had missed because I was not with him as he grew up. I would never see him crawling and then staggering into his first steps. I had no real idea of how he learned to cope with his blindness and how he discovered he had unsuspected talents. I wished I had been there when he began to play the piano. I wished I had been there when he defeated his first sighted opponent at chess. Come to think of it I would probably have been that person. He would probably have just laughed and explained to me where I went wrong. I could have helped him with so many things and I was not there.

    I thought gloomily that it had been the same with Sam. Mind you it was hardly my fault that my wife had kept me away for so long. How different would all our lives have been if she had not? I had come into his life when he was eight and I had also missed his early years. Sam had needed me at that time and I still wanted to be part of Sam's life now, to see him go on through university and beyond. But with Piers I could not pretend it had been anything else but my fault and I was only too well aware of that. I had walked out, whatever the complicated and difficult situation I found myself in, and that was tough to live with. Now, sitting there and looking at the sleeping boy, I realised that over the last few weeks my life had changed yet again. I had grown very fond of him and I was now desperate to make up for all those missing years. It was not a matter of salving my conscience. He needed me and I needed him. I suppose I wanted to be part of both my sons' lives and unfortunately I could not see how I would manage that.

    I tried to ring Alice but the number was engaged. I thought about leaving a message but when I tried I found my phone battery had gone flat. I was rather relieved as knew if I did get through I would just get an earful and I would rather not have to listen to her shouting at me down the phone. Next morning, as I was getting dressed, I was surprised to get a call from Jonathan. He asked if I could bring Piers to London that day as he had a free studio and would like to book a pianist and do some trial recordings. In for a penny and all that, I thought, and agreed at once. I knew what Alice would say, so I decided to wait until I was at the studio before I called her. That way it would be too late for her to scream at me and tell me to take him back.

When Seb and Piers did not return I began to get worried. I rang Seb's mobile but it was switched off. By the evening they still had not appeared. Not surprisingly I became extremely concerned and began to wonder if Seb had had an accident. I rang the police and the local hospital but they said they were no reports of anything like that. Another hour passed silently by. The increasing anxiety I felt was becoming hard to bear and made me really angry. How could Seb do this to me when I had been so reasonable with him? I began to wonder whether he had abducted him. I dismissed the idea as silly. Why would he do that? He would not want the responsibility. He enjoyed the odd day out with Piers and I was pleased about that, but I could not seriously believe Seb wanted more than that. It would be much too demanding yet what other explanations could there be? Eventually, I rang George Dale who was sympathetic but not very helpful.

"He's probably had a puncture or something," he said.

"Why hasn't he rung?"

"They could be in a mobile phone dead spot or the battery has run down. Do you think Piers is in any danger?" he asked.

"No, not really," I was forced to admit. "It was just that Seb took him out and has not brought him back as he said he would. I don't know where they've gone or what's happened. Frankly, I'm worried he might have abducted him."

"I know Seb and I'm sure he wouldn't do anything like that," he told me. "He's not that silly. He'll bring him back soon, you see. I think you're worrying too much. There will be some simple explanation. I'll ring around the emergency services and tell you if I find out anything."

I did not sleep at all that night and when they did not appear by lunchtime the next day I vowed that I would never allow Piers to spend time with Seb again. Ellen tried to reassure me and said much the same as George. She gave me one of her herbal drinks to calm me down and I fell asleep. When I awoke it was early evening and still there was no sign of them. I tried not to panic but I felt such overwhelming pain inside me that I could hardly breathe. The anguish was dreadful. As darkness fell I became desperate, even thinking that Piers might have returned and was somewhere around in the woods or in one of his other haunts. I rushed up to the cottages and searched frantically to no avail. Back in the house I imagined I heard his voice and hurried to his room only to find his empty bed. Despair was tearing my mind apart and I alternated between sobbing and furious anger. I could think of nothing except the revenge I would eventually wreak. But unexpectedly, early that evening the telephone rang. It was Seb.

"I got your message," he said.

"Message?" I screamed. "Where is he?"

"He's with me of course. I'm really sorry but it all took much longer than I expected. The photographic shop in Waterbridge had closed down so I had to go on to Stowe Minster where I knew of a good one. I've had a beautiful portrait taken and I'm sure you'll love it."

"But that was two days ago!"

"Yes, I know, I'll explain about that."

"It better be good."

"While I was in Stow Minster I took him to see the cathedral."

"And I suppose while you were there you just popped in to see Mark."

"Yes but what's wrong with that? He's my oldest friend and I wanted Piers to meet his sons. I'm sorry what with one thing and another it all got a bit too late to get back. Piers was rather tired so I took him back to my flat. I tried to ring you several times yesterday but the line was always busy. Then my mobile packed up this morning and it took me a little time to get a replacement." He was such a liar!

"I don't give a damn about your mobile. I don't believe you. Where is he?"

"I told you. He's with me and he's having a great time. I can assure you I did call yesterday evening but you were engaged every time I rang. I'll put him on in a minute. We've been getting on so well and I'll be going back to America soon. He's only been with me for an extra day, that's all. Surely you don't begrudge me that. I won't be able to see him for months."

"You had no right!"

"I know that's what you think but I don't happen to agree. I asked you whether he could spend a short holiday with me but you said no. He should spend more time with me."

"You get him back here back at once or I'll call the police!"

"Don't be ridiculous. I simply wanted to get to know him better that's all. Is that so wrong?"

"Have you any idea of what you put me through?"

"I'm sorry about that," he replied. "But there's some really exciting news."

"I'm not interested in the rubbish you come out with. I don't have to argue with you about it. I want him back here today."

"That's not possible."

"Why not?"

"We're too far away. I was ringing to tell you I would definitely bring him back tomorrow and, as I said, there's some really exciting news. When I was at the Cathedral School I met a record producer. He asked to hear Piers sing and was so impressed he wanted to record something straight away. This morning he telephoned and asked me to take Piers to his recording studio in London today. It's where we are right now. They've just finished recording. The producer thinks Piers could be really big with the right promotion. It was an opportunity for Piers I couldn't turn down, could I? He might make a lot of money from this."

The bastard just saw Piers as a money making opportunity. He must have had this in mind all along. I was almost speechless. "Make money?" I gasped. "You're just exploiting him."

"No, you've got it wrong. I'll open an account in his name and the fee and royalties will be paid into that. I don't want a penny. I just want his talent to be recognised. It could make a huge difference to his life."

"In that case why didn't you tell me about it?"

"I've already told you. I tried but my phone went kaput."

"Don't lie to me. You could have borrowed another."

"There wasn't time."

"So you thought you would just take him to London and not tell me."

"If you want the truth, I knew you would say no."

"Why would I do that?"

"Because it was my idea."

"That's absurd. If you'd just rung and explained, I'd probably have agreed."

"That's easy for you to say now, but I don't think that's likely."

"I give up. I want to speak to Piers." I whispered.

"Of course," he said and put him on. The sound of my sweet child made me feel absurdly emotional and I started to cry.

"Hello, Mum, what's the matter?" he asked.

"Nothing, darling, it's just that I really, really miss you."

"I'm in London," he said. "It's very exciting; I've had a fantastic time."

He chatted away telling me about the recording session and how much he had enjoyed being with his father. That really turned the knife. "See you tomorrow," he called and gave the phone back to Seb.

"I'll bring him back first thing tomorrow I promise," he said. "The record producer wants us to meet a film maker he knows at the BBC later, so we have to stay for a while. If he can get Piers a TV spot, the CD will sell by the thousands. After that it will be too late to travel back."

I was so angry I screamed. "TV appearances! You can't do things like this without asking me! It will ruin his life!"

"Don't be so melodramatic. Of course you have the final say without question. However, the whole experience has been very good for him. It has boosted his confidence no end. I promise I'll bring him back tomorrow. I'll call you later, anyway. I'll let you know what they say."

He rang off and I started to sob with the fury and frustration I felt. Ellen came in and saw my tears.

"I heard the phone ring," she said.

"That was Seb. He makes me so angry." I told her what he had been up to.

"Why on earth didn't he tell you?"

"That's Seb, I'm afraid. He never tells me more than he thinks he has to. He thought I would object. I doubt if it occurred to him that I would be out of my mind with worry."

"I'm sure you're right. What are you going to do about it?"

"I've no idea. What makes it really difficult is that Piers told me he really likes him."

"That's something, I suppose."

"Huh! I'd like to tell Seb to go away and never come back but Piers would be very upset if I did that. I can't bear it. That bastard is slithering his way into the Piers' affections with expensive presents and treats. "

Ellen put her arm round my shoulder. "Don't fret so," she murmured. "Piers loves you and Seb cannot buy his affection whatever he gives him. A child's love is freely given. Seb may come to understand that one day. In any case I'm not sure that's what his motive is. It's probably far more complicated than that. He may be thinking about what he never had as a child."

"I doubt it," I said. "Seb thinks everything can be bought. He's put me through hell these last couple of days. I'm frightened he'll try to take him away from me sooner or later."

"No, no, he won't," she replied. "He knows he'd lose everything. For Piers' sake you need to try and get along with him. The reality is that he's Pier's father and nothing can change that."

"I don't think I will ever forgive him, if that's what you're suggesting."

"No, but you need to come to terms with the part he now seems to want to play in Piers' life, and that can only be done if you can put to one side your anger and bitterness. He can't undo what he did. He should have been here with you watching Piers grow and caring for him and he knows that. He has to live with his past actions but you don't. You have done brilliantly in the way you've brought Piers up. Seb did not and he's finding it difficult to face the truth of what he did. None of us like admitting what we do is wrong, especially if we know it was really quite unacceptable. You need to find some resolution of what happened for yourself. I don't think you have yet. If you help him with this you may be able to."

"But he's just getting away with it scot-free."

"No, he can never do that," she replied. "It will be with him for the rest of his life."

"At the time I was very angry with him for leaving me, although in some ways I didn't blame him. I wasn't easy to live with either and I felt extremely inadequate, wicked even, for having produced a blind child. It was a quite dreadful experience but ten years on, until he returned I had learned to accept what had happened, or at least put it well in the past. Now I can't bear the way he's brought it all back."

"You may not feel like it now, but in my experience, understanding, forgiveness, or whatever you like to call it, is your only choice. Anything else will damage you more than it damages him."

Of course I knew deep down what Ellen had said to me was morally and practically right. Acting on it was a different matter. All I could think about was his duplicity as well as his heartless selfishness. The anger seethed inside me. I wanted to punish him for the torture he had just put me through. Whatever Ellen thought I was sure he had conveniently forgotten that he had ratted on us all those years ago. That was impossible to accept.

Piers telling Alice he was having a great time, which I have to say was quite unprompted by me, was a real slice of luck. It must have slipped through her defences. I had feared she would try to ban me but after what he said I knew it would be difficult for her to prevent me seeing more of him. I returned to the studio where the technicians had just finished listening to what they had recorded and were closing down the equipment.

"I'd just like Harry to take some photos of Piers for the album," Jonathan said, waving towards a man festooned with cameras and lens cases. While they were doing this he introduced me to his friend from the BBC who had just come into the studio.

"This is Tim Cameron-Burke," he said. "Why don't we all go and have coffee. I'll get my secretary to look after Piers until the photographer has finished."

"Is that OK with you, Piers?" I asked.

"It's fine, Dad," he said. That word again. It made me feel quite emotional.

We left Piers in the studio and adjourned to a cafe next door. As we sat down my mobile rang. It was Mark.

"Good news," he said. "I've spoken to the Head and he's considering taking on Piers because of what I told him about his talent but only if he can be given the right support. You'll have to pay for it."

"That's wonderful," I replied. "The money is no problem. It's the least I could do."

"How did Alice react?" he asked.

"Well, we haven't been back to the farm yet. We had to go to London pretty well straight away to record some tests."

"But you must have spoken to her."

"Of course, only a few minutes ago as it happens. I haven't discussed his schooling with her yet. I thought I would leave it until I was certain he had a place."

"Well don't leave it too long; it's now in your court. Don't let me down."

It was proving to be a fantastic day, although I realised I would have to work on Alice. Tim asked where Piers lived. I told him it was with his mother on a farm in rural Wiltshire, and explained she was a painter and had her studio there. He looked very interested.

"I'm making a series about gifted children," he said, "and from what Jonathan has told me about Piers I think he would be absolutely perfect. How would you feel about it?"

"Fine by me but I'll have to check it with Alice," I replied.

"Is that your wife?" he asked.

"We never married," I said. "We discussed it at one stage but she didn't want to."

"I see. How interesting. I collect modern art. What sort of pictures does she paint?"

"She used to do abstracts when we first met, but she now paints landscapes of the countryside around where she lives. She also paints portraits. She's become extremely successful."

"Brilliant. It gets better all the time. Tell me about Piers."

I gave him an undeniably vague account of Piers life emphasising how clever he was and how he was about to start at Stowe Minster and skating over my own minimal role in his life so far.

"Alice and I split up some years ago and she's only recently allowed me back in his life. Piers and I are just getting to know each other again," I told him.

"That's happened to so many of my friends," he said. "The pressures of modern life I suppose."

"To be honest," I replied. "Just between the three of us, his mother doesn't see life in quite the same way as the rest of us. It can be difficult to live with an artist if you know what I mean. I think I understand her a little better these days and we're getting on fine right now. I say this in confidence. It is not something I wish to become public knowledge. I'm just telling you so that you understand the situation. What went wrong is not important. Piers' wellbeing is what really matters to me now."

"Of course, I quite understand."

"Do you think you can do something with Piers?" asked Jonathan.

"I'm sure I can. Tell me a little more about yourself, Seb."

I did so and I suppose I put myself in as positive a way as possible. I left out some detail, it's true, but who does tell other people the whole truth about their lives? I don't know anyone. Most people do not even tell themselves.

I drove Piers back to my flat that evening. I suppose I could have taken him to his home but I wanted a few more precious hours with him. He slept most of the way and would not wake up. I had to carry him in to the house, put him to the bed and cover him up. I left my cases in the car. I could collect them in the morning.

"God he was a weight!" I told Rachel who had seen us come in.

"You're so good with him," she said. I sat with her and explained that I was taking him back to Alice next day. Our little holiday was over.

"You'll miss him," she said. There was no doubt about that.

Next morning after breakfast my phone rang. It was Tim from the BBC. He wanted to come and film an interview with me and asked would Monday week be convenient? I told him that would be fine and gave him my address.

"Piers won't be with me," I explained, "he'll be back with his mother."

"That's fine," he replied. "We want to film him at the farm and I'm sure the setting would be perfect. That would probably be later that week. Could you talk to Alice about it?"

"Of course," I said, "I'll be seeing her later." I rang off. I was not looking forward to telling her anything about the filming. I knew precisely what she would say.

Seb did not ring me back from the recording studio as promised but I cannot say I was surprised - ever the Mr Reliable. I thought they would just turn up in the middle of the following morning. That night I could hardly sleep with the anxiety. I awoke feeling bleary eyed, and as I waited I sat in the kitchen excitedly chatting to Ellen and feeling ridiculously nervous. About ten o'clock the phone rang. I thought it must be Seb but to my surprise a woman, whose voice I failed to recognise, addressed me by name.

"I'm Rachel," she said. "Seb and I were colleagues a long time ago. He's renting a room in my house while he's over here and your boy has been staying with him. I thought I ought to ring you."

"Why?" I asked. "Is anything wrong?"

"I'm not sure. He told me last night he was taking Piers back to you first thing this morning but he's just gone to London Airport. I saw them drive off. When I asked him why he was going there he was extremely evasive. He said he had to meet a flight from Los Angeles but I'm not sure I really believed him. I went into his room to shut a window and came across two passport sized photos of Piers. I couldn't find his laptop and there were not many clothes in his wardrobe. Furthermore, his cases weren't there. This could mean something or nothing and maybe he was telling the truth. I just don't know."

My heart started racing wildly. What on earth did she mean?

"Are you sure he's not coming here first?" I asked.

"No but he said he had to rush or he would miss the flight," replied Rachel. "He could have meant an incoming flight, I suppose."

"Are you suggesting he's snatching Piers, then?" I croaked, barely able to ask the question.

"I don't know. He seems obsessed with the boy. He just might."

"Oh my God! What should I do?" It was a stupid, lame question.

"Ring the police," she said.

"What would I tell them? We don't know anything for certain. He might be coming here afterwards. They wouldn't listen to me, anyway," I breathed. "They always take the father's side. This is dreadful!"

"Well, you could go to the airport, I suppose. You may be in time. I'll look up the flight times and ring you on your mobile in a few minutes."

I rushed to my car and set off like a mad woman, hurtling along the country lanes. My phone rang and I screeched to a halt.

"I've checked on the flight times," said Rachel. "You need to go to Heathrow Terminal Three. Most flights to the US go from there. There's a flight going to Chicago at twelve but he would probably have been too late for that. There's another at two o'clock to Los Angeles. That could be the one. He lives near there doesn't he? You'll easily be there before that."

I calmed down a little and drove more sensibly until I noticed the fuel gauge was registering empty. I panicked again screeched to a halt in a petrol station and nearly put in diesel. I told myself firmly I had to try to keep calm. Fortunately, the motorway was not too busy and at half past twelve I turned into London Airport, went straight to Terminal 3 Departures and checked the indicator board for that flight. The passengers for the Los Angeles flight had not yet started boarding. I asked the girl at the check-in desk if she could tell me whether Seb and Piers were on the passenger list. They were not. There were a lot of flights to other places in the States but I decided it had to be either Los Angeles or San Francisco. I asked about later flights and she told me there was a Virgin Flight at six. But why would they have rushed off so early for that one? 'I will kill him, I really will,' I thought. I wondered where else he could be. Perhaps he had not gone to Heathrow at all. He might have been deliberately misleading Rachel and gone to another airport. If so I would never find them. I tried to calm myself and think clearly. He might have been telling her the truth about meeting someone. I should at least look in the arrivals hall. I rushed there. It was very crowded and I could see no sign of them. A flight arriving from Los Angeles was announced and I stared at the indicator board. It had been delayed by an hour but was now going through customs. I again scanned the crowds waiting by the barrier rail where the passengers come through. Then I saw them. They had their backs to me and Seb was talking to

Piers. I screamed inwardly with relief and walked calmly towards them. When I was a couple of yards away Seb looked round and saw me. He looked very surprised. I ignored him and called out Piers' name. As he turned I seized him in my arms and covered his face with kisses.

"Stop it, Mum," he laughed. I took no notice and kissed him again. "Stop it, it's embarrassing," he protested. I let him go. Seb stared morosely at me and then smiled weakly.

"I'm so glad you've come, Alice," he said. "Did you get my message? I left one on your answer phone as soon as I could, I assumed you were out." I was completely taken aback and shook my head. The way he could twist the truth was amazing. "I had to come here first." he went on, "It was quite unexpected. I was going to bring him back later. You needn't have come all this way."

"I'm here now, so I can take him," I replied, feeling completely dumfounded.

Someone called out his name. He turned back to the barrier rail to be kissed and hugged by an elegant looking woman in her early forties. With her was a young man, probably in his teens, who Seb also greeted in a familiar way. They all seemed to know each other very well indeed. They moved off towards the opening in the barrier and he followed.

"Who's that," I asked.

"Jackie's my boss's wife," he said. "Her father's just died and she's come back for his funeral. I received an Email at breakfast asking me to meet them so I felt in the circumstances I had to come here first. Sorry if it's caused a problem but I really had no choice did I?"

"And the young man with her, is he her son?"

"That's right. That's Sam."

He looked anxiously in their direction as they came towards us pulling their cases. She gave Seb another hug and kiss then looked quizzically first at Piers and then at me.

"You must be Alice," she said offering her hand. "Seb has told me so much about you." I was surprised that she knew my name and I laughed nervously.

"Pleased to meet you," I replied.

"I'm taking them to her parent's house," explained Seb. "Her family live not too far from here," Seb explained.

"You never told me Alice was so pretty," cooed Jackie.

"As Jackie well knows," laughed Seb. "I always did have an eye for the ladies."

"And who is this?" she asked, indicating Piers.

"Piers," he said. "He just came along for the ride."

She nodded looking faintly surprised at Seb. "You are a dark horse," she said. "You never said much about him."

"You know I did, I told you about him only a few weeks ago," he replied.

"Yes but you left out quite a lot," she said.

For a moment Seb looked like a cornered weasel. "We really have to go now," he muttered.

"Hello Piers, nice to meet you," Jackie went on, shaking his hand and ignoring Seb's obvious attempt to avoid any further discussion.

"Piers has been spending a few days with me to give Alice a break," Seb told her. His gall was amazing. I could not believe what I was hearing. "I was going to return him this morning," he went on, "but instead I had to rush directly here and pick you two up. Alice kindly offered to come to the airport to collect him. It was so nice of her."

"It certainly was," Jackie murmured. "Thank you Alice. I appreciate it."

I was too astonished at Seb's explanation to think of what to say. The middle of an airport was clearly not the place to have it out with him. Right at that moment I did not care a damn about his pathetic lies. I just wanted to take Piers home so I turned to go. However, Piers, who had been holding my arm, suddenly announced that he needed to go to the toilet.

"Can someone take me?" he asked.

"Could you show him where it is, Seb?" asked Jackie, quickly intervening. "Alice can't really take him into the men's room, can she?"

"I need to go as well," said Sam, who up to that point had not proffered a word. Piers took Seb's arm and the three of them disappeared into the crowds on the shopping mall.

Jackie smiled at me.

"I wanted a quick word with you on my own," she said. "What has Seb told you about us?"

"He said you were his boss's wife, that's all, and Sam was your son."

"That's all true," she said. "But it leaves out quite a lot that you need to know. For a start were you aware that he and I were married once?"

I shook my head, scarcely able to comprehend what she was saying.

She continued: "Has he never told you? I thought not. You must have noticed that he's inclined to tell what he thinks you should know and is somewhat meagre with the rest."

"I certainly have."

"Well, let me tell you some more of the bits he's left out."

She recounted the story of their failed marriage and how they had met up again ten years ago to arrange a divorce.

"But instead we all got on surprisingly well. He told me nothing about you so I thought we might give it another go. Instead of getting divorced I joined him in the States. I suppose predictably it didn't work out. To be fair to Seb, that wasn't his fault. He did try hard but I fell in love with someone else and that was that."

I felt stupid and naive. My brain was in free fall as I tried to make sense of what she had told me. When he went to America I had always thought it was entirely my fault. What an idiot! As for the young man who was with her, exactly who was he? I was confused and asked her who his father was.

"Sam is Seb's son of course, didn't you realise?" she answered.

Her words went through me like a crossbow bolt and I barely heard the rest of what she was saying. All those indelible, searing words he threw at me about Piers not being the son he wanted, not being the son he could play football and cricket with, were clearly just pathetic excuses. All the time Seb was living with me he already had a wife and son who must have been close to his ideal of what a son should be like. And he had never breathed a syllable about either of them to me! I felt completely crushed.

"When did you have Piers?" I dimly heard her ask.

"He's ten," I answered.

"Ten? He must have been born before we went to America then."

"He was."

"I had no idea Seb had another son at that time," she said. "I only found out by chance that Piers existed at all. He told me very little and never uttered a word about him being blind! How could he have abandoned you both?"

"I don't know. I was completely shattered by it."

"I'll bet! How long were you together?"

"Almost two years; he left me when Piers was about nine months old."

"No! The bastard! How could he have done such a thing?" Jackie almost spat the words out. "It beggars belief. God, I was well rid of him. Wait till I tell Carl. Not that telling him will make any difference. He'll take Seb's side. Men always stick together. If I may ask, why did he leave you?"

I told her what Seb had said to me about Piers and she seemed genuinely appalled. Before I could say any more, Seb returned with the two boys and said they must rush. I just wanted to go as far away as I could and hide.

"It was great having Piers for a couple of days," Seb purred. "He and I had a superb time, didn't we?" Piers enthusiastically agreed and Seb gave him a hug. As they parted, to my chagrin Piers looked rather upset.

"When am I going to see you again, Dad?" he asked. The word sent yet another flash of pain searing my breast.

"Soon," I heard Seb say, "soon. Thanks for coming to fetch him, Alice. It was so thoughtful of you."

With that the three of them moved swiftly away leaving me upset and confused. All I could think about on the drive back was his deceit and duplicity. I wanted to erase him from our lives completely. I did not get the chance for he rang me as soon as I returned to the farm saying he was really sorry he had caused me so much worry.

"How did you know where I was, anyway?" he asked.

"Rachel called me."

"Oh yes, of course," he said. "I had to rush. I only knew first thing this morning I had to meet them."

"So you keep saying. Why didn't you ring me?"

"I did but you were out."

"Rachel didn't seem to know why you had gone to the airport. She rang me because she was concerned."

"I see," he replied. "And you, both of you thought I was up to something."

"I'm sorry," I replied, "but you should not have taken him away for several days without telling me in the first place. I was worried sick. What did you expect? For all I knew you might have taken him."

"Now there's a brilliant idea. I don't know why I didn't think of it!" He sounded furious.

"It's not unknown", I replied. You read about cases in the papers all the time."

"Well it's not on my to-do list I can assure you. And you say Rachel rang you to tell you she suspected I was going to do this?"

"Well not exactly. She found some passport photos of him in your room."

"Did she now? And you both put two and two together and made five. You knew I was going to have him photographed professionally. What she saw were samples for me to choose which photo to have enlarged. I've had one framed for you. She had no right to snoop round my room."

"She said she saw a window open as she was going out," I replied.

"Oh yes? I'll have to have a word with her."

"Just go back to America and leave us all alone. We were perfectly happy until you came back."

"Sorry," he replied. "That's not possible. I could not do that to him now that we're getting to know each other properly. He'd be very upset. Is that really what you want? Do you think he would understand? I don't think so. Look, I have to ring off now, they're calling for me. I'll get back to you after the funeral and we can talk some more."

TWELVE

Being accused of planning to abduct Piers made me furious but I quickly calmed down and reflected on the day. I thought I had handled a tricky situation at the airport reasonably well in very difficult circumstances. Alice arriving was quite a shock, and I suppose it was a desperate measure to tell her Jackie was my boss's wife and not mention she was also my ex-wife, but it was hardly the time or place to discuss such delicate matters. Alice must have also assumed that Sam was Carl's son not mine, which was a stroke of luck, and what with her being cross with me for spending a couple of extra days with Piers, I felt that all in all it was far too complicated to talk about in public. I would tell Alice next time I saw her. Neither Jackie nor Sam said much on the drive and I thought I had got away with it. Wrong, Seb, wrong again! That evening, when everyone else had gone to bed, Jackie brought the matter up.

"Piers seems fond of you," she observed.

I should have sensed the danger. "I guess so," I replied. "He's a lovely kid."

"Alice told me a lot about him," she said. "It was, how shall I put it, very illuminating."

"Was it now?" I replied. The warning bells started to ring; had Alice been blabbing I wondered? It was time to make my escape. "Look, I'm feeling rather tired. I need some shut eye."

"Sit down, Seb and listen to me," she snapped. I resumed my seat. "You never mentioned that Piers was blind."

"I thought I had," I replied.

"You know perfectly well you've never said a word to me about it. Too embarrassing was it? You would not want your American admirers to know that you abandoned your blind son and his mother, would you?"

"You make it all sound so simple. It was not. You've no idea how difficult it all was."

"Possibly, but there was something else you failed to mention when I arrived that made me even more angry."

"And what might that be?"

"At the airport you did not introduce Sam as your son. Why not?"

"Didn't I? I thought it was obvious who he was."

"Seb" she said, wearily. "You must think I have an IQ in single figures."

"You're in no position to criticise me," I replied. "For a start, you didn't tell me about Sam for eight years! He grew up without any idea of who his father was and all that time you said nothing to either him or me. I had no idea he even existed. How was I supposed to feel about that? I can tell you it was very hard to deal with. Once I did know, you've got to agree I've been a good father to him."

She sighed. "I know you have, Seb, and I am grateful for it. But you left poor Alice here on her own to cope with a blind child. You're quite something, Seb."

"That's easy for you to say. You're so righteous. You condemn me without hearing my side of the story," I replied.

"OK, so now's your chance."

"For a start, Alice and I had little in common and at the time we weren't getting on. It wasn't working and we both knew it. We were both very miserable and I could see nothing but unhappiness if I stayed with her. Piers was a very difficult baby and I had problems relating to him. He always wanted her never me. Then you and Sam came back into my life and it changed everything. I suddenly discovered I was responsible for another son who clearly needed me and what's more actually wanted me in his life. You've no idea how powerful that feeling was. Piers scarcely knew who I was. So there I was suddenly with two sons. It was obvious I could not bring both of them up. What was I supposed to do? I chose Sam. It was after all what you wanted, wasn't it?"

"So it was my entire fault?"

"Yes, in a way, you were certainly a major part of the equation."

"Oh come on, be honest," she replied. "It was not me. It was obvious that Sam was the only one you were ever interested in. Why do you think we never got it together again? You were actually quite pleased when 1 took up with Carl. You know that's the truth." She looked almost pityingly at me and sighed again.

"Perhaps I should go," I said, getting up again.

"No, sit down. That's not the answer. Sam would be terribly upset if you did. Just be a little bit truthful with us now and again, that's all I ask."

"I'm sorry," I said, resuming my seat.

After a long pause she asked. "Why did you really come over here and make contact with Alice and Piers after all this time?"

"I know it sounds really unlikely but what I did ten years ago has haunted me ever since. I thought about them all the time and realised what a disaster I had made of everything. I wanted to try and put it right. I wanted to be a proper father to Piers, just as I hope I am to Sam. I found out a lot about myself - about both of us really - when I met him."

"What do you mean?"

"It's very personal."

"I need to understand, so just tell me."

I felt embarrassed. I don't really know why but these things are so very difficult to talk about. I took a deep breath:

"I suppose I mean love", I muttered. "When I met Sam, I found that he clearly needed me and I needed him. For the first time in my life someone wanted to love me simply for who I was and for no other reason. I had discovered the uncomplicated, straight forward love of my child. Is that so difficult to understand? You did not love me but he did. I now feel the same about Piers. When he was a baby I did not love him. I don't know why, but I did not. Now I do. I just have to find a way of making it work for all of us now."

"So, just go back to them after the funeral and be honest with Alice. And you must tell Sam about his half-brother yourself. He'll understand."

"Will he?"

"Of course he will. He should get to know Piers. Why don't you bring them all out to California soon for a little holiday to see us? You've got to return before long anyway."

"Alice's never going to agree to that. Anyway, she doesn't know who you and Sam really are. "

She laughed. "Is that right? I told her at the airport. I've told her everything about you, me and Sam."

I was horrified. "You've really screwed everything up," I snarled. "Alice will never talk to me again. I wanted a little more time to break it to them gently so that I could at least put things right with Piers."

Jackie shook her head in despair. "I give up. You're never in the wrong are you? If you want a decent relationship with Alice and Piers you'll have to begin by explaining to both of them exactly why you went to America and about your relationship with Sam. Alice will be angry with you but she might just understand in the end. Tell her the truth for once in your life or you'll have no chance. You're not a bad man, Seb, just a hopeless one."

And with that she rose and bade me good night. I thought I had got off rather lightly.

Next morning, I lay in bed looking at a brilliantly sunny sky. It was a wonderful warm, fresh, pristine summer's day of the kind you only get in England. I could hear the others moving around getting ready for the funeral. I was none too sure what I should do after the previous evening's conversation with Jackie so I did not have breakfast and stayed in my room. We had to be at the church for the service at midday so there was plenty of time. I had just finished dressing when Mark rang.

"The Head has confirmed that the school will offer Piers a place subject to an interview with him and would like to see him with a view to starting in September," he told me. "They had been in touch with the authorities who would provide much of the support needed. You need to ring them and discuss it."

At least something was moving in the right direction. The down side was that it would cause another argument with Alice. I knew she would be upset at me even discussing a place with the school but now I knew I had been completely justified. Sam called out to me so I went to down stairs talk with him. I started to tell him about Piers but, to my surprise, he interrupted me:

"I've already worked that out," he said. "I guessed he was your son at the airport. Why have you never told me about him?"

I shrugged my shoulders. "I should have, I know but I'd completely lost touch with them. I thought I had no part in their lives. Then I came here on holiday a few weeks ago, went to see them and found that I got on well with Piers and that right now they need my help. I'll try to explain everything to you one day but, what with the funeral, now is not a good time."

"Are you going to live over here?"

"Nope, you needn't worry about that."

"But you have a new family over here now," he objected. "How do Mum and I fit in?"

"I will always be there for you, you know that. You're my son. I'll just have to come over here a little more often but I will live for most of the time in the States. Don't worry, I'll still see a lot of you. I'm not giving up on you that easily so don't think you can escape. I have spies everywhere!"

My switch to levity seemed to break the tension and he moved on to what he really wanted to discuss with me, namely the pros and cons of which university he should choose. He told me he wished to major in modern history and thought he might like to go to Columbia University in New York. Or should he try for a place at an English University as he was born here? He thought Durham might be nice. I was a little disappointed that he did not want to continue with computer science but at his age it was his choice. Jackie came into the room and interrupted the conversation.

"I've just spoken to Carl," she told me. "He said the Gemina 6 Operating System launch has been set for September. Professor Zuckerman thinks you have had enough time to sort out your family matters. He says you are a key part of the team and has told him he needs you back next week." She paused and looked at me with a wry smile. "At least old Sammy Zuckerman loves you anyway."

Why do some women think they can pass moral judgement on you just because you once had a relationship with them? She would do so forever, I could see it in her face. Not surprisingly, I was relieved when a couple of days after the funeral I took them to London Airport to see them off. As they disappeared though passport control Sam waved to me and gave me a smile. I knew he was on my side at least. Ultimately, I did not care what Jackie thought.

As I left Heathrow my thoughts turned to when I last saw Alice. I have to admit that, in spite of being a little annoyed when she put in an appearance just at the wrong time, I felt almost sorry for her. She had looked angry, vulnerable, lost and very pretty all at the same time. It was a dangerous combination and I had thought about her a lot since then. When she was furious and feisty with me, which was most of the time, I could not help noticing the sparkle to her eyes and the bloom on the skin of her cheeks. Was I beginning to feel something for her again? It seemed unlikely, yet she looked so tired and defenceless. That alone can be ridiculously appealing in a woman. I needed to be careful if I was not to make yet another big mistake. I knew that my culpability could affect my own feelings so, for the moment, I resolved simply to try to put matters right between us, leave it at that and go back to America so that they could live their lives as they wished. That idea was short lived. I could not just go back and leave Piers thinking that I did not care about him. What would he think of me? I could not bear the thought. Furthermore, the time that I had spent with him had convinced me even more that his talent should be developed in a sympathetic environment and that was clearly at the Cathedral School. He had a lovely voice now but that would break in a three or four years and he might not have one at all.

He played the piano well but the competition in that area was phenomenal and his chances of making a living as a concert pianist were remote. So his intellectual faculties needed to be developed and that would not happen at the farm. Somehow I had to persuade Alice of this.

Once back in my flat I saw the small photos of Piers were still on the table next to the bed and it occurred to me that there would be no harm in applying for a passport and a visa for him. I was on his birth certificate and as his father I could sign the application so why not? So I obtained the forms and sent them off.

A few days later I unexpectedly received a phone call from the secretary at a firm of London solicitors, Truelove & Cash. She said the firm had been trying to trace me for a long time and that they wished to write to me and send me some documents. She declined to tell me what it was about saying it was confidential and anyway she did not know. I gave her my address and she said they would write in a week or so. It was all rather mysterious.

For the next week I debated whether or not to ring Alice again but put it off. I knew she would still be very miffed with me and I had no wish to face her until she cooled down. It would be difficult enough to talk to her about the Cathedral School even if she was in a good mood. I browsed the internet for information about Leber's disease and came across a reference to successful trials in a hospital in Philadelphia for treatment using gene therapy. Had I found my trump card? I could take him to America for gene therapy. It might restore his sight. She could hardly refuse that.

THIRTEEN

I could scarcely believe what Jackie told me about Seb at the airport. What a bastard. I was so angry I thought of little else except his shabby, dishonest betrayal of all of us. Ten years on he clearly had not changed and I really hated him. One night I had even a dream in which I was convinced he really had abducted Piers and taken him back to America. He just laughed cynically at me when I demanded his return, saying Piers preferred to live with him. I felt unbelievably angry and woke up crying, my face running with tears. As I lay in bed I imagined all sorts of ludicrous ways of erasing him from my life. I could ambush him, but the idea of me standing in a hedge then stepping out, shooting at him and inevitably missing made me giggle it was so comical. Perhaps I should pay a hit man? Where would I find one, in the dingier areas of Swindon? It was equally risible. How else could I do it? I visualised myself like Nero's wife Agrippina preparing a goblet of arsenic. Deadly Nightshade grew near the cottages - that would do - very traditional. Ideally, what I needed was something that caused a death that looked like natural causes and was untraceable, something that produced a heart attack, convulsions or something like that, and something that would not act too quickly so that he departed this life elsewhere. The idea was so far-fetched and silly it made me laugh. I tried to go back to sleep but could not so I got up and went to the kitchen to get a drink of water. Feeling wide awake, I went across to the barn where Ellen prepared the herbal remedies and simply out of curiosity I started looking through some of her old books. I was amazed just how many wild flowers were poisonous. Even the Foxglove growing in the garden could be deadly. She must have heard me or seen the light for she came in and asked what I was doing there in the middle of the night.

"I'm trying to find a way to poison the bastard," I replied.

"You shouldn't joke about things like that," she said.

"I'm not," I said and smiled sweetly.

"Very funny," she said, but she did not look at all amused. "You should go back to bed; it's four in the morning."

"I wish I could find a way of making him leave us alone. We were perfectly happy until he turned up."

"I know that it seems unfair and he's really aggravating, but he's not all bad. At least he really seems to care now about Piers, if somewhat late in the day."

"That's what I am worried about. Piers talks about Seb a lot but he'll let him down just as he lets everyone down. I had begun to think he might have changed but I was wrong. After the last few days he's proved he cannot be trusted."

Ellen sighed wearily. "I do understand and I would probably feel the same," she said. "But you really mustn't think like that. He's a very mixed-up human being. I think he's struggling to come to terms with what he did to you both and blundering around trying to undo it. But he can't because he knows he behaved in a way that was indefensible. It is not easy for any of us to face the truth about our shortcomings."

"I suppose I'd better try and sort it out in a civilised way then," I replied.

"Surely, the best way, no matter how it grates, is to at least try to get on reasonable terms with him, not fight him all the time. You need to talk to him and try to understand him. He needs your forgiveness."

"Forgiveness?" I was incredulous.

"That's right. What happened is in the wreckage of your past and in a sense it does not matter to you now. It's gone and you have moved on. He has not. He needs help from you to deal with it, which ultimately means he needs your forgiveness. Only you can do this. More importantly you need to forgive him for your own sake. You hold all the cards and in time you will realise that the bitterness and anger you now feel will not give you peace of mind."

Wise words maybe, but they are easy to say if you are not the one who has been betrayed and not so easy to accept if you are. As I went to bed that evening I went into Piers' room and stood watching him for some minutes. Suddenly he called out.

"Are you going to send me to school?" he asked.

"No, why do you ask?"

"I want to go to school like other boys. The one I went to with Dad was great. I'd like to go there," he said.

"I'm not sure it's a good idea," I replied. "Aren't you happy learning at home?"

"I suppose so. But I can't sing in the choir here. I'd like to do that."

"Well, I could see about you joining a local choir if that's what you want."

"No I want to go to that school. You can do music all the time. I would love to do that, and I made friends with a boy called Peter. I haven't got any friends here."

His last remark went straight to my heart and I began to waver a little.

"I know it's not easy, darling, but just going for one day on a visit is quite different from going every day. Stowe Minster is much too far away in any case."

"I could sleep there like the other boys."

"I don't think so. You would hate that."

"No I wouldn't; everyone was really nice to me there. They didn't treat me as if I was a zombie like they do in the park. I'd love it there."

"It might seem exciting at first," I replied, "but I'm sure you would get miserable and miss us all."

"But I could come back here at the weekends."

"I doubt it. You'd probably have to sing in the Cathedral choir on Sundays."

"But you could come and hear me and take me out to tea. Some of the boys told me their parents did."

"Look it's late. You should be asleep. I don't want you to go and that's final. In any case you can't just go to a school like that, you have to be offered a place and it costs a lot of money."

"I might be given a scholarship. Peter told me he was."

"You only went there on a visit and I've already said no. Go back to sleep."

"Can we talk about it tomorrow?"

"No, be quiet. I'm going to bed now."

"When then?"

"I'll think about it."

"Please, Dad said I could."

"Did he now? Well, it's not possible."

"Why not?"

"I don't want to talk about it anymore."

He sighed and lay back. "I wish my Dad lived with us," he said.

"Well he doesn't."

"Why not?"

"Look you're driving me nuts with your questions. I'm not going to discuss it with you. Go to sleep!"

"I don't care, I want him to live here," he replied. "He's always nice to me."

"And I suppose I'm not."

"You tell me off all the time. You won't listen to me. It's not fair."

"Stop sulking and just go to sleep."

"I'm not sulking." He looked cross and without saying another word he closed his eyes and turned away. Behaving like this was unlike him. It was becoming just as I feared. Seb was driving a wedge between us. It would have been so much easier if Piers had hated his father but the opposite seemed to be true. The fact that Seb left us all those years ago did not seem to matter to him. However, what Piers had said about the school puzzled me. I thought Seb's visit had just been a social one. What exactly had been discussed? I talked to Ellen about it next day.

"Why don't you ring up Seb and ask him," she said.

"I couldn't do that! I'd probably just end up screaming at him."

She laughed and said that no doubt I would find out in time anyway. Later she told me that she thought we both needed a nudge.

"So I've invited him to supper on Monday," she said.

"You've done what?"

"You need to sort things out with him for all our sakes."

"I'll probably kill him," I replied.

"Well at least that would settle it once and for all!"

Ironically, the next day I did get my answer when the postman delivered a large envelope addressed to me. It was from the Cathedral School offering Piers a place and contained the application forms. They had to be signed by both parents and there was also a direct debit agreement. A letter from Mark was enclosed. He said that Seb had agreed to pay the fees and asked me to get him to sign them. I should also make an appointment to bring in Piers to see the Head. I was furious. Seb must have planned this all along and had never breathed a word about it. I wanted to burn the letter at once but instead, immediately rushed to the barn and showed it to Ellen.

"You said I had all the cards," I said. "This is one I didn't have. I told you he couldn't be trusted," I said. "He had no right to do this. You said I should forgive him. How can I when he still does things like this behind my back?"

Ellen looked wearily at me. "I know Seb could not have found a worse way to handle this and has only succeeded in upsetting you but maybe you should consider it," she said. "Piers is growing up fast. The world outside is beckoning and he will be part of it sooner than you realise."

"I know but not yet. He's just a little boy."

"Not for much longer. He'll get very good teaching there and he'll make some friends."

"You think I should send him there, don't you?"

"It doesn't matter what I think, it's what's best for him that matters."

"But he'd have to board there unless we moved."

Ellen shrugged. "You know I love Piers as if he was my own," she said, "and I would miss him terribly so I can understand your reluctance to let him go. If he was mine I wouldn't want him to face the world too soon either. But the time is coming when he needs to be independent and I'm not sure it can be done here just by us. This might be the opportunity."

"I don't think so."

"Don't dismiss everything Seb says. Just because you don't like him, it doesn't make him wrong. Have you discussed going to the cathedral school with Piers?"

"He did tell me a little about it last night."

"What did he say?"

"He said he really wants to go."

"Well, maybe you should let him try it."

I returned to the farmhouse and put the envelope in my bedside table drawer. Although I disagreed with her, talking to Ellen had helped. She never said anything without good reason and I tried to think of what positives there might be. I pictured him in his uniform. He would look rather cute and it would be easy for him to make friends. I could understand he would like that but what if he was bullied or could not cope with the life there? That often happens in public schools. Not only that, the prospect that he would not be living here with us most of the time filled me with a dreadful feeling of emptiness. It was yet another example of the way that Seb was forcing his way back into our lives and putting me in an impossible position. Far from wanting a compromise I hated him all the more.

Later I went to my studio and put a blank canvas on my easel. What I really enjoyed about painting was that I could shut out the real world. My agent had told me she wanted more pictures of Piers as they still sold well but I was reluctant to paint any more. I needed to find new ideas and I had struggled in recent weeks. But now, out of nowhere, they had started flowing again. My first idea was to stylise the landscapes and paint what I saw in a more abstract way, taking the basic patterns of light, colour and shadow that I saw around me. I went outside and sat on the garden bench roughing out ideas in a sketchbook what I could see in those terms. In one drawing I put Piers in the picture dressed in a chorister's surplice in the ruins of an old church, and I could see that it would work. I went back into my studio, faced the blank white surface in front of me and began to mark it out.

The following Monday, Seb arrived at the appointed time clutching a bottle of expensive French wine and I am afraid that just the sight of him almost destroyed any idea of compromise. I took a deep breath and made an effort to observe the conventions of a good host. He gave me the framed photograph of Piers. Ellen was much taken with it and put it prominently on her sideboard. She joined us for the meal with Piers and it was almost like having a normal family supper. True I was rather tense but Ellen did her best to help by keeping the conversation going and asking Seb about his life in America. He said it was a wonderful place where, if you wanted it enough, anything was possible through your own efforts. It sounded like the end of the rainbow to me. Piers was fascinated by Seb's account of life there and asked him when he would take him. Seb glanced at me with a nervous smile and said he would try to arrange it before too long. I nearly choked. After the meal Piers went to his room and Ellen disappeared leaving me alone with Seb.

"You're still talking to me, then?" he muttered.

"Obviously! After what Jackie told me, I thought you would have done the decent thing and slunk off back to the States with your other family."

"I'm deeply sorry about that but she's only told you half the story. I bet she failed to mention that she left me after little more than a week and then told me nothing about Sam for eight years. Think about that! I had no idea I had a son when I first met you."

"I'm not interested in your tale of marital woe," I cut in. "It's too late. I'm more interested in why you took Piers to the Cathedral School to talk to them about a place there."

"I didn't. It just came up in conversation with Mark."

"Do you think I'm a fool? I don't believe you. Of course you took him there to try and get a place. Now I've had a letter offering him a place! How dare you arrange something like that without consulting me?"

"All right, the truth is I thought you wouldn't even consider it."

"And now Piers' head is full of it. Why do you have to interfere in our lives all the time?"

"I just want the best for him. What's wrong with that?"

"Nothing, except that I don't happen to agree with you."

"If it's what he wants to do, why not?"

"He's not going there and that's that."

He shrugged his shoulders.

"OK fine. So be it. But he's such a clever and talented boy. It's a shame to deprive him of the opportunity."

"He's doing just fine here."

"Yes, I agree but now he needs to spread his wings and find out who he is. Away from here he's nervous and needs reassurance all the time. He's growing up and he must learn to cope with the outside world."

"Do you think I don't know that?"

"He may find it alarming - frightening even, but he can deal with it. He won't do that by staying round here all the time. You don't realise it but you're smothering him."

"Utter rubbish. He was quite happy until you came back. And another thing; why did you take him away for several days without my agreement? It was a dreadful thing to do and it put me through hell."

"I'm really sorry about that but someone had to do something."

"You should have discussed it with me. It was unforgivable!"

"Look, the way he clung to me all the time showed he needs self-belief almost more than anything. I think the whole experience of those few days did him a lot of good. Once he stopped being a frightened little boy he really enjoyed himself. Meeting other children at the school who are musical like him and the trip to London helped him enormously. And, frankly, you might not like this, but he loves spending time on his own with me."

"You've spoilt that," I said, "I let you see him as often as you liked, but after all this it just proves I can't trust you anymore. You could have called me but you did not."

"I tried to but either your phone was engaged or switched off," he protested.

"So you say but I don't believe you."

He shook his head. "Please, I don't want to keep going over all that again. If I am to be part of Piers' life, and I know that is what he wants, I would very much like to wipe the slate clean and start again. Can't we do that if only for him?"

"No that's not possible."

"So why did you invite me here tonight?"

"I didn't, Ellen did."

"So that's it then."

"Yes."

Finally, I thought I had got through. He stared down at his glass, then lifted it to his lips and finished it. I thought he would stand up and go but he did not.

"I just have Piers' future at heart," he said. "Maybe I went about it the wrong way but my coming back into his life is helping him. Please at least acknowledge that at."

"Perhaps," I replied, beginning to feel rather weary of this conversation.

"Any wine left in that bottle?" he asked.

I filled his glass, opened another bottle and helped myself. To my amazement, as if the previous conversation had not happened, he proposed a toast to a new beginning. I ignored it, looked at his face and in the fire light noticed his receding hair line and unhealthy pallor. It was difficult to imagine how I had ever found him attractive, let alone made love to him. Of course, for the next fifteen minutes he talked about himself, playing the mea culpa card to perfection, telling me all about the shock when he had discovered he had another son who also needed him and the dreadful dilemma he had faced.

"What could I do?" he asked. "Whatever I did, it hurt somebody."

"Why didn't you tell me about this at the time?" I demanded.

"I was frightened to. I thought it would really mess things up between us," he replied.

"Leaving me did that for sure."

"I know, and in hindsight I should have told you. I thought I could find a way out of the mess but in the end it wasn't possible, which is why I left."

There was another awkward silence. He was talking as if it was all down to circumstances that were outside his control and not really his fault. At that moment I really wanted to punish him, to make him realise the full extent of what he had lost when he left us and could never have again. "You know I really loved you very deeply then," I said.

"Did you?" He examined his wine glass as if it was a crystal ball and he was trying to see his past. "I suppose I've never believed deep down anyone would love me like that, not really love me."

"Just listen to yourself now. You're full of self-pity."

"It's not self-pity. It's the truth."

"Well you threw it all away," I replied.

He said nothing and looked at me morosely and I realised that for once he had told me what he truly felt. His talent for making a real disaster of his personal life was quite remarkable. He looked extremely downcast and I almost felt sorry for him so I was quite unprepared to what came next.

"Look Alice," he said suddenly, "there is an answer."

"To what?"

"For you and me"

"There is no you and me," I replied.

"Just listen to me for once. There could be. What about us getting together again? I think we could make a go of it this time. I've been a bloody idiot and I admit it. I'm older and I hope wiser now. What do you think?"

He fixed his beauteous eyes on me and waited for me to reply. It was laughable. My sympathy for him vanished in an instant. The alcohol and the firelight must have softened his brain.

"I don't know what you mean," I gasped.

"I just thought you might like to get married, that's all."

"Get married!" I was dumbfounded. He must be completely drunk! I could not believe that his self-delusion could have reached such a depth! He imagined I would take him into my life again, into my bed. Never in a billion years! "I don't think so," I said.

"Piers would like us to. He told me the other day."

"That's hardly a good reason is it? Don't keep using him. Answer me this. How could I ever trust you again? Marry you? Don't be ridiculous."

"But I thought after what you just said we might…"

I just shook my head in disbelief.

"Fair enough," he continued, "but don't say I didn't offer."

I laughed. "An offer, is that what it was? Let's talk about something else," I said. "It's embarrassing."

"Fine," he replied, "Anything you like. I just want us to be civilised about things. You can be so unreasonable."

"That's funny coming from you."

"OK, OK, how many times do I have to apologise?" he asked.

"I don't want your apologies. If it wasn't for Piers I'd tell you to go and never come back."

"Where do I stand with him, then?"

"You can see him once a week when you next come over but only here at the farm," I said. "No more days out."

"Very well. I'm sorry. But you may have to change your mind about that after you've heard what I've found out. Have you heard of gene therapy?"

"Of course."

"Well I've been researching it on the internet. Gene therapy is being used in America as a treatment for his condition and it could restore his sight. They've been doing research and having wonderful results. There's film on the Internet of blind children in a Philadelphia children's hospital walking round an obstacle course before and after treatment. The improvement they made was amazing. I could fix it up and he could come out there. I would look after him. He'd be fine and I promise I'd bring him back. He may be able to see again. We can't refuse him that possibility, can we?"

"This is what I mean," I said. "You suddenly throw something like that at me. I would need to know a lot more about it before I even considered it."

"Sure thing," he replied, "I quite understand. It would be a wonderful thing wouldn't it?"

"If it works."

"So what do you say?" he asked. "Why don't you come with me or let me take him for treatment to the States as soon as I can fix up to see the medics?"

He really thought I would agree to this! "Let you take him to America?" I said furiously. "I wouldn't dream of it."

"Why not?"

"I'm not letting him out of my sight after what you did."

"At least you've got sight," he said.

"That was cheap!" I snapped. "He doesn't need doctors experimenting on him with quack remedies."

"That's ridiculous. They're eminent eye specialists who really know what they're doing."

"I don't care who they are. They're not messing around with Piers and risking what little eyesight he has."

"But it could change his life immeasurably," he said. "If you do nothing he's definitely going to go completely blind."

"Are you saying that because he's blind he is somehow a lesser being?"

"No, not at all, I'm just trying to think of what's best for him. You must see that."

"I can't say I do," I replied. "He's used to it now and he has a life that is perfectly valid."

"Of course it is, but think of what seeing properly would do for him."

"Do you know what the success rate is?"

"I don't but it has to be better than doing nothing."

I drank the rest of my glass and poured myself another. I was not used to drinking so much. It made me feel distinctly odd and as he went on I hardly heard what he was saying. I thought he muttered something about applying for a passport and that he would arrange everything. What did he mean by that? Was he planning to take him there anyway whatever I said? I suddenly felt extremely hot. I'd had enough.

"Just go," I said, and took another large gulp of wine

"I sometimes despair of you," he replied. "Why will you never listen to me?"

"Why do you think? Look, I'm tired and I'd like you to leave."

"If that's what you want," he muttered, and picked up his coat. "You'll see sense in the end. One day you'll thank me."

I collapsed back into my chair, shut my eyes and thought I heard the outside door close and his footsteps die away. I felt totally exhausted, my mind in a confused whirl. It did not help that I had drunk far more than I intended. Marry him? Absurd! Send Piers to America for gene therapy? It was a ridiculous idea. But if there was something in it, how could I refuse the opportunity of restoring Piers' sight? Seb was being incredibly devious and putting me into an impossible position. And now he said he had obtained a passport. If that was so, there would be nothing to stop him taking Piers for good. I felt sick inside at the thought but tried to calm down. Thankfully he had departed. The house sank into comforting silence. I felt at peace at last and started to drift off thankful to be rid of him. But when I opened my eyes, to my horror there he was standing in front of me asking for a nightcap.

I felt an almost overpowering fury at this monster in my life. He was going to take Piers away from me and he simply had to be stopped. I knew how to do just that. I found the brandy, poured him a glass and went into the kitchen. The little preparation I had made was on the store cupboard shelf, clear, crystal, pure, as if it was quite harmless like water. All I had to do was put it into his drink, he would slide into oblivion far from here and I would be released from the torture. I poured it into a small jug and carried it back in the living room. He held out his glass and I emptied the benevolent liquid into it. It was all too easy. He sniffed it and swilled it around. I could not take my eyes off him as I watched him warm the glass in his hands. He took his first sip. To my relief he seemed to notice nothing unusual. Then it hit me. What had I done? I stared in horror at him as he took another sip. My heart was thumping as I saw his face screw up with pain. His expression changed and his burning eyes bore into me. He knew. I was terrified he would drop dead right there in front of me, but he seemed to recover and started talking to me, telling me that he loved me, the words crashing around my head. I closed my eyes and much to my relief his voice seemed to fade away as I slipped into comforting oblivion.

When I woke I heard the clock strike one and I was very thankful to see that Seb was no longer there. Then my relief turned to near panic. Had I really tried to poison him? Surely not. I must be going mad. I would not willingly hurt anybody let alone kill them. But are we all inherently capable of such things? You read all the time about normally decent men and women who commit appalling acts of savagery. Is it in everyone? I don't know. I closed my eyes again trying to shut it all out, feeling deeply upset. When I opened them again I noticed there was no sign of the drinks tray or any brandy glasses on the table in front of me. If I had done it surely they would still be there. I felt hugely relieved. It must have been one of my terrifyingly realistic nightmares. It had to be. Even so, I was shocked at what it revealed about my darkest, innermost feelings. Before I could gather my thoughts Ellen came in carrying a hot drink.

"He's gone, then?" she said. I nodded and she gave me the mug. My hand shook badly as I put it down. Fortunately she did not appear to notice.

"You look exhausted," she said. "You'll feel better in the morning. This will help you to sleep."

"What is it?"

"It's a very old recipe of camomile, valerian and other herbs. How did you get on with him?"

I laughed. "He was a bit of a pain but he asked me to marry him!"

"Good heavens! What did you say?"

"What do you think? I told him no way!"

"How extraordinary."

"I can't believe he thought I'd say yes."

"Perhaps he didn't."

"Why ask me, then?"

"I've no idea. It could be a roundabout way of showing you he needs your help and understanding."

"I wish you wouldn't keep talking about understanding. I understand him only too well. He thinks what he did was for the best. He's full of self-justification and self-pity. No, I'm sorry but I don't think what you suggest is possible. He'd think I was a silly, weak-willed woman. He'd just think he'd won."

Ellen shook her head. "What he thinks doesn't matter very much."

"But he walked out on us!"

"Yes he did. But it was a long time ago. Have you ever really come to terms with the blame and guilt you experienced? Isn't it far more important to do that than to be angry with him all the time? How does it help?"

With that she went to bed and I was left sipping the drink she had made me, still mulling over everything. I soon fell into a dreamless sleep and it was early morning by the time I woke again. I went for a long walk along the top of the downs and watched the sun rising behind layers of thin cloud. I could see the grey, etched landscape stretching out into the distance and with little houses, a church steeple here and there and several magnificent oak and sycamore trees, their branches half in deep shadow and half brightly illuminated in the early morning sun. It made me feel that I was part of something much larger and in so many different ways greater than I could ever imagine. I sat down on a tree stump and again went over the previous evening and somehow it now made a crazy sense. My dream had shown me things about myself that I would rather not acknowledge.

It was damaging me and I needed to find another way of dealing with it. Of course I did not really want him dead, not even subconsciously. In hindsight, his marriage proposal seemed rather pathetic and he had looked crushed and deflated when I rejected it. Perhaps he thought I would fall on my knees and forgive him. I wondered what sort of unreal world he lived in. I realised how weak and brittle he was underneath all that bluster and lies. He wanted to be in control but lacked real belief in himself. For the first time in weeks I felt calm as I realised Ellen was right. I held all the cards, I was the one in control. I could accept or reject his ideas. What he had said about gene therapy and sending Piers to school no longer seemed like threats but matters that I could deal with on their merits. Perhaps I would send him to the Cathedral School. Ellen clearly thought I should. I decided to reconsider the matter and felt a huge wave of relief. I knew the nightmare of Seb's return was behind me, at least until the next time I saw him.

The cloud had lifted and the early morning sun warmed my shoulders. As I returned along the bridle path valley I could hear the distant sound of Piers singing, his beautiful clear voice blending exquisitely with the birdsong. As usual he was in the garden next to my studio sitting on the seat. The dog was lying in front of him.

"Come on Piers. Let's go and have breakfast," I called.

"I'll be down in a minute," he replied.

I waited by the farmhouse gate as he came along the path and put my arm around him giving him a kiss.

"What's the matter, Mum?" he asked.

"I just wanted to kiss you, that's all."

"Can I go to America one day with my Dad?" he asked.

"Who knows, perhaps one day? You needn't worry about that for now. Why do you ask?"

"I heard you two talking last night. I'm really pleased he came back," he said.

I took his hand. "I know you are," I replied.

FOURTEEN

Of course I never expected Alice to accept my marriage proposal. I don't really know why I asked and I was surprised she took it seriously. Frankly, I was amazed she was even speaking to me after the airport fiasco let alone asking me to supper. But that's women for you. I enjoyed the brandy, it was an excellent Courvoisier and, as Alice was somewhat worse for wear and had fallen asleep, I left when Ellen came in and started clearing up. I had never been able to decide whether I liked Ellen or not. She was pleasant enough to talk to, even sympathetic, but there were times when the gaze from her sharp intelligent grey eyes made me feel that she understood everything about me. This made me feel somewhat ill at ease, as you might imagine. I had contemplated sweet-talking her to try to get her on my side but I realised she would see straight through that. So I always had to be careful what I said to her.

As for Alice, I was rather annoyed but not surprised she would not to listen to me about gene therapy. Still, I had a contingency plan. I had obtained a visa for Piers for medical treatment and had booked an open flight for him. Of course simply taking him with me was very much a last resort, not at all something I actually wanted to do. In any case I was sure that Alice would see sense in the end and it would not be necessary. Refusing to send him to the Cathedral School was equally unreasonable. I had used my influence to obtain the place, he would clearly derive enormous benefit from it and I would pay the bills. So why object?

Next morning, just as I was leaving my rooms the letter from the solicitors Truelove & Cash I had been expecting arrived. I was in a hurry so I put it in the glove compartment deciding I would open it later. I told Rachel I was going back to the States later that day and paid her a year's rent so that I had a base. I said I had to get some jabs and would return later to collect my cases before going to London Airport. But I had other plans. The flight was not until very late and I wanted to see my son for one last time, preferably on his own, before I returned. It looked like being a pleasant warm day so I decided I would watch from the hillside above the farm and wait for an opportunity. He often went into the garden or on to the hill on days like this. I did not want to just knock on the door and have Alice shout at me again.

Ellen started to clear the breakfast away. She had noticed that I was rather pre-occupied so she left me to finish off my coffee and went across to the barn saying she had to get on. Last night's dream still haunted my thoughts. My mood had changed from optimism to a terrible feeling of uncertainty. I was tortured with the idea that perhaps it had not been a nightmare and that I had really tried to poison him. I remembered the image of his distorted face and a wave of nausea swept through my body. I ran to the toilet, knelt down with my head over the pan and spewed uncontrollably into the water. My stomach heaved again and again but little else emerged except foul tasting liquid.

"Are you alright Mum?" Piers was standing at the door.

"I'll be fine in a minute, just go away and leave me alone," I snapped, instantly regretting my irritation with him. I heard him go outside and a minute later he returned with Ellen. By this time I had recovered somewhat and was sitting back at the kitchen table with my head in my hands feeling awful. Ellen put her hand round my shoulder and bent forward.

"Are you OK," she asked.

"I've just been sick," I said. "Too much wine, last night, I'm not used to it."

"I'll give you something that will help," she said and vanished again. Suddenly I felt an almost overwhelming urge to cry and fought hard to stop. What if I really had done it and Seb was now dead? What a disaster that would be for all of us! My life, our lives would be wrecked. I started to sob. Piers put his arms round me, told me not to cry and started kissing me saying it was all right he was there. Ellen came back carrying a glass with an amber coloured liquid in it.

"Drink this," she said.

"What is it?" I asked.

"Just drink it," she insisted.

I did so. It felt clean and purifying and I felt a little better. "Could you go and get some marjoram for Ellen, Piers?" I asked. Piers looked doubtful but agreed and went outside.

"I think I've done something really terrible," I said as soon as he had gone.

"Don't be silly," she replied. "What could you have done?"

"I tried to kill Seb," I said.

"What rubbish!"

"I did, I made some poison in the kitchen when you were out and put it in his brandy."

She laughed. "Rubbish," she said, "I don't keep anything that you could possibly have used. When Seb left he looked perfectly all right to me."

"But it was slow working and ….."

"No buts. You've just got a terrible hangover and a wild imagination. You must have dreamt it. I suggest you go back to bed for a couple of hours and sleep it off."

Piers came back in with the marjoram and Ellen asked him to help her collect some more herbs. I took her advice and retreated upstairs. I slept for an hour or so and woke feeling a little better. Nevertheless, although I knew it was silly, I had a ridiculous urge to know whether Seb was really all right. I picked up the telephone and called Rachel.

"Could I speak to Seb?" I asked.

"I'm afraid that's not possible. He's gone to see the doctor."

My heart thumped wildly.

"Gone to the doctor?" I repeated, mechanically. "Is he ill?"

"Don't worry he's right as rain. He said he was going to get some jabs. He's going back to San Jose today. Didn't he tell you?"

"No he certainly did not."

"He's booked on a flight from Heathrow. He said he would call back later and pick up his things. Shall I give him a message?"

"No, don't worry. You're sure he was all right then?"

"Yes he was. Did you think you had poisoned him or something?"

"Very funny," I replied. "It was just that he didn't look too good when he left."

"Was your cooking that bad?" she laughed.

"Probably."

"Rich food and too much to drink, I should think. No, he was chirpy this morning, full of the joys and all that."

"He was definitely all right then?"

"Yes, I told you he was fine. Sorry, I must dash, I have to get to work and I'm late."

With that, she rang off. I sat there feeling irrationally relieved and reassured. Then I started to worry again. Supposing it was working more slowly than I had anticipated? I shuddered. Get a grip, I thought. I stared at the cupboard where I'd hidden the poison. Of course, how stupid! I could just look and see if it was still there. I went calmly across and moved the pots I had put in front of it. The bottle was still there. As I picked it up I saw it was virtually empty. I must have put all of it in his brandy. My insides screamed with nerves at what I must have done and my hand shook uncontrollably. A tiny amount of the liquid spilled on to my hand. Why had it not worked? I froze, and then I don't know why but I sniffed my fingers. They smelled of nothing. That wasn't right. I cautiously licked my hand and it tasted of nothing. The liquid was water. I thought I must really be going mad. I could remember making the poison quite clearly yet what I tasted was definitely water. What on earth was going on?

Ellen came in carrying some papers and I guiltily put it down. She did not appear to notice.

"You look a little better," she said.

"I don't feel it." I replied and could not stop myself asking: "Did you clear away the glasses last night?"

"What glasses?"

"The brandy glasses on the little table."

"Why do you ask?" Was she being deliberately evasive?

"I just wanted to thank you."

She looked at me rather sharply. "Brandy glasses? That nonsense again! Yes I did wash them. You were asleep so I took pity on you. Seb was leaving and you were clearly exhausted. But I can assure you he looked very well."

I had to know about the bottle. "What about this?" I said holding it up.

"Oh that. I saw it in the cupboard a few days ago and didn't know exactly what it was so I poured it away and washed the bottle out. I think it was just water, that's what it smelt like. I don't like unlabelled bottles lying around."

Her explanation made little sense to me. Ellen always noticed everything. Had I imagined the whole thing or had she discovered what I intended to do and prevented me ruining all our lives? If so she would certainly have told me so unequivocally. That's what she was always like. Perhaps she was right earlier. I must have fantasised or dreamt the whole thing.

"You must think I'm going potty," I muttered.

"Well, it can't be easy," she murmured. "Your life has been turned upside down in the last few weeks. You're just finding it difficult to deal with, anyone would. Look, there's something I need you to do. Could you put these in the accounts?"

"Of course," I said, smiling ruefully.

She gave me a book of invoices and carbon copies of her orders.

"Are you feeling all right now?" she asked.

"It couldn't be better. I just spoke to Rachel. She said Seb's flying out today."

"That's a relief."

"But why didn't he tell me last night?"

"He probably just forgot."

"I doubt it. Why can't Seb be straight forward with us?"

"I've no idea."

"I sometimes wonder what makes him like he is."

"What do you mean?"

"You never know what he's really thinking. And he always has to try and manipulate things so that he appears to be in the right and you're in the wrong."

"I know a great many people like that, I'm afraid. It usually stems from low self-esteem."

"He hardly lacks that, he's very successful. It's his private life that's always in a mess. The only people he seems to be able to relate to closely to are his sons. God knows why but they adore him. He seems unable to make it work when the relationship is more equal. Why should he be like that?"

"Perhaps he has something buried deeply within him," she replied. "Who knows what that might be?"

With that enigmatic remark she said she would talk later as she had to finish the orders. I cleared the table and for a few moments sat there still thinking about what Ellen had just said. Seb had once told me, true it was with great reluctance, about his father vanishing and his mother dying when he was very young. At the time I wondered if he was making it up, playing the sympathy card, but he had convinced me at the time it was true and I think he was being honest for once. I tried to get him to tell me more about his childhood but he always evaded the subject by saying he could not remember very much and refusing to elaborate. Why? I suspected there was a lot about what happened to him he still kept hidden away.

I parked at the top of the downs and made my way along the bridle path to the little grove of trees. The farm seemed very quiet. I could see Goldie sniffing around in the yard but no sign of Piers. For a time I had refused to admit even to myself that I had returned to England because I was fascinated by the idea that I had a son who might be very gifted. Now, in my heart I knew it to be the truth.

Was that so wrong?   What father would not have done the same? But things had changed.   Now that I had got to know Piers, his gifts seemed unimportant.   He was simply my son and I felt quite emotional about him.   Perhaps it was a mixture of guilt and a realisation of what I had missed.   Sam had also needed his father at that age and naturally I responded to that.   Sam had offered me unconditional love, something I had never before experienced and that was hard for anyone to say no to.   Jackie said that I was only interested in him and never in her.   That was probably true as well, but rich considering the way she had never given our relationship a chance and gone off with Carl.   Not that I particularly cared.   It was probably never going to work.   Why had I left Alice then?   Was it simply because I had fallen out of love with her?   No it was vastly more complicated than that.   True my relationship with her was collapsing but the presence of Piers seemed to be completely wrecking our lives.   Should I have made more effort to deal with that? Probably but in truth, deep down, I did not want to.   Now things had changed.   Ten years later Sam was doing brilliantly and my consolation was that I knew my coming back into his life had a lot to do with this.   I could do the same for Piers if Alice would let me. Maybe I had gone about things the wrong way with her but the fact remained he needed both of us.   So far she had rejected my help at every turn and, whether I liked it or not, that was how things stood.

    I walked a little further along the ridge, through the small grove of trees and, as I emerged, I saw Piers sitting in the place where I first talked to him.   He heard the sound of my footsteps, turned and smiled.   Somehow he knew it was me.   I called out and, ludicrously, waved.   Just as with Sam, I had become part of his life and he had changed mine.   Whatever lay ahead I intended to be a proper father to him no matter Alice thought.   I sat down beside him and he reached out taking my hand and grinning broadly.   Telling him I was going back to America was not going to be easy.

    "Look there's something I have to tell you," I said.   "I'm afraid I've come to say goodbye but only for a short time.   I'm afraid I have to catch a plane tonight." He looked rather crestfallen and said nothing for a good minute leaning into me, resting his head on my chest.

"When am I going to see you again?" he whispered after a little while.

"I can't say but it won't be long, I promise. I'll take you to America one of these days and you can stay with me."

"I don't want you to go," he said, and took hold of my hand. "I don't know when I'll see you again."

"Soon," I said, "I promise."

Neither of us spoke for a little then he relaxed and sat back gripping on my hand ferociously.

"You say you'll come back but you went away once before and didn't," he said. "Don't go now, please. I might never see you again."

"Of course you will," I replied. "Now that I have found you I'll always be back. You're my son and I'll really miss you."

"It's not fair," he said. "As soon as you come to see me you go away." Tears were glistening in his eyes so I hugged him again.

"Life's not fair," I told him, quietly. "The sooner you learn that the better." It was what my Granny used to say to me. He looked even more upset and turned away. "Look, I don't want to go back and leave you," I went on, "but I'm afraid I have to. Let's not sit here feeling sad, I've got a real treat for you. I've hired a terrific sports car, it's incredibly fast. Would you like a ride in it?"

He agreed at once and took my arm as we made our way back along the bridle way to the lay-by. Then a crazy thought entered my brain. If I wanted to take him back with me, here was the perfect opportunity. Just get him into the car and drive. I had a visa and a passport for him and it ought not to be too difficult to find a flight for both of us. I could reach the airport in little over an hour and get us both on an earlier flight before Alice realised he was gone. The idea was clearly completely mad and I tried to dismiss it from my thoughts. But it would not go away. We reached the road and crossed to where I had parked.

"Here it is," I said, and guided his hand on to the passenger door handle.

"What car is it?" he asked.

"It's an Alfa Romeo Sports Coupe," I told him. "It's like being in a racing car."

"Fantastic!"

I helped him into the passenger seat, went round to the driver's side and sat in next to him. I could feel incredible excitement and nerves in the pit of my stomach. I could take him back to the States if I wanted to. All I had to do was to start the car and put my foot down. There was nothing to stop me.

"What do you think of the car?" I asked.

"It smells rather peculiar," he replied.

"All new cars smell like that," I explained. Was abducting him what I had been subconsciously thinking about for a little while? I could do all the things for him that Alice had rejected. She had called gene therapy the work of quack doctors but doing nothing was not an option. Gene therapy might not work but I could not bear the idea that he would go blind because I failed to act. What was there to lose? I could also find a school over there that would help him. I'm sure they have fantastic facilities in the best ones. My nerves fluttered wildly. It was now or never, time to decide. I started the engine which lolloped over with an impressive sound. I realised that I needed to calm down and try and think clearly so I put off the decision. I would take him for a short drive and then decide.

"Fantastic sound," I said.

"It's really exciting, I love it," replied Piers, laughing.

"Let's go then. Let's go, go, go!"

The car pulled away with impressive acceleration and Piers shouted "fantastic!" as he felt the car seat push him in the back. I hurtled towards Wootton Bassett, swerving round a tractor, whizzing past buses and roaring past other cars when I could. Then my subconscious mind made the decision for me and the lunacy completely gripped me. I had to take him with me. In a few more minutes I was on the motorway. I put my foot down and the car accelerated very quickly. Piers was giggling and laughing with excitement.

"We're doing a hundred miles an hour," I told him.

"Is that fast?" he asked.

"Too fast," I said, "I was being a bit naughty but I just wanted to show you what it felt like." I slowed down and saw the sign for the turn off for Marlborough approaching. It was the real decision time. I could go straight on and we would soon be at London Airport. There was nothing to stop me. Yet doubts began to fill my mind. How was I going to explain it to him? Could I really convince him it was for his own good? I was not sure. I knew that he trusted me completely and it might wreck that. And what if he refused to get out of the car at the airport? I could hardly drag him by the collar. Even if I persuaded him to come with me, which I doubted, I could hardly force him to go through customs and immigration if he did not want to go. It would also have been a dreadful thing to do to Alice and she really would never have forgiven me. Had I not already caused her enormous pain? Was that really what I wanted? No, it was a crazy idea and I needed to think things through a little more clearly. It would be much better to talk to her again about gene therapy and schooling, perhaps when I came back later in the year. So I turned off the motorway and took the road back to the Marlborough Downs.

I t did not take me long to do the invoices. As I finished the telephone rang and man whose voice I failed to recognise asked for me.

"I'm Tim Cameron-Burke from the BBC," he said. "Could I come and see you this morning? I met Seb and Piers when they came to the recording studio in London. Did he tell you about my series on gifted children?"

"He did mention it," I replied.

"I'm sorry to contact you without any notice. We were due to film at Stowe Minster Cathedral School today but there's been an outbreak of measles and I've had to postpone it. As a result, I have a crew down here doing nothing so I was hoping we could film some sequences with you and Piers instead. I'm sorry, I know it's a bit of a cheek," he said, "but I didn't want to waste today and I would greatly appreciate it if we could."

"Well, all right, it's fine by me. But Piers isn't here at the moment."

"I know, I saw him in the distance. He was walking on the top of the downs with Seb. They were heading your way. I don't think they'll be very long. I'll be along with the crew shortly if that's OK."

I can't say I was thrilled to hear that Seb was back again. I still did not trust him but I suppose he had had the jabs and wanted to see Piers before he went back. A few minutes later Tim arrived. We had coffee and Tim explained a little about his series.

"It's often said by educationalists that gifted children are the product of pushy parents. For some children there's some truth in that but my research also shows that for others the opposite is true. That's to say when a child with an obvious gift appears he somehow makes the parents feel they have to provide him with what he needs, not the other way round. Yehudi Menuhin's story of smashing the toy violin he was given as a small child and demanding a proper one is an obvious example."

"How does this relate to Piers?" I asked. "He's just a normal little boy who can sing a bit and play the piano."

"Well he's a little more than that. Yes he sings well. But that's a gift isn't it? He can also play the piano brilliantly and that's also a gift. And it doesn't stop there. I'm told he has a phenomenal memory and can play a game of chess in his head. These are all undeniably gifts."

"He likes playing chess," I conceded, "but it's just a game as far as he is concerned. He plays in his head because he can't see properly, that's all."

"Of course, but few ordinary chess players can play a whole game in their head. Most blind players can't either. They normally use a special board and pieces they can feel."

"Yes he has natural ability but he does these things well because he's had good teaching."

"That's exactly my point. I agree a gifted child also needs good teaching but surely, without those natural gifts, would not all that teaching be useless?"

"Possibly."

"Piers fits the profile shown in my research for the series perfectly. I think that many gifted children are born with brains that simply work better than yours and mine. It's as if God, Mother Nature or whatever you like to call it has bestowed on them grey matter that works much faster and more accurately than for the rest of us. I think Piers is one such child and I would like to tell his story. Obviously his blindness makes it doubly interesting."

"Can you tell me a little more of what's involved in the filming?"

"Of course I will. First of all I'd like to talk to you about your experience of bringing him up, the challenges you faced, other people's attitudes, prejudices that sort of thing and how you met them. I would also like to talk to Piers, find out how he perceives the world that he can't see, how he deals with that and also film him singing and playing the piano, perhaps playing a game of blindfold chess and whatever else he does."

"Ok that's fine but I don't want him to be made to feel he is an oddity because he isn't. He's a normal little boy who simply can't see."

"Absolutely, I completely agree. Could you begin by showing me around the farm? I need to get the feel of the place and perhaps you can tell me a little about yourself as we go. Seb told me you're an artist. I collect modern art. May I see your studio and some of your work?"

I took him up the path to the cottages and showed him into my studio. He admired my paintings, said all the right things about them. He particularly liked the one of Piers lying on the couch. He said he would certainly like to buy it after the filming. I suppose he thought he would get it cheap. I told him he should talk to my agent. My latest painting was on the easel and he peered at it.

"That's interesting," he said. "I like the formal garden in it, quite unlike the natural landscapes in your other pictures. Who's the group of people just sitting round a garden table and the white figure lying in the ditch at the bottom of the hill?"

"Oh it's just an idea."

"And I like all those crows. Aren't they a symbol of death? What does it all mean?"

"That's for you to decide," I said.

"Very mysterious," he muttered.

We went back into the garden and I saw the film crew had now driven into the farm yard. Three men were unloading equipment. Tim said he would like to start by interviewing me sitting on the garden bench near the studio. He shouted down to the crew to bring their equipment up to the cottage.

"What do you know about blindness?" I asked him.

"Not a lot, I confess. As a student I was much taken by an HG Wells short story called 'The Country of the Blind.' In it the hero comes across a whole community of totally blind people deep in the South American mountains. Their reaction to meeting a sighted person was fascinating. When he told them what he could see, they thought he was having delusions and that his eyes needed to be removed to cure him. It's a thought provoking idea don't you think?

"It is, but what has it to do with Piers?"

"Well it would be fascinating to hear what Piers makes of the world around us. For example, what does he think of things that he has never seen, such as clouds, look like? What does he think you look like?"

"He knows what they are and that they're floating in the sky. But you'll have to ask him, although I think he has a pretty good idea."

"And of course I would like to hear your story. I filmed Seb yesterday," he said. "He told me about the difficult time you've both had."

"That's true," I said. Why had not Seb mentioned anything about this yesterday evening? I wondered what highly coloured version of the truth he had invented to make him the hero. At least I could put Tim right about that.

"He's a human kind of guy for someone so brilliant, don't you think?" asked Tim.

"I suppose he is."

"I meet plenty eggheads in my job. They're usually a bit strange but he's one of the pleasantest I have come across."

"Do you think so?"

"I do and he's so interested in the boy's future. It's great to see these days when so many parents are too busy to bother. He says he wants Piers to go to Stowe Minster Cathedral School. A clever boy like him would benefit from all that specialist music teaching, wouldn't he?"

"Possibly," I replied. "But he seems to have done well enough so far, being educated at home."

"Yes he does,' he replied. "I suppose I was pretty average compared with some of the people at my school but I was lucky enough to go to Oxford and it wasn't so much what I learned there but the people I met and the doors it opened. I have a history degree and you might not think it would be much use in the modern world but it got me an interview with the Beeb and a good job in television. I doubt I would have done so without it. Who knows what Piers might want to do with his life? Whatever it is he'll stand a much better chance if he goes to a school and if possible on to an Oxbridge university."

"Do you think so?" I asked glancing up at the hillside. I had begun to feel anxious and was hardly listening. Piers ought to be back by now. Where were they?

"Of course you have doubts," I heard Tim say, "anyone would in your circumstances. But I think you'd find he's tougher than he looks and would be able to deal with it."

I dumbly agreed, wishing this man and his film crew would go way so that I could go and find him. Tim chatted inconsequentially as the crew set up their equipment around us. The sound recordist fixed a radio microphone on to my blouse and the cameraman said he was ready. But I was not. I was just about to tell them that I had to look for Piers when in the distance I heard him singing. He was above us on the escarpment.

"That must be him," Tim said, "I'd know his voice anywhere."

"He loves it up there. He says he likes the view."

"But he can't see."

"I think when he says things like that he means he likes the feel of the wind in his face and the sounds and sense of space he finds on top of the downs."

"But how does he get right up there?"

"I don't know. His eyesight does vary from time to time. Sometimes it improves and then it deteriorates. I think he must be going through a good patch at the moment. He can also tell a surprising amount just from the sounds he hears. He has learned to listen in a way that I don't think the rest of us normally do. He's lived under this hillside for most of his life and I think he can almost see it in his head."

Tim looked impressed and gazed across the wide valley.

"It's wonderful here, a truly lovely place," he said. "Are you ready Frank?" he asked the cameraman who nodded.

"I'd like you to pan from the valley and tighten in on Alice," he said. "After a minute or so I'd like you to widen to a two shot, and then play it by ear." The cameraman nodded and practised the shot before saying he was OK.

"Hang on a minute," said the sound recordist, "I can hear a dog barking. Could we wait till it stops?"

Goldie came bounding along the top towards us, jumping up and making a big fuss of Piers. We walked through the spinney and sat down on the grass bank.
"I like sitting here," he said, smiling at me, the warm wind ruffling his blonde locks a little.

"Sing me that folk song again," I said, "the one I heard the first time I came. I'd love to hear it once more before I go back."

"OK," he said and looking straight ahead started to sing, his voice pure and clear, the tune of 'Down by the Sally Garden' ineffably sad, and sitting there with him it made me think about the family life I had always dreamed of. It had not been possible with Jackie and Sam, and I had thrown away the one I could have had with Alice. How miserable it must have made her when I left. It was too late now. It could not be undone. Oh God, I was feeling sorry for myself! Perhaps that was it. I was far too absorbed in what I felt. At least Alice was giving me the chance to love Piers and be a father to him. You couldn't buy that. I was very lucky she was so forgiving.

Piers finished singing and I noticed he was looking a little dejected.

"What's the matter?" I asked.

"If you're going away when will you come and see me at my new school?" he asked.

"What new school?"

"Where I went with you."

"Have you spoken to your mother about this?"

"Yes",

"Has she said you can go?"

"No but you could persuade her, couldn't you?"

"I'm not sure about that but what exactly did she say?"

"She said she would talk to me later. She usually says that when she's going to say no. But you said I could go, so can I? I really want to go. When you took me there my friend Peter told me if you wanted to be a professional musician you had to go somewhere like that. He said he wanted to play in a symphony orchestra when he grew up. I'd like to be a soloist, a concert pianist or a singer, if I can become good enough."

"Why not?"

"I want to go there and try. Can't you tell her?"

"Going to school is for your mother to decide not me."

"But you said I could. Will you talk to her again?"

"Again?"

"I heard you two talking about it last night."

"Did you now?"

"I can't live here on the farm for ever, can I?"

"Why not?"

"Because I can't. It's obvious."

"I'll talk to her, that's all I can promise." I was not exactly optimistic but clearly had a much greater chance of persuading her after what Piers had just told me.

"Shall we go down now and ask her?" he asked.

"OK, why not?"

Piers called out to Goldie who had been sniffing around on the edge of the woods. She came bounding up wagging her tail.

"Will you help me go down?" he asked.

"I thought you and the dog could manage that perfectly well by yourselves."

"We could, but I want you to help me. Will you?"

He seized my arm and the three of us went down the steep slope, the dog running on ahead and Piers hanging tightly, telling me exactly which tree to step round and which bush to avoid. It was just great.

The sound recordist said he could not hear the dog now so he was happy. The cameraman practised the shot again. During the wait I considered what I would say. Seb would undoubtedly have left out anything that was embarrassing or put him in a bad light. My first thought was that I could set the record straight. I would tell him the truth. I suppose I had thought Tim should understand what I had been through not just accept Seb's version. But I began to have second thoughts about the wisdom of saying too much. What good would it do me in the end to have our private lives spread all over the media? It might make a fascinating programme for him but would it be of any real use to us?

"OK to start Alice?" Tim asked. I nodded. "Turn over," he said and the clapper board was banged in front of my face. Tim waited for the camera to pan on to me before he spoke.

"Alice," he said. "Bringing Piers up in this idyllic place, you must have quite a story to tell."

"I don't know about that," I replied.

"Seb has told me a lot about what you have both been through. He says you both found it pretty tough."

"I certainly did."

"So why don't we start at the beginning? How did you meet Seb?" he asked.

"I met him at the first year show at Waterbridge Art College. He came in with his friend Mark who bought one of my pictures. It all followed from that."

"So what did you think of him?"

"At first I thought he was a bit conceited and rather too full of himself."

Tim laughed. "And what do you think now?"

Before I could answer the cameraman, who seemed to be able to see not just what was in his eyepiece but everything else that was going on, pointed at the hillside behind the cottage. Piers was coming down the path and, to my surprise, he was clinging on to Seb's arm. They were both laughing and I could hear Piers calling out instructions as to where to go next. The cameraman looked at Tim who just nodded. He moved his shot across to follow them down the hill.

"We'll talk in a minute," he whispered. "That's too good to miss, a magic moment, real father and son stuff."

Reluctantly I had to agree. After a short while they both disappeared into trees and soon they were standing at the end of the garden, both grinning. I don't know who looked the most like a schoolboy.

"Cut! Hold it a minute," Tim said, and waved a greeting as Seb and Piers sat down together to watch. Piers leant against Seb who put his arm round his shoulder in a very affectionate way. To my surprise, I felt quite pleased to see it. My child's happiness was my priority and it was obvious whatever I felt, Seb was now a major part of that. Ellen was right. For Piers sake I needed to put my anger to one side and make peace with him. When we resumed filming I told Tim that I did not blame Seb for our break up and leaving us.

"What do you mean?" he asked.

"None of us know how we would deal with bringing up a handicapped child until we are faced with it. All sorts of personal issues come up and it's very complicated. It split us up. Seb could not handle it at the time - some people can't. A lot of fathers in his position never come near their child again. At least he is trying now. He understands why Piers needs him and the part he has to play in bringing him up." I knew this was putting a somewhat rosy glow on it but it would have to do. I was certainly not going to reveal too much about what he had put us all through. It might make me feel better for a short time but it would just make matters worse.

They filmed in my studio and around the farm for the rest of the day and departed about four thirty saying they would be back in the morning to film Piers having a singing lesson and playing the piano. Out of the farmhouse window I could see Seb and Piers sitting at the garden table. They were locked in an arm wrestling contest and Piers was putting in a huge effort against Seb's immovable arm. I smiled at the two of them in spite of myself. It was obvious that I had to make the right choice about his future. It was not easy to face but I was beginning to agree that there might be better people than I who could take him forward from now on. The Cathedral School was the obvious place for him to go. Piers had made it clear that was what he wanted. What would he say in a few years' time if I denied him this opportunity? I went to my dressing table, took out the letter from the school and went into the garden. Seb let his arm dramatically fall back and they both laughed loudly.

"You win, you win," he called out.

"I told you I was stronger than you," shouted Piers.

Seb stood up and said he had to go or he would be late for his flight what with the security checks.

"I'm parked up in the lay-by near the bridle way," he said.

"I'll walk up there with you, then," I replied.

"Will you really?" He looked very surprised.

"Can I come too?" asked Piers.

"Of course," I said. "You'd better fetch Goldie."

We slowly made our way up the path to the top of the downs with Piers and Goldie rushing on ahead. The sun was low in the sky and the view across the plain was extraordinarily atmospheric with hillocks, trees and hedges darkly silhouetted and rimmed by the golden light.

"This is an unexpected pleasure," said Seb.

"Don't get the wrong idea; I wanted to make it plain to you after what you said last night that we can't turn back the clock. What we once had has gone forever and can never be revived - too much history. However, I can see that Piers has become very fond of you and needs your support. But if you ever let him down......"

Seb had listened to this in complete silence for once. "What do you want me to do?" he asked.

"Just to go on with what you've started. Come back and see him often, nothing more."

"Of course I will." We had reached the road and Piers was waiting. Seb put his arm round the boy's shoulder. "I'm warning you in advance, Piers," he said. "I'm going to study a couple of chess books while I'm in America so you'll stand no chance when I come back. I want my revenge for that hammering you gave me."

"In your dreams, Dad," laughed Piers.

We crossed to the lay-by. Seb opened the car door and turned to me. "There is one thing I promised Piers I would raise with you," he said, sounding a little nervous.

"I know what you're going to say," I replied, pulling the envelope out of my bag. "I'd like you to sign a couple of documents."

He saw the Stowe Minster Cathedral School letterhead. "You're going ahead with it then?" he asked.

"I've thought about it and perhaps I was a little too hasty. He says that's what he wants to do so he should at least be allowed to try it. I'll see how he gets on and how the school copes with him."

"Does that mean I'm going to go to the Cathedral School?" Piers asked.

"It does," I told him. He threw his arms in the air in elation. Seb smiled at me, signed the papers and we formally shook hands.

"I'm really sorry," he said quietly, "walking out on you both was unforgivable. I've never really understood why I did it. Will you forgive me?"

"I don't know."

I would like to have believed him but I was not sure I could. Time would tell. He reached into the car and produced a mobile phone.

"I've bought this gadget for you, Piers," he said. Piers felt it with his fingers and looked puzzled.

"What is it?" he asked.

"It's a special mobile phone and it speaks the numbers." He pressed a button and a tiny voice called out "seven".

"Hey you have a go." Seb handed the phone to Piers who pushed a couple of buttons and looked delighted with the result. "It's even cleverer than that," Seb went on. "Look, I'll show you how." He took Piers hand. "Can you feel this button?" he asked. Piers nodded. "I've programmed my number into button one. Just press it and keep it pressed for a short time." Piers did so and a few seconds later Seb's phone started ringing. He answered it and the two of them had a short and silly conversation.

"You're spoiling him," I said. "Isn't it going to be expensive to call you in America?"

"Don't worry, the bill will be sent to me. Your number is on button two so he can call you as well. And if you're ever worried where he might be you can call him and find out. Now I really must be going."

"What do you say, Piers?" I reminded him.

"Thanks, Dad, it's fantastic!"

Piers flung his arms round Seb and hugged him tightly. After a few seconds Seb gently loosened the boy's grasp and took him by the hands.

"Look after your mother for me, won't you," he said. "And enjoy yourself at your new school. I'm sure you'll have a great time." With that he gave him a kiss on the forehead, got into his car, started the engine and waved at us.

"Bye Dad," Piers called out, looking rather gloomy.

We crossed the road and paused briefly by the stile to watch Seb's car as it disappeared down the road.

"Cheer up," I said. "You'll be able to talk to him whenever you want to on that posh phone he gave you."

"Yes, I know but I wanted him to stay."

"I know you did," I replied.

"That's a terrific car," Piers said.

"What do you mean?" I asked.

"Dad took me for a drive this morning. We did a hundred miles an hour on the motorway. It was incredible, so exciting."

"What! Took you for a drive! What motorway?"

"I don't know."

The same old Seb taking Piers away without my knowledge! Why couldn't he have simply asked? That was too easy. I sighed. I should be furious with him but what was the point? I knew what to expect by now. He was such a frustrating man. For all the stupid, blundering and inconsiderate way he went about things, he wasn't all bad. He even had a few admirable characteristics. He was highly intelligent, although I suppose it depends on what you mean by intelligence. Furthermore, he certainly could not be accused of being stingy. The money he already spent on gifts for Piers and what he was prepared to pay for his education proved that. All right, Seb was trying to assuage his guilt about deserting us but whatever demons had originally driven him to leave us, I was sure his feelings about Piers were now quite sincere. At least to that extent he had changed. So why did he hide away what was decent within him in a murky sea of deviousness and deception? It was baffling. From what he had told me, his own childhood had been pretty difficult. Perhaps his lies and his deception were an attempt to reconstruct his world as he thought it ought to be. Could that explain him? No that was too simple, and too trite. It was much more complex than that. Without doubt he was a damaged individual. I thought about his solitary drive to the airport and back to his bachelor life in the States. He only had himself to blame for that. I doubt whether I would ever fully understand him and I was very relieved he had gone at least for now. For a few months at least my life could return to normality.

"Come on Piers," I said, "Let's go home."

We started along the bridle way and I glanced up at the sky. Dark clouds were beginning to pile high into the sky. I could see the ragged bottom of the cloud base and below it grey downward streaks as rain approached. We needed to hurry back before it arrived. A buzzard drifted over us and in the valley below a flock of small birds scattered in panic. A stoat ran across the path and scuttled down the side of the escarpment. Down below on the farm next door I could see a group of horses slowly moving round the field as they grazed. Near them a combine harvester slowly cut a pale yellow swathe through the ripened wheat. From the other side of the Marlborough Plain a large RAF transport aircraft took off from RAF Lyneham. It circled and then flew into the distance. Piers could never pilot an aeroplane as I had once dreamed but I felt very optimistic about what he might do when he grew up. I watched him following Goldie, moving confidently along, now way ahead of me, sometimes trotting fearlessly and sometimes stopping to wait. He would be going to boarding school before long and in the meantime I wanted to enjoy as much time with him as possible.

FIFTEEN

As I drove away from the top of the Marlborough downs heavy clouds towered into the sky in front of me and in the distance I could see forked lightning arcing alarmingly down. A curtain of heavy rain was clearly falling and I wondered how long it would be before I reached the storm. I thought about Piers and his insistent pleading trying to persuade me not to go back. His love had become worth more than anything else to me and it made me feel incredibly happy, sad and angry with myself at the same time. I wanted to stay in England but the money had to be earned to pay for his education and I doubted I could do that here. Perhaps I could persuade Gemina to open a research centre in Oxford. There are a lot of brilliant young computer programmers in this country and I could run the team. I must have a word with Professor Zuckerman when I got back.

I was startled by an enormous crashed of thunder and the rain started to deluge down, bouncing off the bonnet of the car onto the windscreen making it extremely difficult to clearly see the road ahead. I pulled into a lay-by to wait until the storm had passed and started fiddling with the radio. Then I remembered that as I left my digs that morning I had received the expected letter from Truelove & Cash. I had put it in the glove compartment of the car unopened. I took it out and inside was a covering letter and an old envelope addressed to me. The solicitor explained that it was from my Granny and been written many years ago. She had deposited it with them with the instruction that it should be only to be passed on after her death. I tore the envelope open and immediately recognised her astonishingly neat writing.

Dear Seb,

I will be with the Good Lord when you read this letter. I wrote it because there are things you should know about your parents and your childhood that I could not bear to tell you when I was alive. It was all too painful. I told you that your father had just disappeared one day. He did not. He went to live with a woman he had been having a secret affair with for some time. She had a young family. He was the 'uncle' I took you to see when you were three but he refused to have anything to do with you. He claimed you were not his child and that was why he had left. All this was completely untrue. However, your parents were a very unhappy couple and it was probably for the best. No doubt this will come as a shock to you but I'm sorry to say there is more I never told you. I'm afraid your mother did not die of cancer. Your father leaving sent her completely off the rails. She left you with me and went to live with a professor of mathematics she had become obsessed with. He was the unpleasant man I took you to see when you were eight. I think she thought you would be able to go and live with them, but she was wrong. He would not hear of it. He had no time for children and was a very domineering man. I'm sorry to say your mother just went along with whatever he wanted. She was in the house at the time of our visit but no matter what I said she would not see you. Later, I did make an attempt to explain the situation to you as delicately as I could, but as soon as I mentioned your mother you became very angry, insisting she was definitely dead and that I was just making it up. I suppose she was dead as far as you were concerned. You were traumatised by the whole thing and accused me of wanting to be rid of you. You were always a very sensitive and complex child. I sent you to the boarding school because I thought they might sort you out. I'm sorry to say your mother died of an aneurism a few years later.

I hope telling you this does not make you too upset but I felt you should know the truth about what happened to you as a child in this Godless world. They did not love you enough. Just remember I did. I loved you dearly.

Goodbye,

Granny

My first reaction was an acute feeling of numbness, pain and complete confusion. A deluge of tears poured from my eyes as quite unexpectedly, I vividly recalled the day she took me to see them. I was standing by myself in the professor's house and listening to the shouting coming from the next room. Through the crescendo of voices I heard Granny tell someone that she must take me *because she was my mother*. It had made no sense. My mother was dead. Why was Granny telling them this? I heard a woman screaming unintelligibly and there was more angry shouting. Granny rushed back in and I was shocked to see that she was weeping, which really frightened me. She pulled me roughly out of the house and when we returned home she tried to talk to me about it and, as she said in the letter, I became very angry. I remember I blocked my ears with my thumbs and screamed at her that my mother was dead and she should not try to say she wasn't. She sent me to bed and the subject was never mentioned again. I had completely forgotten all about it.

Poor Granny; I felt very sorry that she had had to live with the burden of this awful family secret for so many years. This feeling of great sadness slowly gave way to a smouldering, then incendiary rage at what she had told me. My parents could all rot in hell as far as I was concerned. I started the engine, slammed the car into gear and accelerated away at a lunatic sped, full of fury and resentment. Both my mother and father had just abandoned me. I was appalled. My father had denied I was his. What a bastard! He obviously did not love me. Neither did my mother, at least not sufficiently to matter. She was dead but Granny had said nothing about him being dead. He might still be alive. Would I like to meet him and tell him what I thought of him? He wasn't worth the angst, I decided, but laughed bitterly at the thought of turning up on his doorstep and saying 'Hello Dad, I'm the son you did not want.' That would make his day.

It was still raining as I came over the top of a hill and I hurtled down a twisting narrow road. Ahead of me I could just make out a tractor that had come out of a field and was trundling along, its huge wheels throwing mud into the air and spattering it on to my screen, momentarily obscuring my vision. I pulled the screen-wash lever and as it cleared I realised I was still going much too fast. It was too late to brake, so I accelerated round the outside of the tractor only to see a car coming straight towards me. I jammed on the brakes and swung in just in time, almost clipping the front of the tractor as the other car hurtled past in a huge wave of spray. As I straightened out, I was alarmed to find that my car's steering felt oddly light, almost as if it was floating, and I had little control. I tried braking but the back of the car swung sideways and I veered alarmingly on to the wrong side of the road. I turned the wheel the other way and to my relief the tyres regained their grip and I was back in control. I could feel the adrenalin pulsing through by veins making my nerve ends tingle with fear. At the same time I felt absurdly angry and realised I was still thinking about my parents. I needed to forget them and concentrate. I had got away with it and my mood switched to exhilaration. That feeling did not last long as the knowledge that I had never been loved by them carved insistently through my thoughts and blotted everything else out. I felt completely worthless and totally humiliated. Worse still, I had behaved just as badly myself with Alice and Piers and I had no excuse for that. My parents were right. I was totally worthless. Tears, of self-pity I suppose, blurred my vision as I hurtled along and I did not care. I just wanted to die.

    In the rear view mirror I could just make out the tractor vanishing into the grey rain soaked distance. I reached the bottom of the incline and in front of me the road straightened out for a long way ahead. I slipped the car into fifth gear and drove along at a maniacal speed, creating fountains of water as I hit the puddles and scudded over dry patches. I knew I was going much too fast but I did not care. I wanted to die and I was completely overwhelmed by the strange feeling of weird excitement that it gave me. It was a mixture of anger, resentment, bitterness and self-loathing all mixed up in a lunatic exhilaration.

All too quickly I reached the end of the straight section, flashed past a slow sign, and found myself on an awkward curve with an adverse camber that ran around the side of a hill. I changed down and braked to slow a little more but I had not reckoned on more mud on the road. The car started to slide so I tried to turn into the skid. It made little difference. I rushed towards the verge, with the car almost floating once more. There was an enormous thump as I hit the kerb and crashed straight through a hedge. A fraction of a second later I felt a second terrific bang as the car smashed into something very hard, flew into the air and landed with a colossal, metal screaming crump. I blacked out.

When I came to, I could not understand why everything was at such a bizarre angle. The ground was vertical and trees seemed to be growing sideways. I slowly realised that the surreal scene I could see was no illusion. The car was lying on its side completely wrecked. Inside the bent and broken dashboard pressed down on my legs and I could not move them at all. Oddly, though, I was feeling strangely warm and comfortable. I could hear the sound of rain drumming softly on the car bodywork and it was curiously peaceful. It was shock I imagine and surprisingly I did not feel too bad. The airbag had not activated but at least I had not gone through the windscreen. The seat belt and the anti-roll bars must have saved my life. Apart from the sound of the rain it was surprisingly quiet. A pair of crows wheeled overhead and then flew off. I lay there for perhaps an hour, slipping in and out of consciousness and then realised nobody had come to find me in all that time. A few moments before the crash I had wanted to die and it now looked very likely I would have my wish granted. But this was a very lonely spot to die and death did not seem so attractive. I felt an almost electric charge run through me. What had I been I thinking of? I knew my two sons both needed me and loved me in spite of my many failings, and I was extremely lucky to have found even that solace. I could almost feel their warmth and affection. Dying seemed yet another selfish thing for me to do. What I had done was my fault, but what my parents did was not. I must not let it ruin my life and those who had forgiven me. I had to survive. I shouted out a couple of times then realised it was pointless. If nobody was going to help me then I must help myself.

I found I could move one leg but the other was trapped by the crumpled dashboard. I felt down to see if I could break or push the broken plastic out of the way and a searing pain shot though my whole body. I cursed, pulled my hand back and saw it was covered in blood. I decided my leg must be broken and I started to shiver. I suppose it was the shock. I decided I ought to get out but I still did not want to move and wondered idly what Alice would say when I told her that I had not been able to go back to the States because I had crashed my car. 'Just another one of his lies,' I should think! It was obvious I needed to get help urgently and I fished into my inside my jacket pocket for my mobile. I don't know why I had not thought of that earlier. But how could I describe where I was? I knew I was somewhere on the Wiltshire-Berkshire borders but I did not know the number of the road l had been driving along. The answer dawned on me. My mobile had a satnav on it that would give my exact spot. I resumed the search going from one pocket to another but there was no sign of it. I tried to think where I had last used it and remembered that I had put it down on the passenger seat as I drove away from the Marlborough Downs. Perhaps it had fallen onto the floor of the car. I peered down but could see nothing in the blackness. I cursed and started to panic. After a few minutes I heard what sounded like a farm vehicle coming along the road. The driver would be sure to see me and call the emergency services. But he just went past, the sound of its engine slowly vanishing into the hissing of the rain. Another vehicle thundered by on my side of the road sending a wall of spray into the bushes. It did not stop either. Were they blind? Rain started to leak into the car and I began to feel very cold, wet and extremely anxious. Why had nobody come to investigate the crash?

The crows were back in numbers, circling overhead and making a dreadful cawing noise. Why were they gathering overhead like this? What sounded like a bus rumbled slowly by and as its engine died away I realised that the car wreckage must be obscured by the bushes and foliage of the trees and could not be easily be seen from the road. Darkness was falling and I knew I must somehow get out or I would have to spend the night in the wreck. I was not sure I would survive that. I reached into the glove compartment but there was only a map-book, the hire car papers and a torch in there. I switched it on and was pleased to find it worked. I tried the door pocket and discovered a pair of pliers, no doubt left there by some careless idiot at the garage. I took it out but as I set about trying to free my leg the dreadful pain I felt earlier shot through me. This time it was much worse and I fainted. When I recovered consciousness the first thing I saw was a very large crow, perched on side of the car and looking straight down at me. I remembered what Piers had said. The crows were waiting for me to die.

"Shove off you black bastard!" I screamed and waved the pliers at him. It flew off and settled on a branch alongside a row of others. I had no intention of being their supper and I pointlessly shook my fist at them before resuming my task of trying to smash the dashboard.

Ellen was playing one of Eric Satie's dreamlike 'Gymnopedies' in the living room. She had a wonderful touch and the music made me feel calm and relaxed as I sat at the kitchen table sketching out some ideas for my next picture. I glanced at Piers who was sitting at his book reader and he seemed to sense my gaze for he stood up and walked slowly across to me and put his arm round me. His face was a picture of gloom.
"What's the matter?" I asked.
"I don't know," he replied. "I feel very unhappy and I don't know why."
"Well, you probably miss your father. That's natural. It's been a busy day and perhaps you should think about going to bed. You're probably tired. You'll feel all right when you've had a sleep."

"No I don't want to go to bed. I don't feel like it. I'm not just sad, I have a bad feeling."

"What sort of bad feeling?"

"I don't know. Just a bad feeling….about Dad."

"What about Dad?"

"That I won't see him again."

"Don't be silly, of course you will."

"He was really nice to me," he whispered.

"I know," I said. "Look you have nothing to worry about. He'll be back. Come here I'll give you a cuddle,"

I put my arm around his waist, pulled him onto my knee and kissed him. He sniffed a little and I could see tears on his cheek. "Hey," I said, "I told you, he'll be back soon, you see."

"Will he?"

"Of course he will. He's very fond of you."

"I really miss him already you know."

"Of course you do, darling,"

"Why did he have to go away? He really understands me."

"Does he? He has to go back to his work in America."

"But I've got this really bad feeling," he persisted.

Ellen had stopped playing and came into the kitchen. She saw Piers had been crying and came over.

"What's the matter then?" she asked.

"He says he's got a bad feeling about Seb," I told her.

She looked quizzically at Piers.

"What do you mean?" she asked.

"That I won't see him again," he said.

"Why?"

"I don't know. I just want to talk to him. Can I ring him up?"

"Not now, he's probably driving at the moment."

"Please, please."

"He might be at the airport by now," said Ellen. "It could be worth giving him a call."

"Please, Mum," pleaded Piers, squeezing my hand. "I could ring him on my new phone."

He was a difficult boy to say no to so I reached for my bag and took out my own mobile.

"We'll use mine," I said, and I clicked in Seb's number.

I heard the sound of my phone ringing but it came from outside the car. I could see its light flashing in the undergrowth just a few yards away. It must have flown out through the torn soft-top. The answerphone cut in. It was Piers leaving a message. It was difficult to hear his voice properly. I thought he said he wanted to know when I would be back. I screamed in frustration and started to hit and tear wildly at the broken dashboard with the pliers. The effort exhausted me and I drifted off into a fitful sleep for a couple of hours.

When I awoke it was very, very dark. The crows had disappeared but I had little doubt they would be back in the morning. There was no moon and it was very difficult to see anything. I continued to work away at the dashboard but it seemed hopeless. I tried to shift my leg again but it would not move. At least this time I did not faint. I remembered the torch in the glove compartment. I retrieved it, switched it on and shone it down into the foot well. My leg was a real mess with my shin bent at an absurd angle. Fortunately the bleeding had stopped although I thought I must have lost a lot of blood. I began to feel very thirsty and licked my lips to moisten them.

Outside it had stopped raining and through the car window I could see the trees overhead silhouetted against a full moon. I heard my phone ring again and I pulled at the torn soft top to make the hole larger so that I could see out better. The phone's light was flashing and I tried to make a note of the exact direction so that I would know where to go if I could get out of this wreck. I heard the answerphone cut in and this time it was Carl Neumann saying he would meet me at San Jose Airport if I let him have my flight number. I laughed bitterly. It was going to be a long time before I returned to California.

I decided I was wasting my time with the pliers in the darkness, and that I should conserve my energy to keep warm and have another go in the morning. I started to fiddle with the controls on the steering wheel and turned the headlights on. Why had I not thought of that before? Any passing car was bound to see. I heard another car approaching and whizz by. "Bastards!" I shouted. I settled back but no other vehicle went by as night set in. After a little I looked at my watch. It was midnight and all I heard was the eerie, distant sound of an owl calling and the scuffle of small animals as they moved about through the undergrowth. It was not long before I again drifted into an intermittent, light sleep, half awake and half dreaming, in which images of my childhood flickered uncontrollably through my mind. I saw my mother's face smiling and holding out her arms to me, but as I tried to reach out to her, another face screamed at me, a girl's face, contorted and inches from my nose. I was six years old and in my Primary School playground and the face summoned up from the depth of my unwanted memories was Julie Plumb. She was screaming "dead mum! dead mum! dead mum!'

'Shut up, shut up, shut up', my childish voice croaked back her up. I wanted to shrivel up and die. The images faded and I was running as fast as I could, but no matter what I did I could not escape the mob of children pursuing me, all shouting out those terrible words. Then I was hiding in the toilet and soon they were hammering on the door screaming more obscenities. I was shaking with fear and had no idea what to do. It was very dark in the cubicle and I knew I had to escape somehow, but the door crashed open, I was pinned down and I became aware of a searing pain in my leg that was seeping into whole my body. I forced myself to wake up but the dream was still very vivid. Why on earth at a time like this was I dreaming about the horrors that seared my childhood?

A damp mist was hanging over the tops of trees and I could hear the cawing of the crows as they returned. This time they were much bolder and were pecking at the ground around the car. I was going to die before the next dawn came and they knew it. My lips were very cracked and had become quite painful. I felt weak and helpless and regretted all the wasted effort I had put in trying to free my leg. One of them hopped up onto the soft top and looked at me. It was the same big bastard as the previous evening.

"Shove off!" I screamed at him but this time he took no notice. I reached for the torch and aimed a blow as close as I could get to him, hitting the fabric with a bang. This time he did fly off but only as far as a low branch close by where he settled, his sharp black eyes glinting in the early morning light. I closed my eyes, started to doze again and in my mind I thought I could see Alice and Piers looking at me in the wreck. He was crying and I could see his face screwed up with desolation. I knew I was hallucinating and shook myself back to reality. I desperately wanted to be back with them and vowed that I would resign my job in America if I could just get out of this mess.

Piers was not in his room. Normally this early in the morning he would be sleeping. He was probably in the toilet, although I had heard no sounds to indicate this. A cold grey light had started to illuminate the view I could see through his window. Thin clouds papered the sky and I could just make out the lights on the farm buildings next door as the dairymen rose from their beds to milk the cows. The downs behind were darkly silhouetted against the early dawn and I could see the odd crow pecking at the ground in the mist-covered grass of the adjoining field. I listened intently and heard a slight noise coming from the living room. I slowly went down the stairs and saw he was sitting at the table holding my mobile phone.

"What are you doing, Piers?" I asked. "It's five in the morning!"

"I was trying to ring Dad," he said, "But I don't know how to make this thing work. Where's my phone?"

"You won't be able to get him now. He's on a plane in the middle of the Atlantic probably sleeping. It takes hours to get there. You should go back to bed."

"But I want to talk to him. He said I could ring him any time I wanted."

"Yes, but the middle of the night is definitely not a good idea, is it?"

"Well he didn't answer yesterday and I was worried. He hasn't called back like you said he would."

"He probably had to rush for the plane and didn't have time. I'm sure he had his reasons. You'll have to be patient. Now go back to bed."

"I can't sleep."

"Why not?"

"I don't know. It's just that feeling I have about him."

"Look I'm sure you have nothing to worry about."

"Couldn't you just try him again?"

"No. I told you, he's thousands of miles away."

"When can I ring him?"

"Tomorrow."

"I want to try now."

"No, just go back to bed before I get cross with you."

"Where's my phone?"

"I put it away. I'll get it for you in the morning. Now go back to bed!"

He reluctantly made his way up the stairs to his bedroom. I was wide awake so I picked up the drawing pad I had been using the previous evening, put on a coat and wandered out into the garden. I liked the feel of the early morning freshness on my face and I loved sketching the landscape as it changed with the light of the rising sun. There was little wind to disturb the leaves and the air was transparently silent. I could hear the sounds of cattle in the distance and a little bird song. I suppose with Seb's departure I felt very much at peace with myself for the first time for months. I could get on with my paintings now. I made my way up the path towards my studio and stopped by the gate to look back. The old farmhouse, which had been built and added to over hundreds of years, hid its cracks and deficiencies in the dawn half-light and looked very homely in a dishevelled kind of way. I knew I belonged there and I did not want to live anywhere else for the rest of my life. I hoped Piers would feel the same when he grew up. Through the kitchen window I could see the old table and wooden chairs that Ellen's grandparents must have sat around, although back then it would have been candle-lit. There was an extraordinary sense of generations gone by and I felt enriched by it. As I turned to go I saw Piers again come into the kitchen and start to pull the draws of the sideboard out one by one. He was searching for his phone. I watched fascinated. He quickly he found it, took it out of the drawer, sat down at the table and put it to his ear. I felt a momentary flash of irritation that he had defied me and then laughed inwardly at his determination to talk to Seb. The relationship he had with his father was clearly closer than I realised. It was hard to swallow after the appalling way Seb had behaved towards us. Piers lowered the phone, felt it with his other hand then press the button Seb had shown him. He would not get through to him on the plane, of course, but he had to find that out for himself. He was stubborn just like his father.

I could see the light of my phone flashing as it rang and I knew I must answer it. It was my only hope. With a huge effort I wrenched my whole body sideways. My trapped leg somehow twisted free and sent a ferocious shock through my whole body that forced me to stop for a few seconds. I pulled myself through the tear in the soft top and gulped in the fresh air, ignoring the excruciating pain. The ringing ceased. I cursed but I thought I knew roughly where it was. I slowly inched myself away from the wreckage but was forced to stop after a couple of yards and lay there on the wet ground gasping for breath and sweating. After a few minutes I recovered a little and looked round. Behind me the road was not too far away but it was obvious I had no hope of reaching it for a considerable time. The crows had all flown into the trees but I knew they were just waiting patiently. "Not just yet you buggers," I whispered. The dark sky was becoming paler with the rising sun and I began to feel more hopeful. Soon more cars would be on the road and someone was bound to see me. I heard my phone ring again. I was certain it must be Piers trying out the new phone I had given him. Only he would have kept ringing my number. I peered into the bushes to try to see where it was but the increasing daylight had become too bright for the flashing to be easily visible. It made me cry a little in frustration.   I pulled myself together and tried to move in the direction of the sound. It took a huge effort just to make a yard or two and I was soon forced to stop. I was completely exhausted and lay there hardly able to move. One by one the crows came down again from the trees and started pecking at the ground close to me. They knew I had all but given up. I was going to die and I wondered what it would be like. I felt a calm horror at the thought. Would I slowly lose consciousness, disappear into oblivion and know nothing about it? I certainly hoped so. Or would I be only semi-conscious and feel the sharp beaks begin to peck at the soft flesh of my face and eyes? I shivered with terror and closed my eyes. I must have lost consciousness for a few minutes and when I opened them again the large crow was only a foot or so from my head. I shouted in panic and to my amazement there was a loud bang and he vanished from my sight. All the other crows flew high into the sky in a panic, cawing wildly. Standing looking at me was a gamekeeper holding his gun. He walked across, knelt down and I smiled weakly at him.

"You're still alive then," he observed.

"I've had better nights I must admit."

"I saw the crows wheeling around earlier this morning and came to see what all the fuss was about. I heard the noise of your phone ringing. It probably saved your bacon. You're a lucky bugger! You were on their breakfast menu. I've been after that big one for a long time."

"Did you get him?"

"No, he was too near you. I'll hang him on the fence one day, you see."

My phone rang again. He walked over to where it was lying, picked it up and gave it back to me. It was my darling son and I was never gladder to hear his sweet voice.

"Hello Dad," he said. "Are you OK?"

"Of course," I said. "Superb, never been better, and I'm really pleased you rang. But what are you doing up this early?"

"I just wanted to speak to you," he said. "Mum said I should wait but I didn't want to. You'll probably think it's silly but I was frightened I'd never see you again."

"Why ever not? Of course you will. Why would you think such a thing?"

"I don't know, it was just a feeling. I thought something had happened to you."

"No, I'm just fine."

"Your voice sounds strange."

"I'm a bit tired, that's all."

"Are you in America yet?"

"No, I haven't quite arrived. But I would like to speak to your mother when she gets up."

"She's up already. She's gone to her studio. I heard her go there a few minutes ago."

"Well can you ask her to call me? There's something I need to tell her."

"OK Dad, bye."

"Bye, bye son."

The gamekeeper grinned at me.

"You don't look exactly fine to me," he observed. "I've seen a dead sheep look better than you."

SIXTEEN

Piers was still in bed, so I had breakfast with Ellen and we chatted a little about Piers' almost obsessive insistence that something might have happened to Seb. Ellen said that it was only natural that the boy was worried in the circumstances, and she was pleased that Seb and I had at least been able to settle our differences over his schooling. She thought I had made the right decision, which was reassuring, although I still had my doubts. After breakfast I went up to the studio and tried to get on with my painting but it was one of those frustrating mornings when everything I tried did not work. I found it difficult to concentrate and, annoyingly, instead of thinking about the painting my mind kept returning to Seb and his involvement with us. It was fine as far as I was concerned, but only if he did what he had promised and just made occasional visits. The problem was that I knew Piers would not be at all happy with that and I doubted Seb would stick to it anyway. What a difficult man Seb was to understand! I wryly thought about the fact that a couple of times I had really wanted to kill him, particularly when I had that awful nightmare about poisoning him. That would fade in time but I did not like what it revealed about me.

At about twelve o'clock I gave up on the painting and as I made my way down the path and back to the farmhouse I was surprised to see a police car driving up the lane. It stopped outside the gate and George Gale got out. I waved and ran across to meet him.

"George, how nice to see you."

He grinned and kissed me on both cheeks continental style.

"Can we go in?" he asked. "There's something I have to tell you."

I took him into the kitchen and made him a cup of tea. Ellen was still in the barn and Piers had still not appeared.

"It's about Seb," he said. "He was involved in a nasty car accident last night."

"Oh my God is he all right? Was he badly injured?" I felt quite shocked.

"I'm afraid so but I understand he'll be all right. He's now in Swindon hospital with a broken leg but that beautiful sports car is a write-off."

"How on earth did it happen? Was anyone else hurt?"

"No, there was no other car involved. He must have been driving far too fast. He skidded on a muddy road, overturned and ended up in the middle of a copse. Worst of all he was lying there all night badly injured and nobody found him until this morning. " I immediately thought of Piers' anxiety about him and his persistence in trying to call him. How could he have known? What would he say? "I assume you will go and see him fairly soon," George continued, "so I've brought his case, which I retrieved from the car boot. I also found this on the floor of the car."

From a folder he produced a slightly crumpled envelope and gave it to me. As I thanked him, I heard a noise behind me and looked around to see Piers standing on the stairs still in his pyjamas.

"I heard voices," he said. "I thought Dad might have come back."

"Sorry it's just Sergeant Gale," I told him, and explained about the accident. He started crying and then really shouted at me.

"I told you something bad had happened to my Dad," he screamed, "but you wouldn't listen to me. I kept telling you but nobody would listen."

"Piers", I replied. "Don't shout at me. You can't talk to me like that! It's very rude."

"I don't care," he cried, and rushed back up the stairs slamming his bedroom door shut.

I followed him up the stairs and through the bedroom door I could hear him sobbing. I started to open it but he screamed: "Go away, I hate you. It's your fault. You wouldn't listen to me." I decided to let him calm down and retreated down the stairs. George was staring at the floor.

"I'm sorry, George he's not usually like this," I told him

"He doesn't mean it," he replied, "he's very upset. He's just frightened he'll lose his father. Look, I'd better go". I thanked him again and he told me not to be too concerned about Piers behaving like that. He had seen it many times before with his own kids.

"Don't worry," he said, "he's ten, isn't he? It only gets worse from now on!"

With that cheery thought he departed and I was left thinking about Piers' uncharacteristic outburst, the premonition he had obviously had and wondering what it might mean. Most likely it was simply anxiety as George had suggested.

The envelope George had given me was on the table and I saw that it was addressed to Seb in very neat handwriting. It was torn open and as I picked it up the letter fell out. I'm sorry to say I could not resist the temptation to read it and I was deeply shocked at what it said. Poor Seb, no wonder he was screwed up.

In hospital I thought a lot about the letter Granny had written to me and wondered what had happened to it. At least I now understood what had been going on when she took me to see the professor and the woman whom I now know was my mother. Of course I felt bitter they had rejected me but it was all too late now. It could not be changed and I decided I should forget them and get on with my own life. That was easier said than done. I thought a great deal about my father now that I knew what had really happened to him. As a child I had I fantasised that he had been killed on some obscure secret service mission. I knew I had made it all up but I really believed my own story and it had protected me until now. It never once crossed my mind that he simply did not love me and had just walked out. Now I knew differently, I had no idea how to come to terms with it. I should hate him I suppose, but it is hard to hate someone who never really existed in your life, at least at any meaningful level. Perhaps I should do some research to find out if he was alive but what good would it do me? I very much doubted that he would say how sorry he was and ask me to forgive him. I decided it might be better not to inquire too deeply. Who knows what else went on in their lives? Consequently the questions remained. Nevertheless, as the days wore on I became less enraged by the treatment my parents meted out. I began to realise that I could either let the resentment I felt ruin my life or move on. None of it was my fault so why let myself become obsessed about it? It was easy to tell myself such things but actually very hard to be so rational. I might get there in time, I told myself, as another wave of bitterness slowly dissipated. Fortunately they became less frequent as time passed. I felt I was fine but in reality I was not. The horrific nightmares about my childhood returned. Those screaming, leering faces chanting 'dead mum,' frequently caused me to wake in terror. Why was I still haunted by what happened in my childhood? I thought I had put all that behind me years ago. A psychiatrist in the hospital tried to help me. He suggested I should have therapy when I left but I never took it up. I did not like the idea of someone prying into my innermost thoughts.

Piers and Alice came to see me. She gave me my case and then handed me Granny's letter. I saw that it was open so I asked the obvious question.

"Have you read it?"

She hung her head. "I'm very sorry but I have to admit I did," she replied. "I do apologise, it was unforgivably nosey."

I was pleased she had read it. At least she now knew just what I had gone through as a child. In truth I was so thrilled to see them I just laughed and told her I would have done the same.

"I thought it had got lost in the car crash," I explained. "I was going to show you it anyway if it turned up."

"So you forgive me then?" she asked.

"Only if you give me a hug," I replied.

Piers just stood there grinning as she told me that on the night of the accident he insisted that something bad had happened to me. He had defied her to make that crucial phone call. How did he know? A sixth sense perhaps? Alice said it was because he was a Chime Child. I was amazed she still believed such junk. Whatever the reason, it saved my life. Maybe I was just plain lucky.

She was more sympathetic than I expected. I suppose she thought I could do little harm immobilized and in a hospital bed with my leg in traction. Nevertheless, when I was discharged it still came as a surprise when she agreed to the doctor's request that I could convalesce at the farm for a few weeks. Piers had come with her and I noticed him smile triumphantly. I was sure it was his idea.

I wrote to Professor Zuckerman and told him I wanted to stay in England and start a research centre over here. Soon afterwards Sam and Jackie came over to see me. Jackie told me that Zuckerman thought it was a great idea. He was happy to fund it and that I should run it.

Sam just laughed when he saw me all plastered up and said he always knew I was a lousy driver. It was great to have him around again. He and Piers spent a lot of time together and it was clear they liked each other. "It's great to have a kid brother," he said. "Why didn't you tell me about him sooner?" Why indeed? He told me he might try for a place at an English University so he would see us more often. Surprisingly, Jackie got on very well with Alice which was mostly, how shall I put it, delightful, perhaps? Except that the two of them sometimes made me feel rather like a dead insect pinned to a botanist's board. Was that a guilty conscience on my part? I don't think so. More likely they just enjoyed ganging up on me. One morning Jackie paid me a visit. After we had chatted for a short time about very little she suddenly said:

"I've been talking to Alice about you."

"Is that so? I'm not sure I like the sound of that."

"I hear you asked her to marry you not long ago."

"Did I? I suppose I did. I imagine you both had a good laugh about that."

"Of course but I have to admit I was rather surprised."

"Well no doubt she also told you she turned me down."

"Yes, but what did you expect?"

"Exactly that."

"So you weren't disappointed then."

"Not at all."

"Supposing she'd said yes?"

"There wasn't the slightest chance of that."

"And what do you think now?"

"The same thing."

"Well, I'm not so sure. Give her time and she might feel differently."

I stared at her, wondering if this was some game they had both set up to get back at me.

"I very much doubt it," I replied.

"We'll see," she said. A few days later she returned to America but just before she left she told me to remember what she had said.

"I don't think so," I replied. I just thought it was part of her revenge game.

However, Alice continued to be very kind to me and I was enormously grateful for that. Perhaps they had not been playing a game as I had suspected, or at least Alice was not in on it. She really was my angel and in spite of my misgivings I knew there was a serious risk that I might fall in love with her again, if I hadn't already. However, I had no intention of making a fool of myself so I kept my mouth firmly shut about my burgeoning feelings.

At the end of August I had recovered enough to start hobbling around the farm and late one afternoon I made my way up to the seat in the studio garden where I sat in the warm evening sun idly contemplating the view over the Marlborough Plain. There is something about spending time looking at distant landscapes that encourages you to mull over your life and try and make sense of it. As I sat there, for the most part my thoughts were a whirl of disconnected and contradictory questions for which I had no answers. The accident had really frightened me. At one stage I was sure I would die and end up as crow food. And if I had gone what would people say about me? Oh yes, a clever man but he was a real shit for walking out on Alice and their blind son. Of course it was an oversimplification of what happened and it was certainly not how I wanted to be remembered. Yet I could hardly deny it was true. How could he have done that they would ask? What a bastard. The thought depressed me. Few people would understand. I still didn't really understand myself. I had loved Alice for a while and then I did not. Now I do. What a mess.

It went wrong ten years ago but why? I tried to remember the details of exactly what happened to split us up, but all I could recall was the gradual feeling of alienation towards both Piers and Alice that slowly engulfed me. I could no more prevent it than stop breathing and I still guiltily remember the immense relief when I finally left them. I knew it was wrong at the time and I have felt terrible about it ever since. It was also true, as Jackie had once said, that I sometimes hid behind a veil of protective lies. But doesn't everyone protect their cosy view of themselves because what else can we do? Face the unblemished truth? That's an almost impossible thing to do.

The sound of the piano ceased and a few minutes later I saw Piers emerge from the farmhouse and make his way up the path towards me. I called out and he came into the garden and sat down on the bench next to me. I slipped my arm round his shoulder, he smiled at me and we sat in silence. There was no need to say anything. The studio door clicked open and Alice, who had been painting all afternoon, came out.

"Are you two feeling hungry?" she called.

"Starving," shouted Piers

"I'll go down and get the supper on," she said.

"We'll be down in a few minutes, then," I replied.

I watched her go down the path and thought about the time when we first came here and she had tried very hard to persuade me to buy the cottage. I was wrong then as I usually was where she was concerned. But things had worked out well for her in the end so I did not feel too bad about it.

Piers, who normally babbled away, was unusually quiet. He was due to start at the Cathedral School in a couple of days and I suppose he was feeling a little apprehensive. He also knew I was moving out fairly soon. When I had told him he was rather upset. He argued angrily with both of us about it but in the end he seemed to accept the situation. But I was wrong.

"Dad," he suddenly asked. "Have you liked living here with us?"

"Of course, I've loved it."

"Well if you loved it, why can't you and mum just make it up and live here?"

"I don't think it's possible at the moment."

"Why not?"

"It just isn't."

"What about me? Don't I matter?"

"Of course you do. I promise I'll come and see you at the school. I'm going to be living much nearer to it than here and I'll be able to come and see you at weekends and sometimes in the evening if you want. You'll love it at the Cathedral School. You can get on with your music studies and make lots of friends. You want to do that don't you?"

He nodded gloomily, stared thoughtfully into the distance and for a few minutes said nothing. I hoped that the cross-questioning was over. It was not.

"Why did you leave mum and me?" he suddenly asked.

"I thought I'd explained that to you once."

"Yes but I still don't really understand."

"It was a bit complicated. I'd lost my job at the time and the only one I was offered meant I had to go to America to work. Your mother would not come with me and we couldn't agree on what to do. I had to earn the money to support us and, as I just said, it was the only job I was offered so I felt I had no choice. But even when I was away, I thought about you the whole time and I'm really glad I came back to see you."

I know it was the usual mixture of what actually happened and flannel and I know it left out a lot but I thought it would suffice, until he came up with his next question.

"Yes, but was it really because of me?"

To say I was shocked at the directness of this would be an understatement. My insides burned and fluttered with nerves. I would end up telling him the whole truth if I was not careful.

"No, absolutely not, don't be silly," I replied, weakly. "Why would you even think such a thing?"

"I wondered whether it was because I was blind."

The accuracy of his question completely disconcerted me. Had he worked it out? He might have done, he was clever enough. What should I say? 'Yes that's right my son' and try to explain. I dare not risk it. I was terrified of what he would think of me.

"Of course not," I managed to whisper.

He turned his head towards me, perhaps noticing my unconvincing tone of voice.

"I think that my blindness was the real reason," he said firmly.

"Is that what your mother told you?"

"No, she said I had to ask you about it."

I looked at his innocent boyish face, his expression flickering with anxiety and doubt. It was obvious he needed to know the truth and I needed to tell him. I could not conceal it any longer.

"Yes, what you said was right, it was your blindness." I whispered.

"I knew that was the real reason," he said, quietly.

I waited for the angry reaction I had feared. But he simply looked miserable and said nothing while I tried to think of some way of explaining what had happened, other than the lame half-truths I had already given. I could not. I had failed him and his mother and that was the pathetic truth. I just stared at the ground. "You must think I'm a dreadful father." I muttered, "I'm really sorry,"

"No, but just saying sorry does not tell me anything. I still don't really understand why my blindness made you leave us," he persisted.

I gazed blankly at the glorious landscape in front of us and somehow it seemed almost an affront to my being there, almost mocking me. Piers had never seen it yet it was clear he felt it, heard it and understood it in a way that I doubted I ever would.

"I am not sure where to start," I said. "It was all very complicated. For a long time I hid behind all sorts of excuses that somehow told me that what I had done was all right. But I knew deep down it was not. Your social worker once told me that it's quite common for dads of children with all sorts of disabilities to walk out. She said some men simply can't deal with it. So I used to tell myself that was really what happened and I was not to blame. Nobody's perfect and all that. But if I am completely honest I don't think it was true for me. It was much more complicated than that. I thought you were not the son I wanted. I thought my child should be perfect and you were not. Why I would be stupid enough to think I wanted a perfect child I have no idea. The truth is that your blindness was at the root of it and because you were blind I made all sorts of assumptions about you that were stupid and wrong."

"Like what?"

"I thought I would never be able to do things with you like playing football or cricket, like other dads and their kids. I also thought you would probably be a bit dim and I wanted a son who would be clever. I know this all sounds shallow and silly but it was what I felt and I don't know why. Somehow everything got out of proportion and I didn't understand what was important and what wasn't. The truth is I have no real explanation that completely makes sense to me, and ultimately I have never really understood why I left. It's what I did and I have to accept that. I can't blame anyone else. I just hope you can forgive me."

He said nothing and stared straight ahead. Of course I blundered on: "Worst of all I thought I could never grow to love you and you would hate me."

He looked sharply at me. "Dad! Stop talking about it. I don't like it."

"I just wanted to say I'm very, very sorry."

"You keep saying you're sorry. You don't have to. I know you are and it's embarrassing. You're my dad. Just leave it. I told you I don't want to talk about it."

"Right, OK," I muttered. He seemed angry with me and I feared the worst.

"Are you still going to go away again?" he suddenly asked.

"I have to go to America for a while but I'll come back soon and live near here so I can be with you, that's if you want me to."

"Of course I do," he said. "You're my dad, aren't you? I like you and it doesn't matter now what you did then." He grinned, leaned across, gave me a big hug then nestled his head in the hollow of my shoulder. I put my arm round him and we sat there for a while without speaking. Then quite unexpectedly he sat up and flung both arms round my neck.

"I really love you, Dad," he said.

I felt like screaming and shouting with elation. A ten year burden had been lifted from my life. I bent forward and kissed him.

"I love you too," I murmured, feeling quite choked.

"Ugh!" he complained. "Your face is scratchy." We both laughed and hugged each other tightly. What more did I want? What more is there than the uncomplicated love of your own child? For the first time I realised the enormity of what had just happened, and what it meant to both of us. He had given me his love in spite of now knowing the truth about me, without asking anything in return. Nothing in my life would ever be better than that.

Down at the farmhouse the door opened and Alice stepped out ringing the bell.

"Come on," I said. "Supper is ready. I'll guide you down."

"No," he said, "Close your eyes and I'll guide you. You can see what it's like to be blind. Just trust me."

He took my arm and led me down the path. It was very scary and I'm afraid I opened my eyes half way down. As we reached the gate to the farmhouse he stopped and laughed.

"You cheated," he said. "I knew you'd opened your eyes. I could tell by the way your walk changed."

I laughed, slightly embarrassed. "Can't fool you can I? I didn't want to fall over and break something else."

"You have to learn to trust me," he replied.

That was truer about more of my life than he realised. As we went towards the farmhouse a group of horses in the next field looked up, neighed and started moving towards the fence. Piers broke away from me and made his way towards them. In the adjoining field a flock of rooks swooped down and landed. A startled partridge shot into the air and flew towards the trees. There was no doubt I was going to miss this beautiful remote place. I went into the farmhouse and Alice smiled faintly at me from the stove.

"He's gone to see the horses," I told her.

She nodded and said the meal was not quite ready. I watched Piers through the kitchen window and recalled his remark about trust. I suppose that's what love is. Would Alice ever really trust me? I suppose she might, one day. Although she had been very kind to me while I recovered and she was friendly enough, she seemed more like a sister. I had told her a few days ago I would move back to my digs when the plaster came off. That was due to be removed next week. She just smiled enigmatically and said "Fine." I may have dreamt about remaining there but I knew it was unrealistic. I had done too much damage and I would have to wait and see. At least I knew she did not want to kill me anymore!

The horses were standing by the fence. Piers was stroking their noses and feeding them carrots. After a short while he broke off and moved towards a small clump of bushes out of which flew a group of tiny birds. They whirled round and round and seemed to have no fear of him. He must have had some seed in his hand for he held out his arm and soon they were perching on his wrist and gobbling it down. Odd that for wild birds. Perhaps the Chime Child myth had something to it after all.

THE END

Copyright © David Hodgson, Beckenham, October 2014.